ADAM

James Bushill

I ought to be thy Adam, but I am rather the fallen angel.

—the Creature, *Frankenstein*

Chapter 1

August 11
2101

The asteroid Metis

Arkolov ran through the tunnel, tracked by a pool of light, his footfalls kicking up puffs of dust that swirled and glittered in the still air. The only sounds were the light tap-tap of his bare feet on the rock floor, the steady bass thump spilling from his headphones, and, somewhere in the distance, a low rumble like an approaching subway train.

Ahead, in the darkness, was the faint green glow of the emergency refuge that marked the turnaround point on this, his favorite jogging route. When he spotted it, he increased his pace.

At first, the pool of light matched his speed. Then it stopped, frozen in place, no longer tracking his movement. He ran on into the darkness anyway. It wasn't unusual for a block of motion sensors to fail. The light would soon catch him up.

But it didn't, so he stopped and returned to the lighted area. He hopped back and forth across the gap between light and dark, hoping to trigger the sensors. When nothing happened, he jumped and waved his arms in the air. Still, the light refused to move.

He tapped a metal spot below his right ear and his music cut out, allowing him to hear the rumble, not quite so distant now, louder with each passing second. It didn't worry him. He knew that sound well.

"Full light. Tunnel Two, Section Niner Zero Seven," he said, gesturing with intent toward the darkened tunnel ahead.

As he did so, the remaining lights switched off, leaving the tunnel in complete darkness. Undeterred, he repeated the instruction with more force, raising his voice and pronouncing each word carefully, "Tunnel Two. Section Niner Zero Seven. Full light."

The tunnel remained dark. He tapped the metal spot again. "The power's failed in Two. Are you receiving?"

While he waited for a response, a strange light began to flicker off the tunnel walls. It caught his eye and he turned to find its source: a bright light in the distance. As he watched, it split to become two lights; the headlights of an enormous mining truck, approaching fast, its bulk filling the whole tunnel, massive tires scraping the rock walls on either side.

Arkolov raised his eyebrows, bemused by the new development. The truck itself wasn't unusual. In the eight-lane Tunnel One, they passed him all the time, roaring along in the center lanes, always careful to give him a wide berth. But Tunnel Two was different. Its single lane was only intended for emergency use. In all the years he'd run this way, no truck had passed.

For a few moments, he stood, frozen in place. Then his training kicked in and he jogged toward the refuge, only a short distance away.

By the time he reached it, the truck was less than a quarter mile behind him, and gaining fast. He pressed the glowing door button. Nothing happened. Given the electrical failure, he wasn't surprised.

Next, he fumbled around in the dark until he found the door's manual control: a long metal handle. He tried to turn it. When it didn't budge, he tried again, putting all his weight into the movement, near wrenching his arm out of its socket. The handle snapped off. The door remained closed.

He looked up. The truck was only a few hundred yards away now, bearing down on him at speed, triggering a rain of dust to fall from the tunnel walls. Even if he sprinted, he wouldn't be able to make it to the next refuge.

Still, he didn't panic. There were other safeguards. When the infrared camera on the truck's cab detected his movement, it would engage the emergency brakes. A voice command would have the same effect. He waved his arms and shouted, "Stop," trying to trigger either of the safety systems.

A tsunami of dust rolled ahead of the truck, diffusing the headlight beams into a cloud of light. It didn't seem to be slowing, so he shouted again, "Stop immediately."

It roared closer. The noise of the truck went from a sound to a feeling, a bass rumble in his chest. He shielded his eyes from the headlight glare and lowered himself to the ground, safe in the knowledge that, even with a full load of ore, there would be plenty of clearance beneath the truck's body.

After he'd stretched out flat on the rock floor, he heard a change in the truck's engine note. Finally, he thought, assuming that the safety systems had detected his presence. But the truck was almost upon him. It was too late now.

A split second later, the truck's engine cut out. The sound was replaced by the squeal of brakes as the giant vehicle skidded along the rock floor, smoke rising from its tires. Dust swirled up around him, stinging his eyes.

When he'd blinked it away, he looked up. All he could see was the dark shape of the truck's body. It had come to a stop directly above him. The tunnel was completely and utterly silent.

A little nervous, despite the ample clearance, he began to crawl forward, eager to get out from under the truck. A second later, the truck's suspension lowered with a sudden hiss and crushed him.

A few minutes later, the suspension raised, the engine restarted and the truck accelerated away, headlights blazing a trail through the dust. Its cab was empty.

Below the cab, hidden in the shadows between the headlights was a logo: the silhouette of a miner holding up a golden pickaxe against a backdrop of stars.

Chapter 2

June 17
2091

Bozeman, Montana
(10 years earlier)

At first the black drone flew straight and level. Then it banked steeply, rolled, and descended in a flat spin toward the farmland below.

As the sun set, two figures crisscrossed the field. The first, Victor Rasmussen, a tall man with tangled hair, glowered at a mangled piece of wreckage as he threw it into his bag. The sticker on it read, "University of Montana and Universal Spacelines—Biopilot Project."

Maria Rasmussen strolled behind him, her jet-black hair blowing in the wind. She knelt to pick up a couple of plastic shards, placed them carefully into her bag, and continued on.

It was dark by the time they returned to their lab, a rusty shipping container on a patch of wasteland at the edge of Bozeman. A short airstrip had been cut into the long grass.

Victor dropped the bags of drone parts on the bench that ran along the right wall. "What now?" he asked.

"It needs more electrodes," Maria said.

"They'll still be connected to rat neurons, and it'll still crash," he said, exasperated.

"This isn't supposed to be easy. We have to be patient."

"We promised them a prototype two months ago," Victor said, as he began to sort through the parts, separating the salvageable from the shards.

"They'll wait," she said.

"The funding's run out."

"Already?" She frowned. "We'll have to ask for more."

"And tell them we blew their funding on an autopilot that can't fly. Good luck," he said. His hands clutched a section of wing.

Maria reddened. "It's getting better."

Victor's fingers whitened as they pressed against the wing's plastic. His words had a fierce intensity. "It's not good enough. If we want more funding, we'll have to show them something more." The plastic cracked. He dropped the piece to the bench. "Something perfect."

"That's impossible."

"With rat cells, maybe." Victor rolled up the sleeve of his sweater, exposing his bare skin. Then he held his arm out to her.

Maria stared at his arm in disbelief. He waited for her refusal. But she said nothing. Instead, she picked up the scalpel and looked him in the eye. He returned her gaze in silence, then winced as she slid the cold blade across his skin, scraping off a thin layer, and dropped it into a test tube. It dissolved into the cloudy liquid inside.

She dropped the tube into a slot on the white machine below the bench. "What if they find out?" she asked.

"They won't. And if it saves them money, they won't care," he replied.

The bioreactor whirred and drew the tube inside, while Maria gestured with her right hand, triggering a sensor in a metallic dot embedded in the skin below her right ear. The dot was a picoprojector, pico for short. It beamed a large display into the air, filling it with graphs and figures. At the top was a line of bold letters, "Time Remaining: Twenty-Two days."

Victor looked at the bioreactor and thought of the cells inside, his cells. Over the coming days, they would divide again and again. Then, prompted by the delicately engineered viruses within, they'd start their transformation into neurons. In every way but one, it was no different to how they'd done it before, but it felt strange. He felt light-headed.

As he put out a hand to steady himself, the fridge door hissed shut and he turned to see Maria holding a bottle of champagne in one hand.

"Happy anniversary," she said, smiling.

When he didn't react, she said, "Did you forget?"

"I'm sorry, I just..." He reached for something in the corner, hidden beneath the bench.

"It's okay. We've been busy," she said, unable to hide her disappointment.

He held something out to her. She stared blankly, then double-taked, noticing the neatly wrapped package.

"Happy anniversary," he said and kissed her softly.

Once she'd unwrapped the gift, her eyes widened in surprise. "Where did you get this?"

It was a hardback edition of Romeo and Juliet, bound in red leather and blocked in gold. The cover marked it as part of a limited run printed for the 500th anniversary of Shakespeare's birth.

He tapped his nose and winked. She laughed and began to leaf through the book, reading her favorite parts aloud while he watched and listened and laughed.

Afterward, they went outside. Victor set a fire while Maria poured champagne. Then the couple lay on a blanket beneath the starlit sky. They traced the courses of asteroids, stars, and satellites with their fingers, and spoke of their wedding as if it were only yesterday, wondering aloud where the four years had gone. But somehow their conversation always returned to the bioreactor and their hope, their excitement. This time, it had to work, they told each other, willing it to be true.

Chapter 3

July 9
2091

Bozeman

Victor watched his cells. They lined the bottom of a glass dish, drinking in nutrients and oxygen from the liquid that bubbled past.

Maria waved a yellow note in front of him. "What do you think?" she said.

On the note, in blue pen, was the name Adam. Victor said, "I like it. It, I mean he, needed a name."

After she'd pressed the note to the glass and stepped back to admire her handiwork, Victor put his arm around her. Maria turned to him. He nodded. She breathed deep and swept her hand through the air.

Six displays appeared. The largest showed the view from the drone's tail. The craft was flying straight and level, high above the fields.

Victor put his hand to the dish's thick metal base, felt behind it for the transmitter connection, found the switch with shaking fingers, and waited, while Maria checked and double-checked the figures on her displays.

She spoke in a hoarse whisper, "Ready."

He flicked the switch.

The only sounds were the whir of the water pump and the gurgle of the liquid swirling through the plastic tubes.

The drone wobbled. Then it rocked from side to side. Sweat trickled down Victor's back as he counted the seconds, waiting for the drop.

Instead, the wobble weakened to nothing and the drone flew on. Maria nudged him. She pointed to a display. Minute control adjustments scrolled down it. He grinned. But her expression suddenly darkened.

The drone's engines had just cut out. It swung into a steep left bank and dove toward the ground.

Victor lunged for the switch as the ground rushed up to meet the craft. Before he could reach it, Maria grabbed his wrist. He scowled. Then he looked up.

The drone had soared up into the sky, its engines back to full power. A stream of commands rushed down the display in an illegible blur.

They stood in awed silence as the craft approached a stall then recovered, banked sharply one way then the other, then performed a series of aerobatic maneuvers: corkscrewing, spinning, and looping.

Finally, it resumed level flight. Victor pulled Maria away from the displays, a manic grin on his face. She laughed and they ran out to the runway, peering into the bright blue sky.

A black dot appeared in the distance to the south and grew until it became the drone. It flew low over the field before making a lazy spiraling turn and coming in for a neat landing, rolling to a gentle stop a few feet from the couple.

Maria's hand clasped Victor's fingers so tight that it hurt. But he couldn't form the words to tell her. His mind was somewhere else. What else would Adam be capable of? He imagined new uses, new possibilities, the good they could do in the world. Adam could be more than just an autopilot. Adam could be anything they wanted.

Chapter 4

August 10
2091

Bozeman

The pico beeped, alerting him to a new email. Victor ignored it and continued to pore over the latest energy use projections. He sat, surrounded by paperwork, in a spot beside the container's metal doors. Maria worked at the other end of the lab, with Adam.

At first, they had shared the teaching duties. But as much as Victor cared for Adam, he didn't have the same rapport with their creation. Perhaps he wasn't a natural teacher. Perhaps they were too close, like siblings.

So now he planned, balancing power use, adjusting nutrient flows, and juggling credit cards, while Maria taught, bringing the world's knowledge to Adam.

A speaker crackled. Victor looked up from his work.

"What light through yonder window breaks? It is the east, and Juliet is the sun," said a voice, full of confidence.

It came from the twin speakers wired into the base of the glass dish, now half-filled by the gray-pink mass of cells. Maria sat on the mattress in front of it, holding up her red copy of Romeo and Juliet to the camera lens.

A rush of emotion bolted up Victor's spine. It was not so much the words that moved him as the realization that it was his cells, their creation, that spoke them, and the pride, pride in what they, what he and Maria had accomplished in such a short time.

He smiled, imagining the spaceline's reaction to an auto-pilot prototype that quoted Shakespeare. Then he gestured to open the email and his smile faded for good.

While he read and reread the words, and checked and rechecked the newsfeeds, Adam continued to speak. "Arise fair sun, and kill the envious moon, who is already sick and pale with grief, that thou her maid art far more fair than she: Be not her maid, since she is envious; Her vestal livery is but sick and green. And none but fools do wear it; cast it off. It is my lady, O, It is my love."

"Excellent, Adam," Maria said. "Now, what are your thoughts?"

Adam tilted his camera. "My thoughts?"

"Yes, why did Shakespeare use the image of the envious moon and the fair sun? Who is he referring to?"

Before Adam could answer, Victor stepped between them.

"What?" she said, a little irritated.

He gestured and the email appeared in front of her.

She read it. "But the contract—"

"They're bankrupt. It's all over the news."

He gestured again and the pico showed her the bailiffs swarming like ants over the shuttles at Missoula and the shell-shocked flight crews trying to hold back the tide. The owners, the ones that had been so keen on their project, were nowhere to be seen. Universal Spacelines was no more.

Chapter 5

August 22
2101

Missoula, Montana

The cold northerly wind blew wavelines into the pollution cloud that blanketed the valley, permanently smothering the sleeping city below, leaving only the tips of the sky-scrapers visible.

To the east of the hidden city, mansions speckled the hillsides. Outside their garden walls, gnarled trees and yellowing grass struggled for life.

Above the mansions, atop Mount Sentinel, the concrete hospital building glowed golden in the dawn light.

Inside, in a darkened corridor, a gaunt man with close-cropped hair and eyelids underscored by rings of shadow slept, his back toward one wall. It was Victor.

A robocleaner glided along, polishing the marble floor. It adjusted its course to avoid him, passing close to the other wall, a dark glass barrier that stretched from floor to ceiling. Behind the glass were hermetically sealed rooms, their interiors cloaked by darkness.

A number of items were laid out along the base of the glass wall: a red book, a wedding ring, a singed piece of paper, and three photographs in carved wooden frames. The photos showed Maria clad in hiking gear, arms aloft, snowcapped mountains filling the frame behind her; the shipping container lab at dawn; and, lastly, the two of them on a pebble beach, flanked by their wedding party.

Together, the keepsakes and the photographs formed a shrine. Each night, Victor would place them in careful order, before lighting a thick candle to burn through the night. Then he would lie in wait for sleep, his body desperate for rest, his mind drifting through the lonely hours.

Sometimes tiredness would triumph and he'd catch a few hours of restless sleep. In dreams, he'd run through a choking cloud, shouting her name. Then he'd wake in a cold sweat, convinced he was in the old house. Before opening his eyes, he'd reach out to touch Maria's arm and confirm her presence.

Instead, he'd feel the cruel touch of the marble floor and the steamroller panic. Fueled by dread, he'd stand and pace the darkened corridor, unable to stop for fear of being overtaken by the rush of whirling, maddening thoughts. But after the first few manic laps, his body would slow as the adrenaline subsided. Only then, as the tiredness rolled over him, could he lie back down and return to fitful sleep.

Every morning, at seven, his alarm would go off and he'd extinguish the candle, dismantle the shrine, return the objects to his bag, and surrender the corridor back to the robocleaner.

That morning, an alarm rang but it was an hour early. Victor woke with a start and gestured to silence it. After his gesture had no effect, he realized that the alarm sounded different. It was louder than usual. Confused, he clambered to his feet in a daze and scanned the corridor with tired eyes, looking for a nonexistent intruder. But, apart from the robocleaner making slow circles at the far end, the corridor was empty.

The rooms weren't. A cold fear swept over him. The rooms. The alarm could be coming from one of the rooms. A shiver juddered up his spine and sweat soaked his palms.

The glass wall had become transparent, backlit by bright lights in the doorless rooms behind the wall. In each of the rooms, a comatose body floated in a cloudy liquid, connected to a stack of machinery by a thick web of wires and tubes.

A display built into the glass gave a detailed readout of vital signs, together with the name of the patient. The name on the display opposite him was Maria Rasmussen.

Victor scanned her readings and breathed a sigh of relief. Maria's vital signs were normal, at least for her current situation. Her heart pumped five times a minute, circulating antifreeze-like fluid around frozen blood vessels.

His relief was replaced by guilt when he spotted the alarm's actual source: the room directly to his right. Its display was flashing an angry red. Inside, an old man lay still, the skin on his face Botox-taut.

As Victor watched, new text flashed up on the display: "Account Terminated. Code Fourteen–Non Payment. Shutdown in progress. Removal commencing in three, two, one." While the text scrolled, the wires and umbilical tubes disconnected from the old man's body, one by one.

Victor sprinted for the end of the corridor, passing the elevator's open door, taking the stairs two at a time and emerging into the stasis unit's opulent entrance hall.

Jim, the security guard, rested his leather work boots on top of a marble reception desk. He was watching baseball reruns on a large projection that floated in midair.

"One of the other patients is dying," Victor gasped.

"Yeah, the alarm goes off here too," Jim said, eyes still on the game, a slight smirk on his face.

"Does the doctor come in?" Victor asked.

"If they could be saved by a doctor, they wouldn't be here, would they? And if they've run out of money, what's left to interest a doctor anyway?" Jim said with a chuckle.

Victor recoiled a little and Jim looked across at him for the first time. "Hey, sorry, didn't mean anything by it. Mind's on the game." He pointed to the projection. Victor turned without replying and headed for the stairwell.

By the time he got back up to the old man's room, liquid had already begun to swirl down through a hole that had appeared in the floor. The body was being lowered through the same hole. The lights in the room had dimmed and the display was blank except for the time of death, neatly recorded to the hundredth of the second.

Victor shuddered. He knew he wouldn't get any more sleep that morning. So, after canceling his own alarm, he blew out the candle and packed it away with the rest of the shrine, leaving no trace of his presence on the marble floor. He took the elevator down, leaving Maria floating, blissfully unaware of her neighbor's passing.

As he passed through the reception area, Jim called out to him, "Hey."

"What?" Victor kept walking.

"The admin asked about you. Wanted to know if I'd seen you around," Jim said. Victor turned, interest piqued.

Jim continued, "I told her I hadn't seen you in years."

"Thanks. What's she want?"

"How'd I know? Why don't you come in office hours and ask her yourself?" Jim said, smiling. Victor returned the knowing smile, shaking his head. At the door, he pulled his coat in tight around him in a vain attempt to shield himself from the rush of freezing air.

But there was no escaping the wind. The hospital building did little to block the elements. It was particularly exposed, sitting as it did, on a manmade plateau cut into the mountaintop.

He put his head down, leaning into the wind. To his right, a cordoned-off parking zone filled most of the space between the building and the edge of the plateau. A row of odd-looking craft occupied the side closest to the hospital.

They were sail floats. Each had a small, open gondola suspended from cables that seemed to be hooked onto a hazy layer in the air itself. In fact, each patch of haze was a huge wing, gossamer thin and almost completely transparent. The wind was catching the wings, straining the steel stays that anchored each featherlight craft to the ground, sending a series of metallic twangs echoing across the plateau, toward the funicular station perched on its northern edge.

A tram waited at the station, its lights off. Victor shivered as he strode toward it, his mind's eye captured by his last view of the old man's face as it descended through the floor.

The image made him shudder. He'd never seen one of them go before. In truth, he'd never considered the possibility, focused as he was on fixes and cures, always next year, every year, always hopeful.

Lost in morbid thought, he hadn't noticed the parking zone's extra occupant: a squat black diesel flyer with a logo on its side, the silhouette of a miner holding up a golden pickaxe against a backdrop of stars.

Therefore, he didn't connect the dots when something bit his hand. He slapped it off and kept walking, missing the sight of the tiny robot mosquito falling to hit the concrete with a crackle and a spark.

Still rubbing his sore hand, he stepped aboard the tram, taking care to close the doors tightly behind him. After he turned a handle at the front of the darkened carriage, the lights flickered on and a large fan built into the window began to turn, sucking in the outside air through a blackened filter. An electric winch at the end of the track clanked and whirred, tightening the cable, allowing the tram to slink off downhill toward the hidden city below.

He picked one of the few seats that wasn't stained or ripped or both, and sat down, watching the hospital building disappear from view as the tram descended the wooded hillside, click-clacking along the rails, swaying with the wind.

At the halfway point, the other tram passed them, heading up, lights blazing from its empty interior. A little further down, they met the cloud-line and the morning light faded to white.

At first, the cloud was thin. The sky had disappeared but the gnarled trunks of dead trees were still visible outside. Once they descended further, the cloud thickened to a brownish smog and the trees vanished.

When they neared the valley floor, the track curved left to follow the southern bank of the Clark Fork River. Once fast flowing, it had been reduced to a muddy trickle flecked with polluted foam, its main flow diverted to quench the thirst of the factories.

After they'd crossed the stagnant water on a narrow steel bridge and dropped the final few feet into the station, Victor pulled a breathing mask from his pocket. As they came to a stop, he held the mask to his face, pressing down until it melded to his features. The mask's ventilation system started with a whistle and a roar.

With only the glow of the carriage lights and the weak mask headlight to guide the way, he strode out into the wall of smog. Like all clouders, he'd memorized the unseen hazards, the buildings, the drop-offs, the potholes, and the sharp corners; but he still moved with a light step, ready to dodge the unexpected.

Halfway along the station platform, he stopped, straining to hear something over the sound of his mask. But the only sound was a low rumble somewhere in the cloud above him. Victor ignored it. He was searching for something else, a missing sound: the sound of the factories, the constant hum that had backed each waking moment since he'd arrived in Missoula. The near silence unsettled him.

Chapter 6

High above Victor, the black diesel flyer rumbled through the cloud. With its stumpy wings and bulbous fuselage, it looked like an oversized bumblebee.

Three figures sat inside its cabin, clad in dark blue uniforms that bore the same silhouetted logo as the one on the outside of the flyer.

Corporal Samuel "Sam" Bielański sat in the copilot's seat, his legs bent awkwardly to fit. He was taking a silver weapon apart, piece by piece, cleaning and polishing each one before putting it away inside a wooden case. The case had a slot for each part. Above those slots were ten smaller holes that held the weapon's unusual ammunition, nine tiny robotic mosquitos. One was missing.

A shaven-headed man, Sergeant Gabriel "Rabbit" Evans, sat behind Sam. His right eye was modified, the eyeball covered by a metal lens. Its silver shutter was closed but his other eye was open, watching the woman in the pilot's seat.

A grinning skull, part of the tattoo on the back of her neck, stared back at him from between thick dreadlocks. Below it were the words, "Légion Étrangère."

The woman's name was Lieutenant Delomie "Del" Campbell. She gripped the flyer's controls and peered out into the cloud. Occasionally she'd gesture with her hand to trigger changes on the projected instrument panel.

One projection showed a map of Missoula, with Victor's location pinpointed by a flashing red dot, along with a detailed readout of his vital signs and speed of movement. Another display showed an infrared view of the land below, centered on Victor as he unlocked the chains that secured his bicycle to the fence outside the station.

As Del watched him start to cycle down the slight incline toward the city, she felt a sudden rush of adrenaline. It brought back memories of other such rushes, huddled in rusty transport planes on sweat-drenched tropical nights, waiting for the signal, the drop through darkness, and the nerve-jangling night vision creep to the target. At the time, it had felt like a waking nightmare. Now, she'd give anything to be back there.

Following a bike through a cloud was no real substitute but at least it beat their usual work, shadowing delivery rocket arrivals and trudging around headquarters, following too-dull-to-assassinate executives, feeling like shooting the place up herself for a bit of excitement.

She would make the most of this while it lasted, she thought, as she unplugged the autopilot and took over manual control of the flyer, dipping its nose and accelerating to follow the speeding bicycle, watching for any sign that Victor had noticed their presence.

He seemed oblivious. She shook her head. Typical belowclouder. They thought they were invisible. The truth was that no one cared enough to see them, unless they burgled a mansion or stole a flyer.

Emboldened, she took them lower still, skimming over the rooftops of Missoula's ramshackle main street, past the neon lights of the remaining shops, the pawnbrokers, electrical wholesalers, and tattoo parlors that still eked out a semilegal living belowcloud.

She banked to follow as Victor swung left off the main drag, heading down toward the river.

"We going to pick him up?" Rabbit asked, interrupting her vigil.

"We'll see where he ends up first," she said, watching closely as Victor chained his bike and climbed the fire stairs at the back of the old Wilma theater building, now a vertical slum, a landmark for belowclouders.

When he entered a corridor on the fifth floor, the signal disappeared abruptly, the infrared distorted by the thick brick walls. Cursing her overconfidence in the technology, Del put the flyer into a low hover and considered her next move.

"What now?" Rabbit said, unhelpfully.

"We'll have to take a closer look," she said. And, still furious with herself, she manhandled the craft into a rushed landing on a street by the river.

A few minutes later, three shadows left the flyer and disappeared into the cloud.

Chapter 7

By the time Victor woke from his second sleep, it was early afternoon. He stretched and rose from the bare mattress on the floor and headed for the tiny bathroom, squeezing past the wall of cardboard storage boxes on the way. They were piled five high, occupying the majority of the already cramped apartment's floor space. One was marked with the letter V. The rest were all marked with the letter M.

After he'd wolfed down a late lunch of instant rice, Victor descended to the ground floor, paying no attention to Sam when they passed on the stairs.

He entered the theater through the stage door and walked along a smoky corridor, passing the open doors of dressing rooms. In some, there were hunched figures sharing bubbling pipes. They didn't look up as he passed.

After the corridor, he reached a backstage bar, where hostesses applied makeup and sipped drinks, awaiting the arrival of their regulars. The brothel madam, Minh, an older lady, sat behind the bar. She looked up from her bookwork.

Victor waved, then continued through the backstage maze until his way was blocked by a thick curtain. He slipped past it and entered the robot repair shop that occupied the theater's foyer.

He looked around, surprised. To his left, where the theater's long bar had been converted into individual workstations, there were three workers, each deep in concentration, solder smoke wisping above their heads. On an ordinary day, there would be twenty workers at the bar and a long line queuing, waiting for a spot to become free. It was unusually quiet today.

To his right, Minh's husband, Quan, sat in his regular seat in the ticket booth. They exchanged greetings in Vietnamese. Then there was a moment of silence before Quan frowned awkwardly and said, "I only have this today," passing him a work order, printed on dot matrix paper. "I saved it for you."

Victor read the work order. It was for a malfunctioning cleaning robot. The cleaning bots, the drinks dispensers, the autolaundries, they were an important side business for the shop, but the repairs were usually left for the least capable workers. Sadly, despite his efforts to improve, that group included Victor.

He looked at Quan. "Thanks for saving this, but—" He paused, trying to think of a tactful way to ask where the other jobs were. On an ordinary day, he would fix anywhere from five to fifteen bots.

"I had to share the jobs. The factories are on a shutdown," Quan said, anticipating his reaction.

"Why?" Victor asked.

"I heard no metal."

"No metal?"

"No metal. Metal comes back, factory reopens, work comes back," Quan shrugged, looking apologetic.

The robot factories provided the shop's main income. Their complex production lines were prone to problems. Officially, the giant assembly robots were repaired in-house by the factories' maintenance departments. Unofficially, the maintenance supervisors had worked out that it was easier and, more importantly, cheaper to send the errant machinery to Quan's shop for the fix.

Victor returned Quan's shrug and went to the storeroom to find the cleaning bot. As he wheeled it back to one of the workstations, he thought about the factory closures. The bosses would be desperate to get the production lines moving again. The factories would restart tomorrow or the day after. The work would return. The hospital would just have to wait a little longer for their money. He wasn't all that worried.

Focusing on the task at hand, he picked up a metal monocle from the bar and pressed it to his left eye. It suctioned itself into place. Then he picked up something else, a tool. It was a titanium-tipped microcutter, valuable enough to be attached to the bar with a steel chain. The tool's light carbon fiber body held the cutting blade, tapered to an edge too fine to be seen with the naked eye.

Victor slipped his right hand into the cutter's handle. It molded itself to his skin automatically, blurring the boundary between body and tool. With his other hand, he opened the top panel on the bot, revealing a solid black circuit board with no visible circuits.

He shut his right eye and opened his left. His surroundings disappeared, replaced by the monocle's filtered vision, centered on the circuit board. As he gestured with his left hand, the monocle zoomed and focused. Once the lens reached half zoom, something changed. The circuit board wasn't black anymore. What had first appeared as solid color was in fact a web of fine wires that crisscrossed the board.

He zoomed further, then stopped, and began to scan the circuits, searching for the source of the robot's problem. While he scanned, his head stayed dead still. Instead, the monocle shifted a few microns with each slight gesture from his hand.

As he worked, the hustle and bustle of the repair shop, the smoke and the chatter, the female newsreader on the projection above him, all faded to black. The monocle had become eye and the microcutter, hand. In these moments, his worries disappeared.

His view continued to move from area to area, up wire capillaries to complex junctions, checking connections, looking for errors. After twenty minutes' careful searching, he found the offending section: a frayed ending with burned insulation, ugliness surrounded by cold perfection.

With studied elegance, using only gesture control, he began to cut out the offending section of wire. While he made the cut, the newsreader on the projection continued to speak. Then one word stood out amid the Vietnamese. That word was "Metis."

With the sound of the word, Victor's head snapped upward and his hand slipped, cutting across a whole swath of wiring, leaving a trail of microscopic destruction.

He didn't notice. He'd pulled the monocle from his eye and transferred his concentration to the projection as it cut from the newsreader to an establishing shot of the tallest building in Missoula, a skyscraper that speared up out of the cloud. A logo was emblazoned on its very top. It was the silhouette of a miner holding up a golden pickaxe against a backdrop of stars. The newsfeed's next shot showed two men facing the camera from behind a curved glass table inside a conference room. The same logo filled the wall behind them.

Chapter 8

As Graham stared out at the sea of reporters, sweat beaded on the back of his neck. This was out of his comfort zone. It brought back school play memories, the forgotten lines and the blank stares of the waiting audience.

Felix, the thin-faced man sitting next to him, sipped from his water glass and scanned the crowded room, raising a finger to acknowledge familiar reporters.

A tapping sound caused a few of them to look around the room, trying to work out who had the faulty microphone. Felix turned to Graham instead, first glancing down at his foot, then back up at him.

Graham realized that the sound was his foot tapping on the ground. Embarrassed, he stopped, then wiped his sweaty palms on his trouser legs. As he did so, a PR man by the door signaled them. It was time.

He cleared his throat and waited for the hubbub in the room to quiet, then looked down at his script. It had been carefully prepared, just not by him. It blurred. He blinked, confused, his mind scrambling for an explanation, painfully aware that all of the reporters were staring right at him now. As the camera lights blazed and the walls closed in, he finally worked it out, making a gesture with his hand to switch his contact lenses into reading mode. The text came into merciful focus.

"Welcome to Pharix Mining Headquarters. Thank you for coming. My name is Graham Stone. I'm the head of operations at Pharix Space Mining." He pointed to the man on his left, "And this is Felix Bain, CEO of the Pharix Mining group."

He paused to let the information sink in, then continued, feeling a little more confident, on a roll of sorts, starting to enjoy the attention a little.

"Over the last few days, various rumors have been appearing in news media. We've called this press conference to dispel them. Rumors of our demise are much exaggerated." He felt smug, proud of his deviation, despite the confused expressions on the reporters' faces.

A sharp look from Felix sent Graham back to the script. He said, "However, we are experiencing minor supply chain issues. Moving forward, we anticipate the full restoration of platinum supply in the next few days."

He turned the page. Belatedly, he realized that there was no page underneath, so he stopped abruptly and looked out blankly at the media.

Assuming it was time for questions, one of the reporters said, "My sources tell me you've been unable to contact the mine for ten days. Is that correct?"

"Well, the actual situation is very fluid but—"

Felix interrupted before he could finish. "Your sources are mistaken. We have been in full communication with our operatives on Metis."

"Is the issue related to the computer?" another reporter asked. Felix turned to Graham, waiting for an answer.

Graham took a deep breath. This was his moment. "It is a supply chain issue; the computer has been assisting us with diagnostics and repairs."

"What is the exact issue?" the reporter asked.

"Unfortunately, that's commercially sensitive information that we're unable to divulge at this time. Our customers can rest assured that the situation is under control and production will be restored as soon as possible," he said.

Felix gave the slightest nod of approval and said, "That'll be all, thank you for your time."

Ignoring the barrage of further questions, they exited through a side door into a wide corridor. Its walls and floor displayed ever-shifting views from exotic locations.

A Himalayan valley dissolved into a Tahitian beach as Graham said, "They know we're hiding something," and tried to ignore the view, despite the fact that it was only his second visit to the top floor in fifteen years at Pharix.

Felix strode ahead, paying no attention to his surroundings. "I don't care about those bottom feeders. I've had calls from the big fish: Van der Veld, Raj Prax, Dana Yang. They're suspicious but they can't get domestic production back online for at least a month. They've got no choice but to wait for us."

"Don't worry. It won't take a month to fix," Graham said triumphantly.

"We're paying six hundred million in nondelivery penalties every day," Felix said, as they headed for a carved wooden door at the end of the corridor. Graham couldn't think of a suitable reply so he stayed silent.

Inside Felix's office, fish tanks covered every inch of the walls, masking the cloud-filled valley outside. Felix climbed a stepladder and scattered food into one of them.

A ringing sound filled the room. The dot below Graham's ear buzzed and projected floating text into the air in front of him: "Incoming call. Lieutenant Campbell." Del's stern face appeared behind the text. He gestured and her face was replaced by more text: "call rejected." After a few seconds it disappeared.

"Sorry," Graham said. But Felix didn't respond. He'd come down the ladder but he was still watching the fish; he didn't seem to have noticed the call.

Once the fish had finished their meal, Felix turned to him. "We've got a week until head office cut us off. They'll liquidate the whole mining division and sell the parts to the highest bidder. Do you think the new owners will keep us on? Have you done enough? A week ago, you told me this was a minor glitch and you had it under control. What's your man doing up there?"

"We haven't been able to communicate with him since the metal supply cut off," he said, his palms sweating again.

"Has your team arrived yet?" Felix asked, his face deceptively calm.

"My team?" Graham said.

Felix slammed his hand on the glass of the tank, scattering the fish. "You've not sent anyone?"

"I couldn't justify the cost. We've been focusing on restoring communications."

"Send a team. Who do we have who can work with the computer?" Felix said.

"No one," Graham replied.

Felix paced the perimeter of the room. "What about the designers? Aren't they on retainer? If not, I suppose this could fall under warranty?"

Graham frowned. "They no longer work for us. One's in the hospital, permanently. The other could be of assistance. We're still trying to locate him. He's disappeared. No job. No address."

"He's dead?" Felix tapped on the glass, startling a large flatfish.

"No, he's paying his wife's hospital bills from a bank in Missoula."

"This is our city. You'll find him," Felix said.

"We have our best team on it. It's just a matter of time."

"You don't have time. Your team will leave for Metis tomorrow morning. Find him by then. Then he can go with you."

"With me? You misunderstood. I'm not going to Metis. I'm needed here. Someone needs to supervise operations."

Felix clapped him on the shoulder. "You're right. I'll handle things down here. This is your problem. Go to Metis. Fix your problem." He grinned, baring his teeth. Graham nodded, indicating agreement where none seemed to be required.

Felix continued, "Keep your team small. I don't want the other transnats finding out. They've been waiting years for an opportunity like this. Go."

Graham left, wiping his sweaty hands on his suit pants as soon as he was out of sight. Once he got back to his own office, five levels below, he returned Del's call. Her face appeared on a projection. She was at the controls of the flyer.

"What is it?" he asked.

"We've found him," she said. "We traced him home from the hospital. He's been visiting after hours."

"Where is he?" Graham started to grab his stuff, preparing to leave.

"Belowcloud," she said, and he raised his eyebrows. "You want us to pick him up?"

He said, "No, pick me up. I'll come to him."

Chapter 9

Long after the newsfeed had moved on to other stories, Victor sat still and silent, deep in thought.

Eventually, after several false starts, two cups of tea, and three of Quan's clove cigarettes, he managed to calm his nerves, and return to the repair.

Once he'd fixed the damage he'd caused, finished the original repair, and sent the boxy cleaning bot rolling noisily back into the storeroom, he checked the clock above the bar. It was four thirty-five, much later than he'd expected. He had to be at the hospital soon.

Before leaving, he collected his pay. Quan handed him the envelope and said, "As soon as the factories open, we'll have work for you."

"It's okay," Victor replied. "It's not your fault." He pointed at the newsfeed before retracing his steps backstage, walking quickly, head down, conscious of the time, eager to get back abovecloud, to the waiting corridor, and Maria.

Once, in an attempt to return to an approximation of normality, he'd tried to stay at the apartment instead, but after a few restless hours sweating through memories on the lonely mattress, he'd given up. If he was to be haunted by the past wherever he slept, he'd rather be close to her, not belowcloud.

Up there was where he had to be, at least until the cure, the elusive cure that, despite the doctor's assurances, never came within reach. There was always another regulatory issue, another holdup, another false dawn, but he kept the faith, and did his best to keep paying the hospital bills.

Once he got back to the apartment, he put his pay with the rest of his cash, hidden behind one of the storage boxes. The time was four forty, not quite time to leave yet.

Technically, visiting hours were three to five. To start with, he had followed the rules. But Jim had taken pity on him and let him stay for longer; first an hour, then a few hours, then overnight. They'd stuck to that arrangement for years now.

Each night, at five, Jim would start the night shift, and Darini, the hospital admin, would leave. At five fifteen, Victor would arrive, checking for the telltale flicker of the sports news before entering the building.

That night, he left his apartment at four forty-five to make the half-hour journey abovecloud. As he descended the fire stairs, he ignored the figure seated on the bottom step, assuming it was just an inebriated local mustering up the will to attempt the climb.

Then the figure said, "It's been a long time, Victor."

Victor's head jerked round. At first, he didn't know who it was. Then he looked past the layer of fat to the familiar features underneath. It was Graham.

"Leave me alone." Victor kept walking, past his bike, toward the front of the theater.

He heard Graham following behind him and the words, "That's no way to greet an old friend."

"You're no old friend. Why are you here?" Victor quickened his pace.

Graham jogged to catch him up. "I should ask you the same question. I knew you'd fallen on hard times but belowcloud? I'm not sure about your new line of work either.

Unlicensed roboengineering. One phone call and they'd be shut down."

"If the metal doesn't come back soon, you won't have to bother." He turned the corner and passed under the old sign that still adorned the theater frontage, rusting and half hidden by cloud.

"The metal is why I'm here. I have an opportunity that I'd like to discuss with you. An opportunity for you to deal with a better class of business associate," Graham said.

"If you're referring to anyone at Pharix then I doubt that. At least down here, they look you in the eye when they stab you," Victor said, scowling. Then he stopped. His path was blocked by the diesel flyer. It blocked the whole street, idling noisily, exhausts belching black fumes.

Graham laughed. "Let us give you a ride to the hospital. We can discuss the proposal on the way."

"No." He hurried away, aiming for the gap between the back of the flyer and a shopfront. Sam blocked his path, weapon in hand. When he turned to walk in the other direction, Rabbit appeared out of the cloud, smiling with polite menace.

Victor sighed, raised his hands in surrender and trudged back toward the flyer. Graham opened the door, still smiling. The other two followed them in.

Sam slammed the door and Del pushed the thrust lever forward. The engine roared as she sent the flyer chugging up through the cloud.

Rabbit and Sam took their usual seats and tried to pretend they weren't eavesdropping on the two men behind them.

Graham shouted above the engine noise, "We have an issue on Metis."

"I know. I saw the news. What's going on?" Victor said, curious despite himself.

"We've lost communication."

"That's unfortunate. What's it got to do with me?"

"We need an expert to assist us," Graham said.

"No chance."

"Mistakes were made on both sides."

Victor's voice started to crack. "You ditched us. You left me to deal with... everything."

"We're a business, not a charity. The contract was very generous. What more could we have done?" Graham said.

"It was our work, our property," Victor shouted, far louder than was necessary to be heard above the engine noise.

"You signed the contract. You sold it."

"Bullshit," Victor said, with finality, as the flyer cleared the cloud layer and soared into the clearer air above the city.

"Enough," Graham said, "We want to resolve things. Our terms are very generous. You'll have the best team that we can provide. We need someone up there that knows the computer."

"Haven't you got any other computer experts?" he said, confused.

"It's your computer."

"What do you mean? My computer?"

"Adam," Graham said, as if stating the obvious.

It wasn't obvious to Victor. He felt the color drain from his cheeks. After a moment he said, "He's alive?"

"Of course. Why wouldn't he be?"

Victor could think of a few reasons. He was almost too shocked to speak but when he did, he spoke firmly, with more conviction than he felt. "I'm still not going up there."

"You've been before."

"Once was enough."

"Don't tell me you're not curious. Adam's grown up since you last saw him. Don't you want to see what's become of your creation?"

Of course he did. But he didn't say that. Instead, he said, "Not my creation. My wife's creation. Your property now. Your business. I'm not interested. Find someone else." Then he sat silent, scowling at Graham as the flyer dropped gently onto the ground outside the hospital.

Del opened the door and checked the surroundings, weapon in hand. Then she returned to her seat.

Victor stood up, ready to leave. Graham blocked the exit with his hand and said, "I'll mail you the offer. Think it over. You could buy a lot of hospital time with that money... How's she doing by the way? Are they any closer to a treatment?"

Victor shoved Graham aside, jumped out of the flyer and strode toward the hospital without looking back. Graham's shouted words followed him, "The shuttle leaves tomorrow morning. With or without you."

He marched toward the entrance, lost in thought, passing a sleek yellow sail float. Just before he reached the entrance door, he stopped, realizing his mistake. It was five minutes to five. That was Darini's yellow sail float and that swish was the sound of the entrance door to the reception area sliding open. He spun on his heel and retraced his steps, heading toward the funicular.

As he walked, he heard Darini's heels click-clacking across the plaza behind him and he put his head down, trying to hide his face from view.

He hoped she hadn't seen him. It would spoil his plan if she saw him now. He would prefer to wait until her emails had moved past friendly requests for payment to threats of cancellation and termination. Then and only then, would he hire a suit and saunter in, professing innocence about the fees, before wheedling them down to a payment plan option. After all, half of the stasis rooms were empty. Unless they were all reserved for future deaths, business was slow. Surely, they would let things slide a little to retain his business.

It was all under control, so long as Darini didn't spot him. He sped up as much as he could without drawing attention to himself. Finally, as he hid on the funicular platform, he heard the click-clack sound stop as she reached her flyer, then the twang of her sail float's stays releasing.

After a few minutes, he felt it was safe, so he looked round and, to his relief, saw the yellow float soaring into the sky, heading toward a cluster of mansions on another hill. He had hoped that the Pharix flyer would also have departed but it still idled on the ground, its door closed, dim light shining from inside, its occupants no doubt puzzling over his movements.

He entered the hospital a minute or so later, passing Jim, who hadn't even had time to switch on the sports news. Jim raised his eyebrows. "She only just left. You can't cut it this fine."

"I know. It won't happen again, believe me," Victor said.

As he took the elevator up, he felt the building shake as the flyer departed, and he took a deep breath, trying to compose himself. The unexpected meeting with Graham had shaken him more than the close call with Darini. Seeing them on the newsfeed had been enough contact. Face to face was too much. And the security. You knew you were in a mining city when the company security forced you into a flyer at gunpoint.

In the corridor, he slipped into his routine, placing the shrine and lighting the candle, but he couldn't sleep. Adam was still alive. He could hardly believe it. Of course, Graham could be lying, but why would they need him to go if not for Adam, up there, alive. What would he be like now? What had he been doing all these years? Victor had so many questions but he knew the answer. It didn't matter what Adam was doing. He couldn't go back there. He couldn't leave Maria on her own.

Chapter 10

When the lights came on, Victor awoke, unaware that it was
still dark outside. There were no alarms that morning, just
the familiar sound of the cleaning bot, but he still rushed
to gather his things, worried that he'd overslept.

Bleary eyed and half asleep, he made his way to the elevator. The display inside told him it was five thirty. He
breathed a sigh of relief. The lighting had come on early
for some reason. He decided to leave anyway. It was only
an hour before his usual departure time, and he wouldn't
get more sleep now that the lights were on.

He strolled past the reception desk and waved to Jim.
Then he stopped dead, the color draining from his face. Jim
wasn't behind the desk. Instead, the heavily made-up face
of Darini, the admin, faced him with a false smile. "Good
morning," she said.

"Good morning," he replied awkwardly and retreated
toward the exit. As he approached, Jim moved out from his
position by the door, blocking the way. Victor looked him
in the eye. Jim shook his head.

"I came in early today to talk with you. We have an important matter to discuss," Darini said.

He glanced at the door again, wondering if he should run.
Surely Jim would let him pass or at least not try too hard

to stop him. But what would happen next? How would he visit again? He decided to stay put for the moment.

"We've recently audited our billing system. Your account is in arrears. The total amount outstanding is one million, five hundred thousand and forty-five." Darini touched the desk and a fingerprint interface appeared on the surface. "We require immediate payment."

The nausea rolled over Victor. His legs felt weak, but he took a breath and held his nerve. He had prepared for this day. Like he planned, he would brazen it out.

He put his index finger on the reader, willing his hands to stop shaking. Text appeared: "Account declined." Victor went through the motions, trying each and every finger on both hands, ignoring Darini's skeptical expression. Each attempt triggered the same message: "Account declined."

He looked her in the eye and spoke in a measured tone, "I don't seem to have the funds to pay the lump sum at the moment, but I can pay regularly. I have been paying regularly. I'll try to get the whole payment together but I just need a little more time. Perhaps we can set up some kind of payment plan in the meantime?" He waited to hear her offer and prepared for the inevitable negotiation.

Instead, she said, "We aren't a charity. We cannot give you the room indefinitely, regardless of your past payment history. Do you have a guaranteed source of income?"

He stayed silent. This was not part of his plan.

"How about extra work? Do you have any other potential source of income?" Darini said, a knowing look in her eye.

Victor didn't reply. He had a sinking feeling in his gut, the feeling of a prison escapee tapped on the shoulder by the law.

She continued, "In light of your past financial record, we're prepared to give you a day's grace to enable you to organize your financial affairs and explore other options, but if the arrears aren't settled by close of business tomorrow, we'll have to shut down your account and repurpose the space for another customer. There's a waiting list."

"You can't just shut her down," he said, looking for sympathy in her eyes and finding none.

"As I said, we're not a charity. As per the existing rules, you won't be able to visit while your account is in arrears. I also need to remind you that visiting overnight is strictly prohibited. I hope we can retain your business," she said, then waited for him to leave.

Victor didn't move. He'd spotted something on the wall behind her, the name and logo of the hospital's owner, Advanced Medical Industries. He pointed up at the sign and said, "Who are they?"

"Sorry sir, I don't understand," she said, her voice tense.

"Who owns the hospital?"

"I believe it's a consortium of several transnats."

"Is Pharix one of them?"

"I'm not sure. I can check for you if you like," she said, her composure cracking a little.

"Don't bother." He left, refusing to acknowledge the sympathetic look that Jim gave him.

Outside, the air was still. The sun wasn't up yet. Victor traipsed across the plaza to the funicular, struggling to put one foot in front of the other, though his face showed no emotion.

He waited until the funicular had passed the halfway mark before letting loose, screaming and shouting, punching and kicking at the seats. Then he lay on the carriage's dirt-encrusted floor and shut his eyes before breaking out into short, sharp sobs. The inevitability of what he had to do became clear, and, as he sat on the floor with his back against the carriage door and a wave of nausea rising in his throat, Victor tapped the spot below his ear and spoke the words, "Call Graham Stone."

Chapter 11

December 10
2091

Bozeman

Snow settled on the laboratory's roof, which was now three containers wide. Flakes also landed on the solar array, which had grown to cover a good portion of the field. But instead of settling, they melted and ran off in little streams, courtesy of the deicing fluid sprayed from a system of rusty irrigation pipes.

There was a knock on the door. Victor opened it to a thin-faced man in an expensive suit. The man seemed unfazed by the long slog through the snow. Victor looked for the Bible and found none. "Yes?" he said, confused.

"Felix Bain," the man said, shaking Victor's hand with unnecessary force. "Can I come in?" He entered without waiting for a response. "I went to MIT with one of your professors, Harmison. He thinks we should fund you."

"We?" Victor said, curiosity piqued.

Felix passed him a business card. It read: "Dr. Felix Bain. Chief Operating Officer, Pharix Space Mining."

Victor said, "Space Mining. I don't—"

"We run the platinum mine on Metis. We've got four mark sevens assisting operations, and about twenty thousand staff. It's wasteful." Felix spat out the last word. "We need to automate. Harmison says your experiment can assist."

"Well, Adam is certainly capable," he said.

"Adam?" Felix asked.

Victor ignored the question. "But I, we, don't want to put twenty thousand people out of work."

"We'd retrench the majority. You can't hold back progress. Just think, once your invention is proven on Metis, you can license it to, well, every government and every company in every country on Earth. It could change the world. And you'd be well compensated." Felix smiled encouragingly.

"Yes, there's costs, that's the problem. He keeps growing and we don't have the funds to—"

Felix waved a hand dismissively. "We'd cover all of that. Obviously, you'll need a little time to organize things here." His eyes surveyed the office. Victor followed his gaze, embarrassed by the mess. The surfaces were strewn with bills and other paperwork. Maria, Adam, and the rest of the lab equipment were nowhere to be seen.

"I'll have to speak to my wife," he said.

"Of course. And I'll have to see the experiment," Felix said, as they put on full-length chemsuits.

Victor let Felix through the biolock first. On the other side of the lock, in the new section of the lab, was Adam's glass container, now the size of a paddling pool. Projections filled the air around it. Maria turned to face Felix.

"You finally replaced your suit." She laughed and moved toward the visitor, about to hug him. Her grin disappeared when she saw the unfamiliar face through the mask. She stepped back. "Who are you?"

Felix stepped forward, business card in hand. "I'm from Pharix Space Mining. Harmison told me about the unfortunate situation with the spaceline. It's sadly all too common with these start…" He trailed off. Maria had turned back to the projections. Felix pursed his lips, unused to being ignored.

Victor emerged from the biolock. "So you've met Felix, he's from—"

"Pharix Space Mining. I know." She rolled her eyes.

"I'd just like him to meet Adam, show him the merchandise, so to speak," Victor said, immediately regretting his choice of words.

Maria frowned. "I'm about to run a simulation. Nineteen sixty-two again."

"How'd he do last time?" Victor said.

"He struggled with the Russian generals' factionalism, but we've done more targeted research and discussed a few strategy options. Of course, there's no guarantee I won't change the variables again." She smiled.

The graphs above Adam showed full bandwidth usage on the fiber connection, as always. Sometimes they'd sample the feed out of voyeuristic curiosity. It would jump between subjects with incredible speed, from ragtime to geology to astrophysics in just a few seconds.

"I'm ready," Adam said. He was always listening.

"Okay, let's go." She tapped a finger to the air. More projections popped into existence. She waved her arms like an orchestral conductor, displaying maps, variables, names, and scrolling lists of Adam's commands.

While the Cuban missile crisis played out on the projections at speed, a day passing every minute, Felix watched, dumbfounded.

After the simulation had finished, Maria and Adam debriefed in low whispers.

Outside, Felix shook Victor's hand. "Impressive. I'll get finance to send an offer."

"I think you misunderstood. We're not selling Adam. We'll build a custom version for the mine."

"If it can resolve nuclear confrontations, a few truck movements will be child's play. We don't have time for special orders. Our offer's for that computer. Take it or leave it." Felix strode away through the snow.

When Victor returned to the lab, Maria was waiting.

"We're not selling Adam," she said, after he'd told her.

"He won't wait for us to build another."

Maria tossed Felix's card in the trash. "Too bad."

Victor sighed and pulled open the bottom drawer of the filing cabinet. He handed the sheets of paper to her: the bills, the overdue notices, and the final demands. At first, he watched her read, watched her expression change. When he couldn't stand it anymore, he went outside, out into the freezing air.

He stared out at the whiteness of the field until his teeth chattered and his whole body shook from the cold, caught between sudden bursts of fury at his own failure and the wave of melancholy that rolled over him every time he thought of the future that they'd planned so carefully.

Footsteps crunched in the snow behind him. Then Maria rested her head on his shoulder.

"Did he like Adam?" she asked.

"He was very impressed. Adam did well. Even after that trick you pulled with JFK's chopper accident." Victor grinned.

"That wasn't an accident. And it wasn't me," Maria said.

Victor's eyes widened.

"He tried something different. I've already spoken to him." Maria shivered.

"He did very well," Victor said.

Chapter 12

March 14
2092

Missoula

A glint in the sky above the spaceport signaled another arrival. A black diesel flyer buzzed around the metal delivery rocket as it floated down through the haze and bumped to a landing on a white X marked on the tarmac.

The rockets landed on the hour, every hour, regular as clockwork. The amount of platinum inside them varied from half full to none.

A huge transport plane sat on the tarmac, the Pharix Space Mining logo on its tail. Its cargo door was open. Workers were loading a shiny new shipping container into the hold.

Victor stood in the entrance to a hangar, watching the workers, feeling detached from the whole process.

A raised voice behind him jolted him out of his reverie. It was coming from the other end of the hangar, from the small office.

Maria stood in the doorway. While he watched, she threw her hands up and stormed outside. He rushed to follow, passing the office door. Graham sat at the desk, looking bewildered.

"What did you say to her?" Victor snapped.

Graham's face was flushed. "I thought you'd explained the contract to her."

"I haven't had a chance to," Victor said. Actually, he'd had plenty. It was his turn to sweat.

A series of twangs caught their attention. He swore and raced toward the side door but it was too late. Her sail float was a hundred feet up and rising fast.

He jumped into his own float and scrambled to release the stays. It sprung into the air, its sail urging it upward.

After he'd gained a little height, he banked left and began to climb a strong thermal rising from the neighboring field. His eyes searched for her float. Then he spotted it, a black speck, five hundred feet above him in the same thermal. His float soared in pursuit, climbing a thousand feet a minute.

He stared upward, ignoring the floats and flyers that cluttered the rest of the sky. Then the other craft stalled a little and dropped to meet him.

Now they moved in equal spirals, climbing in unison. They were above the height of Mount Sentinel now, above the new hospital building with its plaza full of people.

Below, the city blurred amid the haze created by smoke billowing from the factory chimneys on the river's southern bank. The plumes twisted around the cluster of skyscrapers in the new development to the west.

They banked and dropped into a steep dive toward the opposite hillside. Victor's float shook violently. He gripped the gondola with his left hand while guiding the controls gently with his right. Without looking, he knew the other float would be diving alongside him, racing him home.

He pulled a lever, flipping the spoiler out of the back edge of the wing, disrupting the airflow and bleeding off the speed. As his float dropped gently toward the hillside, toward a cluster of huge mansions, he looked up. The other float was already on the ground.

After he'd landed neatly on the manicured artificial lawn behind a concrete and glass mansion, he dragged the float toward the house and attached it to a concrete anchor. She was watching him in silence from the patio at the rear of the house, her jet-black hair billowing in the wind, her brown eyes glistening.

He held his hands up in surrender.

"What else did you keep from me?" she shouted over the wind.

"It's just the legals. The contract's flexible. Nothing's stopping us staying longer than the three months," he replied, moving close to her.

She stepped back. "I'm not leaving him up there."

"I got us the best deal possible," he said, unconvinced now.

Before he could go on, she pressed her finger to the reader on the glass wall and moved inside. Victor followed her into their shiny, barely used kitchen. "He's got to be independent, he's not a child."

"He doesn't understand the world yet," she said in a half whisper as she headed for the stairs.

He shouted after her, "That fiber's been on for months. He's read everything. He knows this world, warts and all."

She stopped on the stairs and turned to look him in the eye. "I trusted you," she said, then continued up.

Before she closed the bedroom door, she said, "Go back down. Go supervise things. It's your plan. I need some time to think." Her eyes were cold.

He stood by the closed door. The control freak in him itched to leave, to check on the preparations for departure.

Instead, he took a beer from the fridge and sat on the white sofa, ignoring the whirring brushes of the cleaning bot as it erased their light footprints from the tiled floor.

He stared out through the glass at the city below, watching as the sun dropped close to the hills, sending diffused golden light over the Missoula valley. Even the brutal concrete of the robotics factories glowed with a heavenly light.

After half an hour, he climbed the stairs. Without speaking, he knocked on the bedroom door. The lock clicked open.

Maria was sitting on the edge of the bed, looking out at the valley below as the sun dropped below the hills, swathing Missoula in shadow, transforming the scene from gold to dark gray black. In the center, the river flowed past factories belching fumes.

"I'm sorry," he said. Then he paused, gathering his thoughts. "I was just trying to get the best deal for us and Adam. They wanted us off Metis in a week. They've got their own tech people. They don't see the need for us." He stopped, then sighed. "I should've told you before we signed, I just couldn't find the right time. It's all happened so quick."

"I know. But we can't keep rushing," Maria said as he sat down beside her. She paused before continuing softly, "I know that we needed this deal. Believe me, I tried to find another way. You did your best." As she spoke, she moved closer to him, reaching out to intertwine her hand with his. It was shaking with emotion. "We have the money to build our own company, to change the world. But I can't just leave him up there. Alone."

He met her eyes, seeing the pain within the words.

"He's still fragile. He's not ready," she said.

"What do you mean?" he said, puzzled.

There was a silence. She looked away. "It's nothing. He has to go."

She leaned in and kissed him gently on the cheek.

He hugged her tightly. "Forget the three months. We'll stay as long as it takes."

Maria nodded gravely. Then she looked at the darkened valley below. "Shall we?"

She stood and pulled Victor to his feet. He did his best to hide his churning emotions, for he'd been dealing much more closely with Pharix, allowing Maria to concentrate on Adam. He had gotten to know the company. If Graham, Felix, and the other administrators were any measure of the ones that ran the mine on Metis, their time there would be a deeply unpleasant experience. But he didn't tell her that. He just followed her outside. And together they glided down to the dark city below.

Chapter 13

March 16
2092

Metis

Inside the elevator, built for thousands of tons of freight, there was only a shipping container, and alongside it, Victor and Maria. As the elevator rose from the spaceport to Metis's interior, neither of them spoke. They were tired. It had been two long days since they'd departed Vancouver, full of nervous excitement.

When their huge lift car had docked at the first floating station, three thousand feet above the city, Victor had been every bit the curious scientist, watching fascinated as their car was switched to another cable for the ascent to the second station. Four hours later, when they'd reached the sixth of the twenty or so cable switches, the novelty of the experience had worn off.

After the long final lift to the top station, all he had wanted was a rest from travel, a few hours in a bed. Instead, they'd boarded the windowless freighter, and he'd spent eleven hours drifting in and out of sleep in an uncomfortable seat, his body confused by the missing gravity.

It had been strange to feel the weight of near full G again once they'd landed on Metis. Victor was just wondering how there could be gravity on an asteroid, and why they were ascending from the spaceport to the interior, instead of vice versa, when the elevator slowed and stopped, and the door opened, revealing a huge tunnel, its twelve-lane roadway bathed in artificial light.

In the outbound lanes, a golf cart-like vehicle was parked alongside a truck. Two men stood beside the cart. The taller of the two, a bald man with a thick red beard, looked up, noticing their arrival. He shouted something to the truck driver, then beckoned them over.

"Mackenzie Fraser, call me Mack," the bearded man said, in a thick Australian accent. He shook their hands in turn. Then he pointed to the shorter man next to him, who wore a neatly pressed blue uniform, "And this is David Arkolov, we call him Arkolov."

Arkolov scowled as he shook their hands. Then Mack gestured toward the cart.

"What about Adam?" Maria said.

Mack pointed to the truck, which was backing up toward the elevator, preparing to load Adam's container. "They'll be right behind us."

As he accelerated the vehicle along the tunnel, Mack said, "I'm the operations manager on Metis, Arkolov's in charge of the Tech department. You'll be dealing with him a lot."

"I expect you'll be wanting to get back on the next freighter, though," Arkolov said.

"Actually, our contract's for three months, and we can stay longer if we need to," Maria said.

Arkolov lapsed into silence for a few seconds, then looked at Mack.

Mack said, "We were told you would need a few weeks at most. Will it really take three months to set up a computer?"

"Adam is a little more than a computer," Maria said, taken aback.

"What's Adam stand for?" Mack said. "They didn't tell us."

"It doesn't stand for anything, it's his name," Maria said.

Arkolov looked incredulous. "His name? It's a computer."

Victor glanced toward Maria. Her face was red. Before she could respond to Arkolov, he said, "There seems to have been a miscommunication. Adam performs the functions of an ordinary supercomputer, and more in fact, but he is, well, more than just a computer. He was grown from living cells and is in many ways more human than computer."

Mack said, "Adam sounds fascinating. I'm very much looking forward to having my first conversation with him."

Arkolov said nothing. He still seemed baffled by the whole concept of Adam.

"What exactly did headquarters tell you about the new computer?" Maria said.

"We got a short briefing from Graham Stone last week. We were told to expect a new computing machine to assist our existing supercomputers...which Arkolov's team so ably manage." Mack looked across at Arkolov and smiled indulgently. Then he continued. "They didn't specify the exact nature of the computer. They just gave us some power use estimates."

"So you weren't given any information about the specific areas that Adam would assist with?" Victor said.

"No," Mack said. "Were you?"

Victor spoke quickly before Maria could reply. "No, they were very vague. I suppose now that they've paid for the technology, they don't want any information leaking about what they're using it for." He shifted nervously in his seat, sure that Mack had noticed his own eagerness to talk for Maria.

Mack's next question made that obvious. He said, "So Maria, what do you think Adam's capable of? What areas could he assist in? For example, could he help with running the truck network and other transport, scheduling the drivers and all that?"

Maria's face lit up. "Well, I think he's capable of just about anything. With his capacity for multithread processing, he's probably capable of running the whole mine."

She paused for breath, then rushed on. "Not straight away, of course. He'll need a few months to settle in first. He could definitely work in driver scheduling, but I think with a bit of training and practice, he could probably run the trucks themselves. He's an excellent pilot, so I can't see why he wouldn't be able to drive well. It's one of the first skills he learned." Seeing the expression on Mack's face, she stopped abruptly. "Sorry, did I say something wrong?"

Yes, thought Victor, cursing his own negligence. He should have anticipated this. He should have warned her.

"No, no, it's just a lot to take in. Adam isn't quite what we expected." Mack stopped the cart at a crossroads controlled by traffic lights. Directly ahead was an unlit single-lane tunnel. To either side was another broad tunnel, eight lanes wide.

After a huge mining truck roared past, their light went green, and they made a left turn, into the rightmost lane of the four.

For the remainder of the journey, no one spoke. Maria dozed and Victor watched the giant mining trucks that passed every few seconds, marveling at their size.

"Here we are," Mack said, after they'd turned right, into a side tunnel. Their way was blocked by a metal barrier within a concrete archway. A guard lifted the barrier and they moved on at slow speed. Above them, an array of cameras swiveled to watch their movement.

Arkolov said, "We take security very seriously in this department. These are state-of-the-art machines." His voice swelled with pride as he pointed out the three cavern entrances on their left.

Each of them was sealed with a huge glass door. A display on each door showed the operating statistics for the computers inside and the temperature. Above each display was the name of the computer. The first was "Archimedes," the second "Aristotle," and the third "Socrates."

"You into your ancient Greeks?" Victor said.

Arkolov looked confused.

"The computer names. They're named after ancient Greeks," Victor continued, wishing he hadn't said anything.

"Oh, the names. Yes, of course. We didn't name them. The manufacturer did. I don't really agree with the anthropomorphism but the names help for parts and admin. Easier to order a capacitor relay for Archimedes, than computer 614-8," Arkolov snorted.

Victor smiled weakly as Mack stopped the cart next to a group of workers in blue uniforms: Arkolov's technicians. They'd reached the end of the tunnel. To their left was the last cavern. The door was open. Leftover fixings on the walls and floors showed that the last occupant had not long been removed. Two marks on the wall showed where the nameplate had been.

Arkolov looked at the blank space wistfully, then spoke to Victor. "What temperature do you need? They didn't tell us."

As the truck carrying the shipping container stopped behind them, Victor looked at Maria. She said, "We've never been temperature-controlled before. We ran quite a small operation back home and Adam didn't seem to mind any temperature. I suppose I can ask him for his preference."

Arkolov looked at his technicians, raising his eyebrows. One of them smirked back.

"Just set it to the default," Victor said, a little embarrassed. "Then once Adam's settled in, we'll wire him up directly to the climate control, let him set it himself."

"I'm not sure if we can do that," Arkolov said. "There'll have to be restrictions on what he has access to, for security reasons, you understand."

"What do you mean?" Maria said.

"I mean, there's twenty thousand men and women who rely on our systems to move them around, to provide air to breathe, water to drink, food to eat, and security," Arkolov said, puffing his chest out. Then he continued, in a lower, more serious tone, "We can't just give your computer access to all the life support systems. Things will have to be firewalled."

Before Maria could reply, Mack stepped in. "We're not quite prepared security-wise but if you bear with us, we'll have things ready as soon as we can."

Victor nodded. He understood. Arkolov was cautious. He just needed to see Adam in action, that was all. After that, things would be much easier. He said, "No problem at all. I'm sure once you get to know Adam and his way of working, you'll understand that he doesn't pose any security threat."

The technicians wheeled Adam's container out of the shipping container and into the empty cavern.

Victor inspected the space, spotting the thick water hose and the bundle of power cables. "Where's the fiber connection?" he asked.

"Like I said, we can't give access without security checks." Arkolov looked to Mack for support. Mack said nothing.

"If he's got no access to the mine's data, how's Adam meant to improve things?" Maria said.

Arkolov looked to Mack again. Mack said, "Can you set up the connection so that it's inbound only?"

Arkolov gave a slight nod.

Mack said, "Okay, do that," then turned to Victor and Maria. "Once we've clarified things with headquarters and completed the security checks, we'll see what Adam can assist us with. I'm sure he'll be a great asset to the mine."

Chapter 14

August 23
2101

Missoula

The battered ethanol burner roared along the highway. Minh dozed in the back. Quan drove. Victor sat next to him, watching the cloud swirl around them, wishing he were back in the corridor. The only sound was the whine of their mask filters.

They turned off the interstate. Victor noticed that Minh's eyes were open now, watching. Her stare unsettled him. But neither of them spoke.

The road widened. They were still the only vehicle. Then something loomed out of the cloud. Quan slammed on the brakes and swerved around the Pharix flyer, which had been parked right in the middle of the road. It appeared to be empty. It was.

They pulled into the taxi rank. Quan switched the engine off. Victor didn't move. There was a moment's silence.

"We'll visit her," Minh said softly.

Victor felt the sudden cold fear again, the dread. "No, you don't—"

"We will." She touched his shoulder. Quan nodded. His face was stern. He started the engine and Victor reached for the door, stepped out, and head down, walked toward the spaceport, fighting back tears.

After he'd wiped his eyes, he turned to wave. But the car had already disappeared.

Ahead was the vast terminal building. Its sheer glass frontage rose into the clouds. As he looked up, someone tapped him on the shoulder. Victor jumped.

It was Rabbit. As his eyemod whirred back into its socket, he said, "Del didn't think you'd turn up. Graham guaranteed it, what's he got on you?"

"Too much," Victor muttered.

Rabbit wasn't listening. He tapped his pico, saying, "He's here," before gesturing to Victor with exaggerated politeness. "Follow me, please."

A set of doors slid open silently as they approached the building. The cavernous interior was sealed from the outside atmosphere but unlit. Signs advertising long-forgotten spacelines hung loosely from the ceiling. Rows of empty check-in desks filled the back wall. No staff could be seen anywhere.

They passed beneath a large advert for Universal Spacelines, and through a door marked "Port Authority Staff only," out into a corridor. It led through a series of unattended security checkpoints to a door marked, "Danger. Airside Area." Rabbit strode out onto the tarmac and Victor rushed to follow.

The shape of the shuttle loomed out of the cloud. Victor recognized it immediately. It was a Boeing star class, a '64 model by the look of the swept wing. This would have to be one of the few left, he thought, wistful at the memories it evoked.

Once, he'd seen a model just like this one, coming off the production line at Everett, unpainted, its silver bodywork glinting in the sun. Victor had been watching from his father's shoulders as he'd explained which parts his team had worked on, listing its revolutionary features with great pride. He'd understood a few words in twenty but felt them all, pride swelling in his chest at the thought of his father having taken some part in the creation of such a beautiful, unthinkable machine.

His nostalgia faded when they got closer. He could see the shuttle Pegasus was no longer a winged beauty, more the weary old shire horse, her bodywork scarred and pitted from long slogs out to the asteroids and Luna—and re-entry after re-entry.

A dreadlocked figure emerged from the cloud. It was Del. Ignoring Victor's greeting, she began to pat him down without ceremony. He frowned but let her continue, noticing the thick scar on her left cheek for the first time. He knew better than to ask her where she'd got it.

After the pat down, she scanned him with a handheld device. It beeped when it detected the tracker in his hand. When she gestured, the metal sting extricated itself and dropped to the ground.

Graham appeared beside them. Del and Rabbit slipped away into the cloud. "Thank you for coming," Graham said.

Victor said, "You didn't give me much room for maneuver."

"We didn't have a choice. You are an essential part of this mission. You know Adam. You can help him to resolve the production problems."

"You didn't need my help before now."

"That was a mistake. I'd like to put the past behind us for the good of the mission and the good of Adam," Graham said.

"And the good of Pharix," Victor said.

"And the good of Pharix, of course. We are businessmen, after all."

"Above all," Victor said.

As they walked toward the shuttle, Graham said, "The deal still stands. I have already contacted the hospital. Your billing issue has been resolved."

"And six months paid," Victor said.

"As agreed. I hope your wife will make a full recovery."

"Thanks," he said, as they passed the open cargo door. Inside, the copilot, a petite woman with bright red hair cropped into a pixie cut, was loading the last of the large storage containers into the cargo hold. Her name was Celeste Morton.

Victor followed Graham onto the shuttle, into the cramped passenger cabin. There were four rows of seats.

A bearded man stretched out in the back row, his bald head resting on his bag, eyes closed.

"This is Mack Fraser," Graham said.

Mack opened his eyes. At first he looked a little startled, then he smiled.

Victor returned the smile, instantly recognizing him. Mack's beard was graying but aside from a few extra wrinkles, his features hadn't changed. "We've met," he said, happy to see a familiar face, especially one he was so fond of.

Mack sat up. His smile faded. "We were all so sad to hear what happened with your wife." There was a strange contrast between his rugged appearance and his soft-spoken words.

Victor bowed his head, his smile also gone, the weight of the years back on his shoulders. "It's good to see you again, Mack," he said, then took a seat in the third row. A faded safety instruction card fell out of the seat pocket. Victor picked it up. Someone had scrawled "Don't Panic" in red ink over one of the pictures.

The security team took over the row in front, putting their headphones in, settling in to their own worlds. Sam was watching a football game on a projection. Del had a pile of ammunition boxes in front of her. She was opening them one by one and counting the cartridges. Rabbit was zooming his eyemod in and out, using a dropper to oil the moving parts, and cleaning the excess with a cloth he'd carefully unfolded.

They made Victor nervous. He didn't trust the security team. He definitely didn't trust Pharix. Already, he couldn't wait for the mission to be over. Why hadn't they left yet?

He found the reason outside. On the tarmac, half hidden by cloud, the two pilots spoke with the ground manager.

Chapter 15

The launch cart supported the shuttle's fuselage, in place of the retracted landing gear. Celeste regarded the rusty cart with a critical eye. She frowned. "Taka. We can't use that."

Takeshi "Taka" Endo, a ponytailed Okinawan, stood beside her, wearing his crumpled captain's uniform. He shrugged.

A voice came from behind them. "You needn't worry. This cart'll hold. It's the tube you want to worry about." It was the caretaker, a wizened old man. He grinned, exposing a mix of brown teeth and bare gums.

"You've been maintaining it?" Celeste said.

"Of course, but I wasn't expecting anyone to use it, see," the old man replied.

Before she could ask another question, Taka said, "So long as you think it'll hold. We'll only need it the once. Is the fuel done?"

"Topped up and ready, sir," the old man said, rounding off with an ironic salute while Celeste fumed.

Taka returned the salute. "Alright. We'll go in five."

"Aye, just give me the signal," the old man said, before climbing into his tractor. It coughed, sputtered, started, and settled into a chugging rhythm.

"Celeste. You ready?" Taka said, as they watched the tractor maneuver to attach to the launch cart.

She sighed and gave him the thumbs-up.

"To the stars!" He grinned and jogged up the stairs, heading straight into the cockpit without a second glance at the passengers. Celeste laughed and followed.

While she waited for the stairs to fold away, she heard a sharp whisper behind her. "You didn't tell me he was coming, I can't do this."

It was Mack. He and Graham stood in the corner of the cabin, out of earshot of the other passengers.

Graham smirked. "You know, I just can't think of any reason why his presence would bother you."

The cabin door locked into place. Celeste headed for the cockpit. But Mack blocked her path.

He grabbed her arm, a pleading look in his eyes. "I need to get out."

She pushed past without a word. She'd taken him for an old miner. He should know better than to get in the crew's way.

As she locked the cockpit door, she heard Graham say, "Looks like you're stuck with us now, Mack. No time for cold feet."

Inside the cockpit, there was an anachronistic mixture of high-tech displays, ancient gauges, broken switches, and rusty metal. Taka sat near the front. Celeste was further back, crowded by computing equipment, her sleeves rolled up, revealing her tattoos, thick-lined Polynesian designs that twisted around her forearms. She scanned checklists, scribbled notes on flight plan paperwork, then flicked switches, checked readings, and thumped flickering navigation displays.

The tractor pushed the shuttle along a taxiway at ponderous speed, moving parallel to the main runway. But instead of turning onto the runway, they went the other way, crossing the remains of the old perimeter road, then passing a row of abandoned houses.

To the left, an area of dead grass marked what was left of the old railway alignment, the rails long gone. To the right was a surprising view—a shiny silver tube, fifty feet across.

The cart's wheels slid into deep grooves in the tube's floor. The old man backed the tractor out and a door rose to block off the tunnel end, leaving them in darkness.

"Passengers prepare for takeoff." Celeste's voice crackled through the PA system, as a low hum grew in volume.

The shuttle and cart began to hover ever so slightly. The lights came on, illuminating the tube ahead. At first, the cloudy air limited visibility. Then the view cleared as unseen fans removed the air, leaving only shiny metal walls that stretched into the distance.

The sound of the magnets built to a deafening bass hum. The cart jolted then stopped, then jolted again and raced forward.

A map next to her showed their progress. The tube tracked the old railway east-south-east, skirting the northern edge of Missoula, then climbing at a steady ten-degree angle, burrowing into the mountainside. They moved quickly across the chart, eating up the miles.

But Celeste wasn't looking at the chart. Her gaze was fixed on the projection, watching the cart, watching it shake and shudder and still hold together somehow.

A tiny circle of blue sky appeared ahead as the doors at the far end opened, sending air rushing into the tube. The shuttle's twin rocket engines started with a throaty rumble that drowned out the magnets.

The engine note built to an earsplitting roar, the exhausts spewing out flame, filling the space behind them with smoke. Full power. The shuttle shook with the force.

Inside the cockpit, warning lights flashed and alarms blared. She elbowed the panel next to her to shut them off.

The end of the tube protruded above the mountaintop, supported by huge metal girders, like a rollercoaster track.

A few roe deer ran for cover as the shuttle shot out of the end, rocketing up into the blue sky, shaking the hills to their foundations.

She gestured, blowing away the bolts that attached the cart, then glanced at the rear camera, expecting to see it gliding back toward Missoula. Instead, the joins finally failed and it smashed into the hillside.

On the other camera feed, the passengers huddled back into their seats as the shuttle hustled itself toward orbit, threatening to shake itself apart in the process, the lighting fixtures wobbling, the chairs clanking. She noticed that the shaven-headed security man had gone white and was clutching his armrests in terror. The older miner was asleep. The tech in the third row just stared out of the window, ignoring his surroundings.

A few minutes later, when the gravity had weakened to nothing, she watched Taka undo his seatbelt, light a cigarette, and float up into the air, doing a slow backward roll. Midroll, he turned his head to wink at her. She held his gaze, missing the message that flashed up on her chart display. It said, "Destination location error. Adjusting course to compensate."

Chapter 16

Ahead, through the shuttle's windscreen, was Metis, the asteroid, their destination, over a hundred miles in diameter.

A broad solar array encircled its entire equator. The panels on the sunlit side glittered and glinted like a million camera flashes as the shuttle passed.

Victor watched the asteroid spin beneath them as they crossed the line between light and dark, entered the sun shadow, and began to skim low over the rocky surface, following its curvature.

The main engines cut out, the reversing thrusters fired, and the shuttle slowed toward the asteroid's spin, until they were overflying the rocks at a relative speed of only a few hundred miles an hour.

It appeared as though they were approaching a jet-black sea, rather than a surface scarred by thousands of tiny meteors and a few huge impacts.

When they flew over the rim of one of those impact craters, their bright landing lights triggered a thousand reflecting twinkles from the wide expanse of solar paneling.

The shuttle shook violently as a puff from a thruster sent it rotating. Once the roof faced the surface, the opposite thruster fired, stopping the rotation dead. Victor's stomach kept moving.

He watched through the window as the rocky surface flashed by above his head. It seemed so close. He breathed deep. Perhaps this was the reason for the lack of windows on the freighter. He had preferred the freighter.

In front of him, Del was attempting to explain their unusual approach to Rabbit and Sam.

She held up one of the safety cards. On the back of it was a rough drawing of a merry-go-round with arrows pointing outward. "The asteroid spins. Just like a fairground ride," she said.

Sam scratched the bullet scar above his ear and frowned.

Rabbit leaned forward, and zoomed his eyemod, as if he thought the concept would become clearer the closer he got.

Del battled on valiantly. "So when you're inside, it's trying to push you out. That centrifugal force feels just like gravity. And once you're inside, you wouldn't know any different." She received two blank looks for her trouble.

"I still don't get why we're upside down," Rabbit said.

Before Del could continue her attempt at a lesson, Victor interrupted. "It's best not to worry about it. Like she said, once we're inside, it won't matter."

He spotted a flicker of anger on her face, but it passed. He smiled at her. "This is why the freighters had no windows."

"Exactly." Del sighed.

Victor saw Mack's wry smile. No doubt he'd heard the same explanations and seen the same confused looks hundreds of times.

Something else caught Victor's eye. Far to his left, a long plume of blue flame streaked out from a high tower, spearing up hundreds of feet into the air, one of a pair of huge ion engines. As he'd found out in their original induction years earlier, the engines had initially been used to send Metis on its long journey to Earth orbit, then to produce the artificial spin, and in recent years, for infrequent orbital adjustments.

He realized that Mack was looking out the window too, transfixed by the flame. He caught his eye.

Mack was shaking his head in amazement. "I've never seen a full burn before. I didn't know we still did them."

They lost sight of the flame as the shuttle dipped closer to the surface, heading toward the spaceport, a steel structure that appeared to be floating high above the crater's center.

In fact, it hung from the asteroid by a cable, pushed out by the force of the asteroid's spin, the centrifugal force that Del had tried and failed to explain. The cable was formed of the same nanotube material as the space elevator, light and incredibly strong.

The spaceport itself was built around the end of the cable in an octagonal shape. Eight prongs radiated from the central anchor. Each one had its own landing area.

As they approached, the bow thruster fired again, slowing the shuttle to a crawl, a few miles an hour faster than spin speed.

With the stars below and the rocky surface above, they came in for a neat landing. Their arrival unsettled a thick layer of rock dust, sending a cloud billowing up around them, hiding the asteroid above from view.

Chapter 17

Victor stood in the shuttle's cargo bay, clad in a light flight suit, his helmet on, a small oxygen tank attached to his arm. The tank only held an hour's supply but they wouldn't need anything like that much. The elevator was only a few minutes' walk away.

He looked around the huge space, far larger than the passenger cabin. On one side, the security team's vehicle, an armored jeep that bristled with weaponry, idled, ready to go, Sam at the controls. Victor had the sudden realization that this vehicle would have cost Pharix far more than six months' worth of hospital bills. I should have held out for more, he thought.

Rabbit and Del stood beside the vehicle, clad in heavy-duty military suits, ammunition belts on, guns in holsters, looking armed and ready for action. Victor wouldn't have admitted it to Graham, but now they were here, he felt a little safer having the military-style backup, even though he didn't see the need for the firepower.

Mack stood a little way away, looking uncomfortable in an ill-fitting suit that showed the roundness of his belly. He held no weapon.

Graham stood near the security team, in a shiny new suit, state-of-the-art, a clear genoplastic helmet molded to his head. Victor noticed a slight smirk on Celeste's face as she looked at Graham's suit. Then, with a grinding, scraping sound that faded to silence as the air rushed out, the cargo bay doors opened.

After Taka had wandered off to check the engines, Celeste waved the vehicle out. It clunked down the ramp onto the dusty concrete floor, sending up another huge cloud of dust. The others followed in its wake.

Del looked around the shuttle suspiciously, never off guard. Rabbit walked with his head down, trying to ignore the asteroid surface above his head. Graham sauntered out like he owned the place, followed by Mack, then Victor.

Victor surveyed his surroundings. To his left was the end of the spaceport, and the stars beyond, tracking across the sky as the asteroid spun. To his right, a series of overhead gantries marked the different lanes for queuing vehicles and pedestrians for the elevators at the center of the spaceport.

A wide lane on the left led to the central freight elevator. Its door took up the whole width of their arm of the space-port. A narrow lane on the right sloped to a level above, slightly closer to the surface, that accessed the smaller pedestrian elevators.

A cloud of dust blocked Victor's view, as Sam flung the armored jeep into a series of doughnuts and skids. Victor could see Del shouting something into her suit mic. She was using a different channel but he could guess what she was saying. Sam brought the vehicle to a halt next to the shuttle, then got out, looking sheepish.

Victor joined Graham beside the freight elevator. A camera above the door swiveled slowly to track his movement.

Graham was trying to work the security terminal on the wall. First, he wiped the dust from the screen, then, real-izing it was blank, he tapped buttons, and knocked on the metal casing, all in vain. Out of ideas, he said, "Open the door please."

Victor heard the pleading tone through his helmet radio and laughed. Arkolov hadn't responded to their calls before, so there was no chance that he was monitoring the radio now. He stopped laughing when a voice boomed inside his helmet, uncomfortably loud, broadcasting on the general channel, "Welcome to Metis," it said. The dialect was hard to place, somewhere between received pronunciation and Canadian.

Victor recognized it immediately. He would never forget that voice.

Mack and Celeste had heard the transmission. They came over to join them. The security team continued to check their vehicle. They were either unable to hear it, or just disinterested.

Graham replied to the voice before Victor could gather his thoughts. "Adam, I presume?"

"Mr. Stone. This is an unexpected surprise. I wasn't expecting any visitors. What is your purpose?" Adam asked, lowering his voice to a tolerable volume.

"Deliveries have stopped. Communication's down. We're getting concerned on Earth," Graham said.

The reply came in a measured tone, the syllables rolling smoothly into their radio earpieces. "That's understandable, but I have the situation fully under control."

"What is the situation?" Graham said, unfolding his arms, relaxing a little.

"Unfortunately, there was an attempt at sabotage. David Arkolov damaged the production and communication systems as well as the main vehicle elevator."

"Arkolov? Why? Where is he now?" Graham sputtered.

"I'm unable to establish the exact reason for his actions, but I suspect that the prolonged time alone here may be to blame. As to his current location, I cannot be sure. He hitched a ride on an unlicensed lunar shuttle a week ago. I expect he has returned to Earth."

"Why didn't you stop him?"

"That option was considered but I wasn't sure of the protocol."

Graham said, "How long until production comes back?"

"Approximately forty-five hours. Communications should be back within fifty-six hours."

"Can we be of assistance?" Graham said.

"Your assistance won't be required."

After that, Graham was silent for a few moments. Victor watched him, knowing that he was trying to judge whether he'd done enough to save his job.

"If you want to wait until the fix is complete, and communications with Earth come back, you are more than welcome to come in and wait in the accommodation block. It's a little rundown but..."

Graham said, "No, no, that won't be—"

"Yes, we'll do that," Mack interrupted.

Graham scowled but he didn't contradict Mack, unwilling to argue while Adam listened.

Adam said, "Yes, yes, you are most welcome. Unfortunately, the vehicle elevator is still under repair so you'll have to use one of the crew ones."

"That's fine. Thank you, Adam," Graham said.

"I'll need a list of your names for my visitor records," Adam said.

Celeste answered first. "Celeste Morton."

"You're coming in with us?" Mack said.

"Yes," she said, leaving no room for argument.

Graham said, "And there's me, Mack Fraser, Del Campbell, Sam Bielański, Gabriel Evans, and Victor..." He trailed off.

"Victor," Adam said softly. "Victor Rasmussen?"

No one else spoke. Eventually, Victor said, "Yes," and all of the cameras around the elevator swiveled to face him.

"It's good to see you again," Adam said.

"I'm sorry it's been so long." Victor felt a sudden swell of emotion and paused. He had so much more to say. But where to start?

Graham's voice interrupted his train of thought. "Okay. I'm sure you're busy. Thanks for your help."

"I'll continue the repairs. All the pedestrian elevators are available for your use," Adam said.

While Victor watched the cameras above them, Graham called the shuttle.

Taka's response came after a long pause. "Receiving."

"I need you to pass a message on to Felix Bain, directly. Don't contact Pharix control. I'd prefer they weren't made aware of our presence here."

"Okay. I'll get hold of Felix Bain, directly. What's the message?" Taka said.

"David Arkolov has sabotaged mining operations and returned to Earth on a clipper. He needs to be brought to justice. Also, tell him production should be back within...a week. We'll be staying on Metis until then."

"Received and understood. I'll call right away."

"Thanks," Graham said, then he tried to radio Del, unsuccessfully at first. He flicked through channel after channel until he reached hers. "We're using the passenger elevator. Take what you can carry and leave the vehicle on the shuttle," he said.

"We need the vehicle," replied Del.

"The freight elevator's busted," Graham said.

"I'm not going in without it," she said firmly.

"Stay out here then and forfeit your pay. Arkolov's gone. There's no one else in there. We don't need it."

Del considered her options, realized she had none, and turned to the rest of her team. "You heard the paymaster. Retrieve your weapons and anything else you want to lug around. We'll put the vehicle back."

Victor waited with Graham and Mack while the security team restowed their vehicle and rushed around gathering supplies.

When Taka finished his checks and went to return inside, Celeste didn't follow.

"What you waiting for, Cel?" Taka said.

"They said I can go with them," she said.

"And?"

"You mind if I go? Or do you want to go, and I'll look after this?"

"Go. I'll hold the fort. I'm a flyer, not a burrower." Taka regarded the elevator door with suspicion.

"Okay, see you later then," she said.

"Don't get lost." Taka waved and closed the cargo bay doors.

She jogged to catch up with the rest of the team, as they made their way up the ramp toward the passenger elevator, led by Graham.

At the top of the ramp, the door was already open. Inside, there were twelve rows of twenty seats each, arranged like cinema seating, facing the wall to the left.

The team filed in, seating themselves in the back row. Victor sat in the middle, in between Graham and Mack. Only Del remained standing, looking around suspiciously, as the elevator door slid along its track, jamming a couple of times before sliding across and closing tight.

After the door had closed, three huge fans built into the roof began to whir and draw oxygenated air in from the asteroid above them. A green light came on by the door.

Mack spotted the light and flicked a valve on his tank, switching the oxygen flow off. The others followed his example. Del was the last, checking and rechecking her own suit's display first.

A screen rolled down the far wall. A holographic figure appeared in front of it, frozen in midair and flickering.

The hologram was a tanned man in a neat suit with bright white teeth. The screen behind him showed the Pharix Mining logo on a black background. He said, "Welcome to Metis, a Pharix Mining Corporation-operated mine. During your journey up, please allow me to take a few moments of your time to convey some important safety messages."

Victor yawned. He'd caught an hour's sleep on the shuttle flight but he was still tired.

The presenter continued, saying, "Remember the mine can be a dangerous environment. We encourage all workers and visitors to be mine-safe. The mine has the highest-quality safety features. There's an automated lighting system."

The screen behind the presenter showed a pool of light following a group of miners as they walked along one of the accommodation corridors.

"The backup generation system makes power failure unlikely but portable emergency lights are located in many locations across the complex."

The screen showed a glass box marked "Chemlights," mounted on a tunnel wall. It contained a series of long torch-like objects. A smiling miner broke the box open and flicked a switch on one of them. Bright light beamed out.

"In the unlikely event of a fire, temporary oxygen venting may reduce the atmospheric oxygen. Emergency oxygen is available."

Another box was shown, marked "Emergency Oxygen." The same smiling miner opened the box and grabbed an oxygen tank backpack and attached mouthpiece. He put it on, took a breath and gave a thumbs-up to the camera.

"We provide the best safety equipment available but we still require you to use common sense. Be cautious. Heavy trucks operate throughout the mine."

A pedestrian light went green and a group of miners crossed a tunnel. A gigantic truck idled, waiting for them to pass.

"You will be further briefed by the health and safety representatives in your assigned department."

Workers monitored a bank of complex displays in a control room, supervising a refining process, ignoring the camera's presence.

The presenter continued, "Metis is the most advanced mine in the solar system, thanks to the skilled workers that make it all possible, the best miners in the system, Pharix miners."

The screen showed a crowd surrounding a gleaming metal sculpture, one that Victor hadn't seen before. It depicted a group of miners holding pickaxes. The sign beneath it read, "Welcome to Metis."

The presenter said, "Once again, welcome to Metis, a Pharix Mining facility. Enjoy your stay and just remember, be mine-safe."

The image of the miners flickered and disappeared. The elevator slowed to a juddering halt and the door opened with a groan. Beyond the door was darkness.

Chapter 18

Del and the rest of the security team were first to the elevator's open doorway. They stopped there, waiting for the lights to come on.

Mack walked straight past them, out into the blackness. As he did so, the lighting came on, illuminating the long, narrow tunnel ahead. It had been cut out of the rock, with no concrete lining. A thick layer of dust covered the floor. He took his helmet off, breathed deeply, and continued on. As he walked, he disturbed the dust, and it hid him from view. "Come on. There's nothing to be scared of," he said. His voice echoed off the tunnel walls.

The security team moved forward cautiously. Graham, Celeste, and Victor followed. The door slid shut behind them.

A layer of gray dust settled on their suits and helmets as they walked on like specters through the cloud. The sound of Mack's coughing could be heard somewhere ahead. From the sound, Victor guessed that Mack had been too stubborn to put his helmet back on.

After a few minutes' walk, the tunnel joined three others and widened, curving to the right, eventually emerging into a larger space, the size of the terminal at Missoula.

As they passed the desks and queue lines for processing and accommodation assignment, Victor stopped and looked through the glass wall to his right. Through its dusty patina, he could see the vehicle elevator and the staging area for waiting vehicles, nine lanes wide, directly in front of him. The space was empty, only illuminated by the faint light that spilled through the glass. The door to the elevator was open, revealing the huge interior. A green light blinked on a panel to one side of the door.

The others had already left the arrivals hall, advancing into another narrow tunnel. Victor didn't notice. He'd been distracted by the huge sculpture on the wall. It was the same one from the safety video. The miners were barely visible beneath the thick layer of dust.

He noticed something next to it, two boxes mounted to the wall, and brushed the dust from the sign above them. It read, "Emergency lighting and oxygen."

He opened the box marked "lighting." There was one solitary chemlight in its wrapper. The adjacent box, marked "oxygen," was empty. The box itself was circled with equally dusty yellow warning tape that optimistically declared "New supplies on order."

He realized he could no longer hear the others' footsteps ahead, and nervously hurried along the tunnel away from the hall, through a cloud of dust that was gradually settling. There was no sign of the rest of the team.

After a short time, he reached a junction where the tunnel divided. The right-hand fork descended toward the vehicle tunnel. The other continued straight. It was signposted "Transit Access."

He panicked for a second, not knowing which way to pick. Then he realized the answer was obvious. Both tunnels were swathed in darkness, but the left-hand one was full of recently disturbed dust.

He wondered at his own stupidity, then remembered that he'd only slept for a few hours in the last twenty-four, and tried to pull himself together, struggling to emerge from his drifting, jetlagged state of mind. Tiredness was fine when he was in his normal routine but now, out of his routine, out of his world, in what could be a dangerous environment, he couldn't afford to be drowsy. He was still giving himself an internal pep talk, his thoughts circling back on themselves, when he caught the others up. They'd been waiting for him.

"Where were you?" Graham said.

"Just looking at something," Victor replied.

"I'm not paying you to look. I'm paying you, all of you, to get production back."

Victor was unfazed by Graham's attempt at toughness, remembering the man's deer-in-headlights look from the televised press conference.

Celeste said, "Don't include me in that. You're paying me and Taka to get you here and home, that's all."

"Well, go back to the shuttle then. If you're here, you can help," Graham replied.

"Please?" Celeste laughed.

Graham scowled, unused to being ridiculed. Del and Mack were already walking on, with Victor just behind them. As they walked, Del spoke to Mack. "Are you sure the transit system will be running?" she asked.

"No, but it'd be a long walk to the accommodation, so it's worth a look," he said.

The tunnel spiraled around and divided again. Only one fork was lighted and that's where they went. After a final spiral, they emerged onto one of a pair of long concrete platforms. It was marked with the word "SPINWARD" in large letters on the ground.

Their platform was lighted. The light reflected off the twin railway tracks that filled the gap between the two platforms. The passenger information signs were off, dusty like everything else, including the peeling safety posters and the silent vending machines. The opposing platform was dark, as was the tunnel in both directions. There was no sign of a train.

"What do we do?" Celeste said.

"Wait. He knows we're here." Mack pointed at the security cameras on the wall. They were all aimed at the group.

"You think he watches all of them?" Rabbit wiped the dust from his helmet visor.

"Why not?" Del spoke in a somber tone, eyeing the cameras with suspicion.

A light breeze picked up from nowhere, and the electric wires above the tracks began to crackle. A low sound in the distance built into a loud hum, and a train of four carriages burst out of the right-hand tunnel. After it braked hard to pull up at the platform, the lights in the carriages came on and the doors opened.

Graham stepped aboard with no hesitation. The others followed, a little more cautiously. Victor looked around the carriage, past the junk-food wrappers scattered on the floor and the stained seats, and remembered when he used to catch the train.

The doors beeped loudly, then shut, and the train accelerated away smoothly, reaching its top speed in less than a minute.

"It's like traveling through a dead city," Celeste said, looking out at the darkened platform of an empty station as they sped through without stopping.

They were visibly spooked by the eerie atmosphere. It wasn't quite what they'd expected. The security team showed far less bravado now they were facing such oppressive surroundings. Only Mack seemed unaffected.

After they'd traveled for fifteen minutes, their journey soundtracked by the air rushing past the train and the whoosh as they passed through stations, the speakers in the carriage crackled to life with a recording. It was the voice of the presenter from the safety video. "The next stop will be station twenty-two," it said. "Disembark here for the visitor accommodation."

Shortly afterward, the train slowed, eventually easing to a stop at a station with one lighted platform. A dust-encrusted poster on the wall read, "Pharix Space Mining—Extracting your future."

The group assembled on the platform, next to another curving corridor, fully lighted.

The train doors shut as soon as they were out and it accelerated away, bound for some unknown destination.

A confectionery machine lay on its side in the darkness of the opposite platform, side smashed in, chocolate bars spilled across the platform and onto the track below.

They left the station in silence. Each one of them wanted to break the quiet but no one spoke. Something about the empty stations and the mindless automatic train left them numb.

Sam and Rabbit checked their weapons and composed themselves. The others just hurried onward, eager to get to their accommodation and settle in, hoping it would be better than what they'd seen so far.

The curving corridor straightened, widened, and opened out into the likeness of a boutique hotel on Earth, except without a receptionist or any signs of life. The floor was strewn with invoices for minibars, pay per view, and VIP services, whatever that meant.

A screen behind the desk lit up as they approached. The text on it read, "Visiting Delegation from Pharix HQ: You have been assigned rooms 101–109 in the executive wing. Please proceed through the doors to your left."

There were no sign of any doors to the left, just an empty doorway with one broken metal hinge still clinging to the wall. They walked through into the corridor beyond.

There were several letters missing from the sign on a cracked door to their right. The remainder read "Ecutv Longe." Inside was a long bar, tables, and leather chairs. A glass chandelier lay smashed in the center of the lounge, a table crushed beneath it. The lines of shelving behind the bar had been emptied of all their spirits.

Graham smiled knowingly at Mack, who refused to meet his gaze. The Pharix delegation continued along the corridor, following the numbered signs to their rooms.

When they finally reached their rooms, they were tired from the journey, and ready to lie down. But that changed when they reached the first room, and looked in, past the smashed remains of the door.

"Make yourself at home," Celeste said.

All of the executive suites were in a terrible state. Clearly they'd been occupied by whoever took the spirits. Bottles had been smashed against walls. Bedcovers were stained or burned. The squiggly line art paintings had been kicked in and left on the floor. Graffiti was scrawled across some of the headboards, and across the walls, and even some of the ceilings. Most of it related to Pharix.

Mack noticed Graham reading a particularly aggressive piece of graffiti, and he laughed.

Graham scowled at him and said, "We can't stay here. Is there nowhere else with beds?"

"It'll have to be in the standard rooms," Mack said. He looked at Graham and asked, "Can you cope?" But Graham didn't rise to the bait.

They traipsed back to reception. Victor flicked switches on a lighting panel on the wall and the corridor on the other side of the reception desk filled with light. At the same time, strange sounds began to echo down the corridor toward them.

Once they'd reached the closest rooms in the standard section, they discovered the source of the sounds. It was the projections in the rooms. Old films and TV shows were blurting out words, an eerie effect, like a haunted hotel, jangling their already stretched nerves.

"This place gives me the creeps," Celeste said, gesturing to shut off the nearest display.

"We've got nowhere else to go," Del said from the doorway.

"So what do we do, wait here for days watching old movies? You saw the bar, it's empty," Mack said.

"What else do you suggest?" Graham sighed. He'd already settled into an armchair.

"We may as well check the communications ourselves while we're here. Maybe there's something we can do to fix them. No harm in having a look," Mack said.

"Adam invited us to stay here," Graham said.

"It's your mine, not his," Mack replied.

Graham jumped to his feet, bristling at the inference that he was taking orders from Adam. "As I was saying, Adam invited us to stay here and I'm sure he expects us to carry out our own investigation while we're here. There may be clues as to Arkolov's plans once he gets to Earth. A man can't hide from Pharix." He looked pointedly at Victor then continued, "I'd like to catch him, he's put us all to a lot of trouble. Now, how does the transit system work, Mack? Do we call Adam again or can we request it ourselves?"

"I don't think it's worth bothering him," Mack said, in a measured tone. He pressed his pico and a top-down map of the mine appeared, a stylized version of the actual underground geography around the circumference: the main transit stops, the spaceport and other important landmarks, the ore processing depot, the factory, the vehicle depot, and other unlabeled caverns.

The others studied the map. For some of them it was the first time that they'd seen the mine's vast scale.

"It's huge," Rabbit said, awe in his voice.

"This is just the highlights. There's lots more of the smaller tunnels leading to the actual platinum seams." Mack moved his hand. Capillary like tunnels and passageways appeared on the map, snaking out from the main tunnel, twisting and turning, less ordered than the main ones, "And then there's the old tunnels." He left the words hanging.

"Old tunnels?" Rabbit waited for Mack to add them to the map. He didn't. "Can I see them?" Rabbit asked.

"Oh, they're not mapped. Maybe some were once, but most of the maps occupied the brains of pioneers, not the picos. It's a vast network," Mack said.

"Have you been in there?" Rabbit asked.

"I used to work in there, but I'd still get lost. You had to be so careful. Every tunnel looked the same. We couldn't spare the power for much lighting. You had to remember the shapes in the rock, the feel under your feet. We still lost miners, mostly the new starters, the ones who thought they knew it all. Sometimes they'd come back days or weeks later, sometimes we'd find them years, decades later. Some we never found." Mack trailed off and stared at the map.

Victor was staring at it too. He hadn't been listening, he'd been looking for something. He pointed to the map, "Where's Adam? In the same place as before?"

Mack went to speak, but no words came out. His face was pale.

Instead, Graham spoke. "Adam was moved. For security, he was told to keep the location secret. But I don't see why his location is important."

Victor said, "I just thought I might like to see him, now I've come all this way. See how he's doing. How he's grown. Back on Earth, you said that—"

Graham interrupted. "Social visits can wait till production's back." He turned to Mack. "Now, how do we get to operations to check comms?"

Mack snapped out of his daze and traced a route on the map. "There's no point taking the train one stop. We can walk down Tunnel One instead. It's only a short way."

"Let's go." Graham put his bag down against the wall of the corridor. He undid his oxygen bottle from his arm and placed it with his helmet and bag on the floor. The others did the same, leaving the helmets that they'd been lugging round the mine and dumping what bags they had. Del refused to leave her bag.

They left, following Mack out of a side door from reception and down a set of stairs into an empty car park. After descending a ramp, they emerged into Tunnel One.

Mack strode out into the darkened tunnel. Multiple lines of strip lights on the roof of the eight-lane tunnel sensed his movement and illuminated the section around him. The others followed nervously, checking both ways for traffic, having seen the size of the truck in the safety video.

"Don't worry. You'll see the headlights miles away. And they'll see you first." Mack pointed up at the long line of red lights in the darkened section of tunnel.

"The cameras are infrared?" Del asked, sounding surprised.

"Of course, we're underground, why wouldn't they be?" Mack said.

Del didn't reply. As they walked, she watched as, unnoticed by the others, each camera swiveled to follow their movement.

After a couple of minutes, they reached the junction with a two-lane tunnel. "This way," Mack said.

A few hundred yards along that tunnel, they emerged into a huge cavern, ten stories high. To their right, a narrow corridor spiraled down to the nearest transit station. Ahead was a parking lot that encircled a black glass structure that rose almost to the roof of the cavern.

The glass panels on its exterior were cracked or missing. The missing panels lay in a smashed pile on the rock floor around the base of the building. In front of the main entrance was a huge Pharix symbol, lying bent and broken among shards of glass. Its former location was marked by a large empty frame high above them.

Chapter 19

The building's interior had a strange atmosphere. There was no damage, no graffiti, and no sign that it had ever been used.

As Mack led them through the maze of corridors, heading toward the comms room, the lights flickered on in sequence, illuminating the abandoned offices on either side.

Rabbit's eyemod whirred in and out, zooming to examine the rooms' contents. Del and Sam's eyes darted around, looking for threats.

Victor glanced around but he wasn't looking for threats. He was just remembering the building as it was before, with rooms full of workers and corridors bustling with activity.

He stopped when he saw Mac standing in the doorway of an office, staring misty eyed at the bare desk and the empty chair. Leaving Mack to his memories, he entered the room on the other side of the corridor, the comms room.

The large room was cramped by the twenty dust-caked communication consoles that lined the walls. Their dials and switches emitted a faint glow. There was a mattress in the middle of the floor. Next to it was a pile of instant noodle packets, a jar of instant coffee, a bowl, a cup, and a kettle.

"Looks like he left in a hurry," Mack said as he joined Victor, Celeste, and Graham inside the room. The security team prowled the corridor outside.

"Those unlicensed shuttles don't hang around. I'm surprised he managed to get one to come here. They make enough running to Luna and back, and that's low risk, so long as you grease the right palms," Celeste said.

"There would have been a lot of platinum in it for the crew." Mack stroked his beard. "Come to think of it, what were you and Taka doing last week?"

She laughed. "If we'd picked up a load of platinum, I wouldn't be working now, I'd be with Taka at his beach house, waiting for a swell to come in. You'd know, you're Australian."

Mack shook his head, "My farm's five hours from the coast. I ride horses, not waves."

While they talked, Victor brushed away the dust from the console screens. Each one had the same message on it, "Unable to communicate with server." He tried different keyboard combinations, attempting to spark the consoles to life.

Nothing happened so he crawled behind one of the consoles and tried to prize the back panel off with his fingers. It wouldn't budge. "I need tools," he called out.

While Graham rested on the mattress, Mack and Celeste searched the room, not expecting to find anything. But to Mack's surprise, he found a large toolbox in the corner by the door. Its top was marked "D.A."

Victor took the screwdriver from Mack's hand and prized the panel off, revealing the circuit board. He called out again, and after Mack had passed him a metal magnifying monocle and more tools, he began to work, delicately altering circuits. Graham, Mack, and the camera on the wall watched his progress. Celeste had wandered off.

Finally, Victor stood up, happy with his work. But when he powered the console back on, he frowned. Another error message had appeared on the screen. "Arkolov's managed to block the whole system," he said.

"How?" Graham asked.

"I don't know. I guess he had plenty of time to think of a way."

"Can't you fix it?" Graham said.

"I'm sure Adam can. But I wouldn't know where to start. I'm more of a hardware than a software man," Victor said.

Unsure of his next move, Graham looked to Mack for advice.

Mack wasn't looking at him. He was kneeling by the mattress, examining the items beside it. "I can't believe he just upped and left."

"Believe it. He's not here," Graham said.

"But why leave now?" Mack stood up and faced him.

"What do you mean?" Graham asked.

"He's been on his own here for years. Why sabotage things now? Why not wait till his contract ran out or you finally took his job away?" Mack said.

"And why sabotage the elevator? That makes no sense," Victor added.

Graham frowned. "Look. I don't have those answers but he's not here. Adam is. Adam says that production's coming back. We have to trust him."

"So what's the point in us waiting? What are we going to do if he can't fix it? It's above our heads, we're no use," Victor said.

"We can't go back to Earth without a fix," Graham said.

"We can. You can't. Worried about your job, aren't you? Felix's still your boss?" Victor asked, a glint in his eye.

"Yes," Graham said flatly.

Victor grinned and said, "I don't envy you. I'd be worried." Mack laughed.

"At least I've still got a job." Graham smirked.

"But for how long?" Victor said, enjoying himself.

While Graham simmered, trying to think of a response, Celeste entered the room. "Graham," she said.

"What?" he shouted as he stood up, stumbled and almost fell straight back down.

"I've found something you might be interested in," she said calmly, a slight smile on her face.

"Where?" he snapped.

She pointed down. "Right here."

"What?"

"The floor, it's clean."

"So what? What's wrong with that?" Graham said.

"This corridor is the only part of the mine we've been in that hasn't been covered with dust. Why's that?" she said.

Her words triggered something in Victor, and he returned to the consoles.

"Maybe a cleaning bot's been round?" Mack said.

"Exactly," Celeste said with a flourish.

"What are you getting at?" Mack said, before Graham's frustration could boil over.

"The cleaning bot has been here and nowhere else in the whole mine. I want to know what had to be cleaned away," she said.

"Like what?" Mack asked.

"I don't know. I'd just like to find out. There's something odd about this setup, this room."

Victor returned from the consoles. "She's right, I didn't think anything of it at first, but the consoles were covered in dust, much more than a week's worth."

"So?" Graham said.

Victor replied, "How would Arkolov have called for a pickup?"

"I'm sure there's other consoles around," Graham said.

Celeste knelt and touched the polished floor. "But why not use the one where he was sleeping, assuming that's his mattress."

"I don't know and Arkolov's not here to tell us," Graham shouted.

There was a few seconds of silence as they all considered the information. All of them, except Graham, had their doubts about the story Adam had told them. Something strange was going on.

Del had been listening from the doorway. She said, "Before we try to work out why, we should check which parts of the building have been cleaned."

"If you spot the bot itself, bring it to me, I can see what its cleaned and when," Victor said, eager to be of use, out of his depth on the communications consoles, though he'd done his best.

The team split up. Celeste went back toward the main entrance, the way they'd come from. Del went with her, leaving Sam to stay with Graham.

Victor and Mack went the other way, walking in silence over the shiny, polished floor. Rabbit followed them at a distance, weapon in hand. His eyemod gave him the look of a military cyborg.

They checked the rooms on either side as they walked. There was a clear line in the doorways, marking a divide between the thick layer of rock dust in each room and the spotlessly clean corridor, only dirtied by the trail of faint gray footprints that they'd created.

The clean trail ended at the back entrance. There was a smaller gap between the building and the cavern wall here, only fifty yards or so. A layer of dust covered all of the parking spaces outside.

"Okay, we'll turn back," Mack said, as Rabbit caught them up.

Victor ignored him and kept walking, diagonally across the concrete, toward an open doorway in the cavern wall, giving the other two no choice but to follow.

As Mack walked, he noticed that the layer of dust was possibly thinner between the building and the doorway. But it was hard to tell.

They had to walk fast to keep up with Victor, who had increased his pace, like a bloodhound on a scent. They passed through the doorway, and into a narrow corridor that had been cut straight into the rock. In his haste, Mack almost walked straight into a white cabinet mounted onto one wall.

There were small bedrooms on either side, designed to be as close to the operations building as possible, for staff on standby in the twenty-four-hour operation. Bare bed frames, empty wardrobes, and faded pinup posters were visible through the doorways.

Neither Mack nor Rabbit could tell what Victor was following. All they saw was dust and footprints in his wake. This corridor definitely wasn't clean.

But Victor could see exactly what to follow. Ahead of him was a light trail of dusty footprints, leading through an archway. A sign above the arch read, "Caution. Look both ways for traffic."

He stepped into the darkness of the single-lane Tunnel Two, triggering the ceiling lighting. A pool of light appeared above him. The tunnel floor was dusty. The footprint trail seemed to have disappeared, but it was replaced by a huge set of tire tracks.

Victor saw the tracks, stopped, and waited for Mack, "Which way was the vehicle going?" he asked.

Mack glanced down at the tracks and pointed to his left. Then he saw something and his eyes widened. Beneath the dust was a faint trail of footprints. He pointed it out to Victor and they started walking, following the trail.

But Rabbit didn't move. He was looking at the tire tracks, deep in thought. "I think we've gone far enough," he said. "We should go back and tell the others what we've found."

"We've come this far. We might as well see where the footprints go," Victor said.

"You can go back if you want. We'll be okay, we're not scared of the dark." Mack chuckled.

Rabbit thought for a second, imagining Del's reaction if he came back without them. Then he swallowed, jutted out his chin, and followed them into the tunnel.

As they walked, Mack said, "These tracks are unusual, they look fairly new, but Tunnel Two is a relief tunnel. It's only intended for use if a rockfall blocks Tunnel One and, well, you've seen Tunnel One. It'd take a lot to block it."

Victor nodded, but he hadn't really understood the relevance of Mack's information.

After they'd followed the trail for almost a mile, they were starting to feel like it was a dead end, thinking that maybe Rabbit was right and they should have gone back. Maybe the others would've found something.

Then Rabbit, who had been racing ahead, keen to get the task over with, pointed at something on the ground. He walked over and knelt by that something, moving the dust away with his hands to reveal a reddish-black stain. Victor and Mack joined him, brushing away more of the dust, revealing several smaller stains.

"Blood," Rabbit said.

"Are you sure?" Mack replied.

"Yes." Rabbit nodded.

Victor was lost for words. He'd been following the trail in a sleepy haze, more out of curiosity than actual suspicion. Now the implications of what they'd found came clear. "Blood," he whispered.

Mack was about to say something but he stopped, spotting another pool of light in the distance. He squinted at it, trying to work out what it was.

Rabbit zoomed his eyemod, spotted Celeste's red hair and said, "It's the others."

A few minutes later, Graham, Del, Celeste, and Sam became visible to Victor and Mack as well as Rabbit. Victor watched the second pool of light merge with their own.

"What are you doing?" Graham said, breathing heavily.

"We've been following a trail. Did yours lead anywhere?" Victor said.

"No, the floor was only cleaned to the first corner. We looked around but we just found dust, so we came to find you instead," Celeste said.

"We found blood," Victor said.

"Blood?" Graham said.

"That's what I said." He pointed toward the bloodstains.

Graham looked down at them. "Where's it come from?"

"It looks as though someone was hit by a truck," Mack said.

"How can you say that?" Graham snapped.

"Well. The footprints, the tire tracks, the blood."

Graham waved his hand dismissively. "We're in a mine, tire tracks are normal, and if it is blood, you don't know where it came from, it could be years old."

Del was down on one knee examining the stains. "It doesn't look years old."

"Then whose blood is it? The only person that's been here is Arkolov, and he's back on Earth right now, living it up with the money from our platinum. Standing round looking at blood spots isn't finding him, or fixing production. So let's stop this ridiculous wild-goose chase and go back to the hotel to wait for the fix." Graham marched off down the tunnel, creating his own pool of light that split from their own, expecting them all to follow.

Only Sam followed. Rabbit waited to see what Del would do. Victor and Mack stood with Celeste. Del continued to examine the blood.

"Maybe he's right," Mack said, "It's just a bit of blood."

"In a tunnel on an asteroid occupied by one man and one computer. Something's going on here," Celeste said.

With that, all of the lights in the tunnel went out, leaving them in complete darkness.

Chapter 20

"What's going on?" Graham demanded, as he and Sam stumbled back through the darkness to rejoin the others.

"The lighting circuit must have tripped," Mack said. "Give it thirty seconds and it'll reset."

After they'd spent a minute waiting in the darkness, he said, "Can someone call Adam and get him to reset it."

Del tapped her pico, said, "Transmit on all available frequencies," waited for the confirmation beep and continued, "Adam, are you receiving? We're in Tunnel Two. The lighting has failed. Can you fix it?"

There was a long silence, then a voice boomed from a speaker some distance away, echoing along the tunnel toward them. "I'm sorry but I can't take the risk," it said. It was Adam.

"I don't understand. What risk?" Del said. There was no response. "What do you mean? What risk?"

The silence dragged out.

"I don't like this." Del called out, "Rabbit?"

"Yes," came the loud reply. She jumped. He was standing right next to her.

"Have you got night vis on?" she asked.

"Yeah."

"What do you see?"

"A load of people milling around a tunnel in the dark."

No one laughed. A light breeze, just like the one in the transit station, rustled their clothing.

Victor felt detached from the situation, so tired that it all felt like just another moment in a strange dream. For once, he'd have been happy to wake up on the cold hospital floor. Instead, he stood in a pitch-black tunnel, hundreds of thousands of miles from home, feeling all the hairs on the back of his neck stand on end, and a chill run down his spine.

"I didn't know you got wind down here," Celeste said.

"You don't. You get vehicle movement," Mack said. "We need to get out of this tunnel."

"What about the refuges?" Rabbit said, looking toward the green glow, only a short distance away.

"No, they're only built for one person. We need to go back. Now," Mack said.

Hearing the urgency in his voice, Del took charge. She was in her element, adrenaline flowing, an unnatural calm in her voice. "Everyone stand still, Rabbit will form you into a line. Once he does, keep your hand on the shoulder of whoever's in front."

Rabbit moved around the figures in the darkness, linking their arms, chuckling to himself. When he reached Graham, he stepped on his foot.

"Watch it," Graham said.

"Sorry," Rabbit replied, his smirk hidden by the darkness.

"Hurry up," barked Del, as he guided her into position at the front of the line.

"Ready to go. You can start moving," he said.

She started to move and the centipede-like chain followed jerkily behind her. Rabbit waited until they'd all passed, checking that the line held.

As they walked he called out instructions to Del. "Bear left, you're close to the wall." Then ten seconds later. "Bear right, you've overcorrected." The column weaved and zigzagged inefficiently.

"Not far to go, keep going," Rabbit said. But he couldn't see the archway yet. As he looked for it, he noticed something else, a strange half-light in the far distance. He wondered if the others could see it too. Perhaps it was just a bit of night vision static.

Then Mack said, "Trucks," with an air of reverence, as the half-light formed into a line of faint white light. The tunnel geography played with their sense of perspective, making the line of light appear to be high above them in the distance.

"What are they doing here?" Graham said.

Celeste muttered, "I don't know. Why don't you wait and ask them?"

"Nearly there," Rabbit said, relieved to have spotted the familiar shape of the archway ahead, despite the dust that clouded his vision, stirred up by a low rumble that shook the tunnel floor. Past the archway, he could just make them out, ghostlike in the dust, a long line of trucks moving fast.

"Hurry up. They're coming," he shouted. The others didn't need encouragement. They'd heard the hum of the engines, seen the light reflecting off the tunnel walls, and felt the sickening feeling of impending doom in the pits of their stomachs.

The column dissolved. They rushed forward, stumbling and bumping against each other, moving as fast as possible in the chaos of dust and reflected light.

"It's there. On your right," shouted Rabbit.

Del was already heading for the archway. Its dark outline stood out against the light from the trucks. She entered the corridor, closely followed by the others.

Rabbit hustled the stragglers in, half blinded by the headlight beams, half deafened by the bass rumble of the tires on the rock floor.

Once he'd checked they were all safely inside the corridor, he went back to look along the tunnel. A huge mining truck was almost upon him. It filled the entire width of the tunnel.

After he stepped back to the safety of the corridor, and rushed to catch up with the others, the trucks roared past, one by one, sending a rush of hot, dusty air up the corridor toward them.

No one looked back. Instead, they trudged on, a little embarrassed by their mad free-for-all dash to safety.

Victor shuddered, imagining the metallic death that they had narrowly avoided, imagining dying out here, 200,000 miles from home, 200,000 miles from Maria. The thought of her, alone, with no visitors, no funds beyond the six months, galvanized him, shook him from his jetlag-like slumber. He had to get out, to get home. This was beyond their control. Adam was beyond their control.

The realization finally hit him. The trucks, they were Adam's trucks. Adam had intended to kill them. But that couldn't be. It had to be a mistake.

Rabbit called out, "Stop," and they all stopped, reaching for the nearest wall to orient themselves. "Mack?" he shouted. The others looked around in the darkness, a futile gesture. Rabbit looked through the settling dust. He couldn't see Mack anywhere.

"Hey," Mack shouted from behind them. He'd been taking it slower than the others, feeling his way along the right-hand wall, searching for something. Then he'd found it, the cracked white cabinet he'd almost bumped into earlier.

He opened it and felt around inside, hoping his hunch was right. It was. Each of the ten slots was occupied by a chemlight.

He pulled one out and shook it violently. Nothing happened. He tried the next one. Nothing. When the third one failed, he threw it away in disgust, cursing the fool who had replaced the used lights in their holders instead of ordering new ones.

The others were making their way back toward him now, Rabbit leading the way. As Mack shook the fourth one, he prepared to tell them it was a false alarm, to tell them to keep moving. But to his surprise, it burst into a steady glow of pale greenish light, enough to illuminate the tunnel around him.

He handed out the remaining six to the others. "Shake them," he said, hoping that two or three would light.

They shook them with violence but only the one in Sam's hand lit up. Mack shook his head, frustrated. "Glad you cut the maintenance budget now?" he said, after he'd spotted Graham's sweating face in the glow of Sam's light.

"How many lights would Arkolov need? Two per staff member isn't bad," Graham said.

Sam passed his light to Del. Mack held on to his. "Hey, I can't see anything," Rabbit said, his eye mod still in night mode, an eye patch covering the other.

"Sorry." Mack moved the light away from him. "Maybe you should take the lead?"

Rabbit looked at Del. She said, "You can check the operations cavern for trucks."

He disappeared into the darkness and Del started after him, checking the others were following, using her light to guide the way. Mack did the same from the back of the group. Celeste walked alongside him.

"How long will the lights last for?" she asked.

"Normally four or five hours. I'm not so sure about these ones, but it doesn't matter, so long as we make it to the emergency generator," Mack said.

"Where's that?"

"In the operations building."

Graham said, "Forget the generator. We'll go straight back to the shuttle."

"How?" Victor said.

"The same way we got here," Graham replied.

"You really think the train will take us where we want to go?" Victor said.

"It did before."

"Adam runs it. He ran it when I was here last. He runs everything. You're supposed to be the boss of all this. Why don't you know this stuff? What do you do all day?" Victor threw his hands up in the air.

"Arkolov deals with the asteroid. I'm in charge of ground operations. We have a huge distribution network."

"How's distribution working with no supply?" Celeste said with a laugh.

Graham didn't reply.

They'd reached the end of the corridor. Rabbit was waiting there. He walked out into Del's light. "Trucks?" Del said.

"No, I walked right round the building. There's nothing," he replied.

"Good." She stepped out into the cavern, walking the short distance to the door of the operations building.

As they followed her across the rock floor, Victor glanced around, then stopped, looking up at a blinking red light, high on the cavern wall. "We're still being watched."

"I know," Mack said, following Victor's gaze. Then the pair of them joined the others at the back entrance to the operations building.

"Shouldn't the generator have come on automatically?" Del said, looking ahead at the darkened corridor.

"Maybe, but it doesn't matter, so long as it comes on when I press the power button. I'm sick of wandering in the dark," Mack said as he tapped his pico and brought up the projected map again, refreshing his memory of the generator's location.

He moved his hand to zoom in on the operations building, tapped the map to select the ground-floor plan, then tutted when he realized that none of the rooms were labeled. He scanned the plan, looking for the telltale outline of the generator. Eventually he spotted it, in a large room on the other side of the building, next to the front entrance. It was only a few minutes' walk away.

They retraced their steps along the clean corridors in silence, chemlights guiding the way. Victor couldn't help but notice more of the glowing red camera lights. There seemed to be one in every corridor and nearly every room. He'd look ahead and then quickly back, catching the cameras adjusting to follow their movement. Adam was watching.

What would he do next? Victor wondered. Maybe he'd just wanted to scare them, he thought, hoping that was the case.

Del arrived at the room first, eager to get the lights back on. She kicked the jammed double doors open to reveal... nothing.

The room was completely empty. A large object had once filled most of it. That much was obvious from the relative lack of dust on a large portion of the floor.

"I don't understand. It can't have just gone." Mack said.

"Part of the overhead reduction program?" Victor looked pointedly at Graham.

"We didn't remove it. The emergency systems were never interfered with," Graham said.

"Or maintained."

"We had one employee. We didn't need to."

While they talked, Mack had been looking through into an adjacent room, filled with bare metal shelving. "All the fuel's gone too," he said.

"Wonder who took it," Graham said, smirking at Mack.

"I wouldn't blame them. You took everything else they had," Mack said.

"So what now?" Celeste said, defusing the sudden tension.

"Like I said before. We go back to the shuttle," Graham said.

No one responded. They'd stopped listening. Instead they were looking out through the door, into the corridor that ended at the front entrance. Shafts of light flickered along the walls. Del crept along the corridor and darted out into the entrance hall to glance out before returning.

"There's not much point sneaking around." Victor pointed out the camera on the wall that had panned to follow her movement the whole way.

Del ignored him. She just said, "Headlights."

"They're here?" Mack said.

"Looks that way," she said.

Celeste turned to Graham. "You still want to walk?"

"How else will we get out?" he replied.

"He might just be trying to scare us, to get us to leave, to go back to the shuttle," Victor said as he watched the lights.

"It's working. I'm scared." Sam laughed despite the tension.

"Why turn the power off if he wanted us to leave?" Del said.

"Let's at least go and have a look. You've got weapons. We might be able to get past them," Victor said.

"I don't know if we have much that'll affect the trucks. Maybe we can shoot their tires out, but I don't know if that would stop them. It's not like there's a driver you can shoot," Del said, sounding a little disappointed.

"We should still look, but first." Victor reached up to the camera on the wall beside him, grabbed it with both hands, and tried to wrench it off its mounting. It wobbled but didn't budge.

"Allow me." Sam waited for Victor to step back, then he pulled out his weapon and fired. Dust fell from the ceiling and when the cloud had thinned, the camera was gone, its wire severed, its mounting neatly cleaved away from the wall. What was left lay sparking on the floor of the corridor.

Even Graham smiled. Mack slapped Sam on the back in congratulations. Victor was already moving toward the front entrance, having noticed that the light was no longer shining in. Del caught him up before he got there.

"Can you cover the light? I want to check if they're gone," Victor said.

Del put her hand over her light, muffling the glow. Behind them, Mack did the same. They stared out into the darkness.

"Looks like they're gone," Graham said, starting to saunter out into the cavern. There were no headlights to be seen.

"No," Rabbit said tersely. He'd been the last to round the corner. He'd stood at the back of the group, thinking they could all see the same as him, forgetting his night vision. He pointed out into the cavern, "There's one, two, three..."

As he pointed, a pair of headlights came on, directly in front of the entrance. As they shielded their eyes from the glare, another set of headlights appeared to their right. Then another set on the left, and another and another, until there were five sets of headlights visible and a glimmer on the cavern roof and walls suggesting more around the other sides of the building. It was clear from the size of the shadowy shapes behind the lights that they were mining trucks. Their outlines were just visible in the gloom, a halo of whirling dust around each one.

Chapter 21

They shielded their eyes and squinted out into the light, counting headlights.

Then the trucks' engines whirred to life and the vehicles began to move, at first in a slow creep, then fast, until they were racing toward the building, suspensions lowered, bellies scraping on the ground, sending showers of sparks flying into the air.

First, the group edged backward. Then, as the trucks accelerated, they ran, hurrying back to the safety of the corridor.

The lead truck smashed into the building and the whole structure shook. A split second later, another truck hit, and another, and another.

Victor threw himself to the floor, as the building threatened to shake itself apart around him. He was quickly joined by the others, as big chunks of plaster dropped from the ceiling, exploding into white dust. He stayed prone, waiting for the inevitable collapse, listening to the sound of smashing glass, as the remaining panels plummeted to the cavern floor.

After the last one crashed to the ground, there was a moment of peace. Mack, his face and body covered with dust, stood up. He held his light up and checked that the others were okay. No one seemed to be injured. As they climbed to their feet, thud after dull thud shook the building.

"They won't stop till the building falls," Celeste said.

"They'll be here a good while then," Mack said. "I was here when it was built, the frame's pretty solid. They might dent it but they won't bring it down."

Celeste gave him a skeptical look. Mack ignored it and, while the others dusted themselves off, he wandered along the corridor, looking in rooms, searching for somewhere to regroup.

A little way away, toward the back of the building, he found a break room. Aside from the ubiquitous dust, it was in fairly good condition. There was a kitchen area, an old sofa, and a dining table. Mack was pleased to see there were no cameras.

He called to the others and they joined him in the room, all except Del, who patrolled the corridor outside, gun in hand.

Graham beelined for the fridge, opening the door, then closing it again in disappointment. Afterward, he opened the kitchen cupboards one by one. They were all empty.

Sam saw his look of disappointment. "Better to be hungry and alive, than full and dead," he said.

Graham's stomach still rumbled. He found himself daydreaming about all the food he could have brought from home.

The sound of water drew him out of his reverie. Sam had turned the tap on. He was watching the flow of water, surprised it was still working.

Del stuck her head in the doorway, curious to find out what the sound was. She turned to Sam in horror, her training coming into play, "Don't waste it. You don't know how much pressure's left." It was too late; the stream of water had already faded to a slow drip.

"Sorry," he said, raising his hands in apology.

"You don't know how long we'll be stuck here. I've only got half a liter in my bag." She shook her head angrily and returned to the corridor.

Chastened, Sam took up a spot by the door of the room, next to Rabbit.

Mack was sitting with Victor, Graham, and Celeste at the dining table. He spoke, his voice punctuated by the thud of trucks hitting the outer walls, "I counted at least ten out there, and there's more round the other side."

Celeste asked, "Do you think we can get past them somehow?"

"Maybe the ones out there, if we're quick... and lucky. But Adam's got a fleet of five hundred to work with. At least that's how many there were last time I was here, I don't know if he's built more since. There's no way we'd make it out past them. It's at least ten miles from here to the elevators," Mack said.

Graham said, "That's why we should use the transit system."

"You still think that Adam will send a train to pick you up?" Victor said.

"If there's no trains, I'll walk. At least the trucks can't get in there."

"But you've still got to walk from the station to the elevators. I'm sure the trucks can get into those tunnels. It's the same problem," Victor said.

"It's not. It's one mile, not ten," Graham said.

Celeste laughed. "You think you can outrun one of them for a mile?"

Graham looked down at his belly, realizing what she was implying. His face reddened.

Before he could respond, Mack interrupted, "Look, we've got no chance out there, so we've got no choice but to hold out here as long as we can. We'll just have to wait until they send a rescue party."

"What about food and water?" Del said from the doorway, looking pointedly at Sam.

Graham shuffled awkwardly. "That won't matter, the plan has a flaw anyway, water or no water."

"What?" Mack said.

"Operations doesn't know we're here," Graham said.

"Someone must know," Celeste said.

"No one in Operations knows. I organized the mission myself. Felix is the only one that knows we're here."

"I wouldn't put my faith in that man sending a rescue party. I'm sure he'd rather let us die than risk the media embarrassment," Victor said.

"He'll send one," Mack said. "Maybe not for our benefit, but for the platinum, certainly."

"But how long will he leave it? He knows we're here to fix things, he won't be expecting this. At best it'll be two or three days before a rescue mission even departs," Victor said.

Graham looked a little sheepish. "It might be longer than that. I got Taka to tell Felix that we'd be here for a week."

Silence. Victor shook his head. Mack looked crestfallen.

"Someone else knows we're here," Celeste said.

"Who?" Graham and Victor said in unison.

"Taka. And he's supposed to call the UN for assistance if I'm out of contact for forty-eight hours."

Graham said, "Why can't you just call him now?"

She sighed. "I would if I could. There's no way of getting a signal through that rock."

Graham huffed with irritation. Victor said, "Did you tell Taka you'd come back out within the forty-eight?"

"Not exactly," Celeste said quietly. Victor looked concerned.

"So we have to rely on a clipper pilot following UN protocol. Great," Graham said, "I'm full of confidence."

Celeste stared at him, trying to look more confident than she felt. But she knew he was right. Taka wouldn't call the

UN unless he thought she was in mortal danger, and even then he'd be far more likely to come in and find her himself. She shuddered at the thought of Taka wandering into the mine on his own, unaware of the danger.

The sneer on Graham's face still irritated her, causing her to snap back, "Better than relying on you. He's not the one who got us stuck here in the first place."

Graham stood up, kicking his chair back. As he left the room, he pointed to Victor. "I'm not the one that built that thing."

Victor leaned back in his chair and sighed. The accusation stung, but he couldn't argue with it. Whatever he thought of Pharix, they didn't build the computer. Graham was right.

A little while later Victor was still seated at the table, deep in thought. Celeste had gone to sleep, stretched out on the floor, undeterred by the repeated truck impacts. She had the spacer's ability to sleep anywhere. Mack was dozing too, sitting upright on the sofa with his eyes closed. Rabbit, Sam, and Graham were outside somewhere.

Victor looked up as Del wandered back in. First, she tested the tap again, hoping for water. Then she took her own water bottle out of the bag and offered it to Victor. He took a few short sips, surprised at her gesture.

She sat down opposite him, untied her hair and began to examine it, one lock at a time. Casually, without looking up from her task, she asked, "Why do you think he's doing this?"

"Who, Graham?" he replied.

She shook her head. "No, Adam."

"I don't know. Back when we first came here, I would have trusted him with my life. In fact, he did save my life once..." He trailed off, lost in the memory for a moment.

Del said nothing. She just watched him, her face softer than usual, as she rolled a dread between her fingers, gradually tightening it.

Victor looked up, surprised at the change in her demeanor. It gave him the impetus to continue. "Ever since the power went out, I've been trying to think of something we did, or something he did, any sign that he was capable of this, but, I just can't," he said, feeling his eyes sting. Then he remembered another detail from the same memory as before, something triggered by the sound of the roaring trucks outside. But that was different. Adam hadn't harmed anyone that day. He'd saved them. There was no point mentioning it, no sense reopening old wounds.

Del went on, almost whispering, "Is there anything in his programming that could explain it? Maybe if you could find that, we could find his weak points, a way to beat him."

Mack had opened his eyes and sat up to listen to their conversation.

Victor leaned forward. "Adam wasn't programmed, so much as guided. Maria was the one who dealt with the teaching and the behavioral side. I was more involved with the logistics, the nutrient feed, the power bills, you know," he said, wishing he'd paid more attention back then.

Del turned to Mack. "Did you notice anything odd about him?"

"I didn't have much contact with the computer, with Adam, either," Mack said.

She was about to ask another question when there was a loud whoosh and a flash of light.

Chapter 22

"What was that?" Celeste jumped to her feet. Victor, Del, and Mack were already rushing from the room to look.

In the corridor, Rabbit and Sam were in battle mode, crouched low by the wall, weapons out. Graham was lying on the floor, still half asleep.

"What is it?" Del said, as she tied her hair back up and joined the rest of her team.

Before they could answer, there was another flash, and then, the unmistakable crackle of flame. Smoke wisped along the corridor toward them.

"Fire." Sam stated the obvious.

"How?" Graham rubbed his eyes and clambered to his feet.

"We'll have to go," Mack said.

"We'll be sitting ducks," Celeste said.

Del started to walk along the corridor toward the front entrance. "What choice do we have?" she said.

"No, wait," Sam said, and Del stopped. "They'll be too fast for us. We won't all make it. We might not make it at all," he said.

"We can't stay here," she said, impatient.

"I'll go out front and create a bit of a distraction. The trucks will move and all of you can sneak out of the back entrance."

Del was a little embarrassed at not thinking of the idea herself, but proud of Sam nonetheless. It might just work. "And how will you get back?" she asked.

Sam pointed at his feet, "I might not beat the trucks over ten miles, but over a few hundred yards, no problem."

"I'll come with you," she said.

"Can you still run at your age?" Sam queried. Del punched him playfully, then remembered the situation and focused. Smoke was slowly filling the corridor.

She turned to the others. "Stay out of sight near the back entrance until you hear us firing. Then wait for the trucks to move." She started walking.

"Wait," Victor said, "if we go out the back we'll be trapped in that corridor."

"The trucks can't get to us there," Del said.

"For the time being. We don't know what other weapons he's got. We don't know how this fire started."

"We'll go out the front, into the transit corridor, at least that's in the right direction," Graham said, happy to steal Victor's idea.

"There's two hundred yards between the front entrance and the corridor. You'll never make it," Del said.

"We will if you create a good decoy. The smoke should help," Mack said, as it billowed around them, thicker than before. The fire was getting closer.

"Let's go," Del said. Sam and Rabbit followed her.

She waved a hand. "No, Rabbit. Go with them, guide them across when it's time."

"Wait, you'll need light." Victor grabbed the two chemlights and handed them to her. "Take them, Rabbit can guide us, you'll need them."

Del handed one of the lights to Sam. Then she broke into a run, heading through the smoke toward the back entrance, light in hand. Sam followed, running with a long loping stride, easily covering the ground.

The others began to make their way toward the front, staying low, below the thickest smoke, feeling their way along the corridor, with Rabbit's guidance.

Once they got closer, they no longer required his vision. A fire in one of the rooms to the left illuminated the corridor. Pieces of burning plasterboard were popping out of the wall and spreading the flames.

The five of them pressed themselves to the other wall as they passed, sweating in the heat that radiated out. Not long after, Rabbit stopped suddenly. They'd reached the entrance. But it was blocked by the side of a huge truck. There was no way through.

"We'll have to find another way," he said, leading them into a corridor to the right.

There was another flash of light directly ahead of them, from the far end of the corridor. They dove to the ground as a huge jet of flame came straight at them, stripping the paint from the walls as it passed.

Now, the whole end of the corridor was ablaze, and when they looked up, they could see the source of the flame.

The wall at the end was gone and beyond it, on the other side of a room was the nozzle of a flamethrower, sticking through the space where a glass panel used to be. The nozzle sprouted from the front of a mining truck. They froze, staring at the truck.

Victor was first to react, crawling along the corridor and into a room on the left before the flamethrower could fire again. "Come on. Get in here," he said.

They crawled along the floor, following him in, out of the corridor of smoke and flame.

Mack looked at the smoke pouring through the open doorway. "Close the door."

"I can't," Victor said. "He'll know we're in here." He pointed toward the empty window frames on the other side of the room, the outer wall of the building.

They lay on the floor, trying and failing to avoid breathing in the thick black smoke that was filling the room, feeling drowsier by the second, struggling to get a proper breath.

Then they heard it, pop, pop, pop. The sound of gunfire from the other side of the building, rising above the sound of the flames. Victor resisted the urge to cheer.

The gunfire intensified. The pop, pop, became a wall of bullet noise. He could hear the bullets ricocheting off the trucks, the windshields shattering. He hardly noticed the smoke anymore, the adrenaline rising again, the fog of war descending.

"Get ready to go," whispered Rabbit as he crept toward the window. He risked lifting his head, hoping he'd be hidden by the smoke. When he turned back to the others, he was smiling. "They're moving, the trucks are moving. They're all going round to the back," he said, excitedly.

Victor suppressed a cough, his throat itching. Rabbit waited by the window. After a few smoke-filled seconds, he raised an arm and beckoned the others over. "Let's go," he said, as a tire exploded on the other side of the building.

While Rabbit helped them over the windowsill and out into the fire-lit cavern, hellish orange in the light of the firestorm, the sound of gunfire died down, then ceased.

Graham was the first out. He stood and checked carefully for trucks, squinting out along the zebra-striped pedestrian walkway that led from the front entrance. Somewhere through the smoke was the transit corridor.

"Go, go, what are you waiting for?" Victor shouted.

Graham started to run, his belly wobbling. Mack and Celeste overtook him easily.

Victor waited for Rabbit and they ran together, Rabbit glancing from side to side, checking the trucks weren't following. Victor focused on following the striped walkway, hoping that the infrared cameras would be confused by the smoke and the heat of the fire.

Eventually, the outline of the transit tunnel appeared, swathed in smoke, and they sprinted for its safety, hearing the echoing sound of truck engines, and imagining the cloud around them to be full of vehicles.

Mack and Celeste made it in first, followed by Graham, then Victor. The first three ran on down the narrow transit tunnel, past the faded route map on the wall, before stopping.

Victor stayed by the entrance, waiting for the fifth member of their group.

Rabbit had stopped, his eyemod whirring, trying to see through the smoke-filled cavern, his gun in his hand. He pointed toward the others. "Look after them, I'm waiting for the other two."

Victor walked down the tunnel toward them, feeling useless without a weapon, knowing that he'd probably be equally useless with one.

Rabbit darted out into the smoke. His eyemod gave him limited visibility. There was no sign of the other two. Then he heard the sound of engines again and a whooping war cry from the other side of the cavern. The trucks were coming.

Rabbit raised his weapon and fired a few rounds, before shouting, "This way, over here."

A few seconds later, Sam and Del appeared in his eyemod vision in blurry infrared, light orange against the bright crimson of the burning building, parts of its structure falling in clouds of sparks to the cavern floor. Behind the two running shapes were ten or more trucks, swerving to follow the zigzagging path of the two sprinters.

"This way," he shouted again, and the two of them changed direction, following his voice. He dropped to one knee and fired his weapon, aiming carefully for the truck tires, firing again and again, bursting the thick rubber tires but hardly slowing the pursuers. The trucks continued on frayed rims, throwing burning rubber in all directions.

Sam and Del were only twenty-five yards away, close enough for him to see them with his unmodded eye. He pointed them in the direction of the transit tunnel and prepared to follow them, still firing in wide sweeps toward the trucks, their neat line in disarray, their windscreens and camera lenses cracked and broken.

But, as he pushed up from his crouched firing position, preparing to make the final sprint for safety, a heavy impact knocked his left leg from under him.

Victor watched from a safe distance. When Del and Sam appeared from the smoke cloud and entered the tunnel, he walked over to meet them, expecting Rabbit to be right behind them. But he wasn't. They stared out into the smoke, willing him to appear.

"There," Sam said, as two trucks appeared from the direction of the building, headlights half blinding them.

Rabbit was crawling toward the tunnel. One of his legs was limp, dragging along the ground at a strange angle, leaving a trail of blood. A truck was bearing down on him, moving slowly, going in for the kill.

Del and Sam fired simultaneously, shattering the windscreen and crucially, the truck's front camera.

Rabbit took advantage of the distraction. With clenched-teeth effort, he pushed up on his good leg and made a stumbling, hopping attempt to reach them.

He only had a short distance to cover, on level ground, lighted by the headlights of the trucks that were converging on his location.

But they were going to be too late. They wouldn't catch him in time, as he growled through the pain and made surprising progress across the ground.

Ten yards to go. Almost there. The rest of the team shouted encouragement. They'd all assembled at the entrance, feeling united, feeling elation at their survival, willing Rabbit to join them.

A long spout of flame shot across the cavern, filling the air with bright orange light. It blinded Victor for a second. All he could see was white light. The image of Rabbit running was so burned into his vision, he thought that he might have made it. Then as his vision returned, the reality set in, brightly lighted by truck headlights.

Mack bowed his head, turned and trudged away. Graham and Celeste followed. Sam stared ahead. He was still dry retching when Victor gripped his shoulders and pointed him in the direction of the others. He shambled away, sobbing softly, eyes wide with shock, hands shaking uncontrollably.

Del stood silent, eyes focused, watching as the huge truck made a slow, lumbering turn.

Victor put his hand on her shoulder. She took a step toward the body on the cavern floor. "I have to get him."

"He's gone now, we have to go."

"I can't leave him here."

"You don't have a choice," he said, as the barrel of the flamethrower that protruded from the cab windscreen, the driver's seat replaced by an instrument of flaming death, turned to face them.

The truck rolled forward, past Rabbit's body, and Victor grabbed Del's arm, pulling her with him as he ran toward the others. She moved free of him. Victor kept running.

Del took one last look back as the flamethrower prepared to fire, then sprinted to catch up with Victor. By the time it fired, they were far enough away and the gout of flame only caused a gust of hot air to wash over their backs. They ignored it and kept running, Del stony faced, her eyes blazing.

Chapter 23

The fiery glow from the cavern receded into the distance behind them, and they were forced to slow and regroup, limited by the twin chemlight beams.

Sam stepped into the light. It reflected off his clammy skin. "What now?" His voice shook.

Mack said, "Stay calm. We're safe here. We'll just stop and—"

Sam interrupted. "You thought we were safe in there."

"Let's go to the station. Maybe there'll be a train there," Graham said.

"For the last time, there won't be a train. Don't you understand what's happening?" Celeste snarled.

"No. Ask him. He built the monster." Graham pointed to Victor.

Victor didn't reply. He was kneeling by the wall, feeling his stomach churn. The shock of Rabbit's death had hit him at the same time as the realization that it was probably his fault.

"Victor," Mack said.

"What?" he murmured.

"You okay?" Mack held out a hand.

He wasn't. But he waved away the offer of help, and clambered unsteadily to his feet.

Graham said, "If there's no train we'll walk the rails. There's no other option."

"I'm not walking on the rails. Trains run on rails. Who runs the trains? I'm not that stupid," Celeste said.

"There's two sets of tracks. If a train comes, which I doubt it will, I'll move out of the way," Graham said smugly.

"What about the old tunnels?" Del said.

"Adam would still find us. He's got cameras everywhere," Victor said.

"Everywhere except the old tunnels," Mack said.

"So where's the nearest entrance?" Celeste asked.

"Most of the holes were blocked up years ago," Mack said.

"We could unblock them," Sam said.

Mack shook his head. "No, they're not marked on the map. The only entrances I know of are miles away from here."

Graham said, "So the station's the only option. Come on, Del."

Without meeting his eye, she walked off into the darkness, holding her chemlight up, with Graham trailing a few steps behind her. The others followed. Sam brought up the rear, his eyes bloodshot, holding the chemlight with shaky hands.

They walked in silence, listening to the rumble of trucks above them in Tunnel One, and watching as smoke from the distant fire wisped through the chemlight beams.

Eventually, they emerged onto the platform of the transit station. Victor had half expected there to be a train waiting, but there wasn't. The station was empty.

He watched as Del shone her chemlight around. Its light played across the smiling faces of staff in the Pharix propaganda posters on the far wall, and glinted off the slick of chocolate wrappers beside a toppled vending machine.

There was no obvious threat, but Del didn't relax. Instead, she tilted her head, listening carefully for approaching trains.

The others watched her, waiting for the verdict. She shook her head. There was nothing coming.

She looked to her left and was surprised to see Graham sitting on the platform edge, preparing to drop to the rails below.

"You're really going to do this?" Del asked.

"Yes," Graham said firmly. He was a little less certain now that he'd arrived in the station, but he betrayed no doubts in his voice. "We've got no other option. I'm not staying and waiting to be burned alive."

Mack shuddered, still shaken by Rabbit's death. Despite the blood in the tunnel and the fire, the danger hadn't sunken in until he'd seen the shock on Rabbit's face in the flame's grim light. "Just wait here. We'll come up with a plan," he said.

"And give Adam time to think of a better one? No. I'm going now. Who's coming with me?" Graham said.

The silence was deafening. The others shuffled awkwardly. Graham looked at Del expectantly.

She returned his gaze with steely determination. "I want to get off this asteroid as much as you do, but this isn't the way. I'd rather be stuck here than walk into a trap."

"You don't get it. This is all a trap. This whole place." He lowered himself down onto the trackbed and walked toward the tunnel to their left.

"Wait, If you're going to walk all that way, you'll need this." Del reached out, ready to pass him her chemlight.

"I'll go with him," Sam said, stepping forward and hopping nimbly down off the platform to the tracks, the other chemlight in hand. Del stepped back, surprised.

"You don't want me to go?" he said, seeing Del's shock.

"This isn't Earth. You make your own decisions here," she said softly.

Sam looked from Del to Graham, to the dark tunnel entrance, and back to her. Then he joined Graham.

"You sure you aren't coming, Del?" Graham said, willing her to join them.

She shook her head firmly. "No. The way out is not through that tunnel. You heard Victor. Adam controls the trains."

Graham shrugged. "Come on, Sam, let's go home."

Sam disappeared into the blackness of the tunnel, loping along between one of the sets of gleaming rails, underneath the electric wires that snaked along the roof. Graham hopped between the two tracks, illustrating that if a train came he could jump out of the way.

The others watched the pair of them leave, wondering if they would make it, wondering if they'd sealed their own fate by not going with them. After the chemlight had become a small point in the darkness of the tunnel, Celeste said, "Maybe they'll make it."

As she spoke, there was a new sound from the opposite direction, in the tunnel to his right. At first, it was hard to make out, then it became clear. It was the electric hum of an approaching train. A light wind rustled the posters on the opposite wall.

Victor shouted after the other two, "There's a train coming. Train. Train."

They were a few hundred yards along the tunnel already. Graham heard Victor's faint shout but he didn't stop.

Sam covered the chemlight and stared back toward the platform, trying to see what prompted the shout. Then he spotted a spark in the distance and heard the crackle of the electric wire. He turned to warn Graham but the man had already disappeared into the darkness.

"Graham. Look," shouted Sam, jogging to catch him up.

Graham's red face appeared in the chemlight glow. "What is it? Come on."

Sam pointed up at the crackling, humming power lines, thinking it self-explanatory. Graham looked puzzled.

"A train's coming," Sam said. Graham responded by stepping over to the other set of tracks and walking away again.

Sam strained to try and hear what the others were shouting, but they were too far away. The shouts seemed to be getting more frantic but he couldn't make it out. He stepped over to the other tracks then watched as the train emerged into the station, its headlights off, but its front carriage illuminated by Del's single chemlight beam.

When his eyes tracked the beam of light toward the other platform, he suddenly worked out what the others had been shouting. He started to sprint away, shouting to Graham, "Run, run, there's two trains."

Behind them, the pair of trains took up both tracks, both heading in their direction, traveling fast, still accelerating.

Sam caught Graham in a few seconds, as the plump man stumbled and tripped through the tunnel.

He pressed the chemlight into Graham's sweating hand with baton-change swiftness. Then he sprinted away, his muscles pumping effortlessly, his feet gliding over the tracks. While he ran, he swept one hand along the wall, feeling for an alcove, for a place to hide.

In his sweating, scrambling, fear-filled way, Graham did the same, mumbling and waving the light around.

As the trains approached, he returned to the center of the tunnel and stood side on, in the space between the two lines. The chemlight reflected off the empty train cabs and he realized there was only a couple of inches between the two. Too late.

Sam didn't try the same trick. He just ran without looking back, even as the vibration of the rails and the crackle of the overhead wires told him the train was right behind him, until he could run no more.

When the last carriage passed the platform in a cold rush of air, with their solitary chemlight reflecting off the windows of the eerie, empty carriages, the others still hoped against hope that the two men had found a place to hide. Graham's scream and the loud thud, followed not long after by another thud, told them that this wasn't the case.

Even after the sound of the trains had subsided in the distance, and the crackle of the wires had died to nothing, no one spoke. No one stood either. They had all slumped against the station wall, each lost in their own thoughts.

Celeste was the first to break the silence. "There has to be something we can do. I don't want to follow them, but I don't like just sitting here."

"That way is trains." Mack pointed to the tunnel, then back the way they'd come from. "That way is fire and trucks. I don't like it any more than you do, but we have no choice, we just have to wait for the captain." He looked at Celeste. "How long will it really be before he calls for help? You sounded pretty confident earlier."

Celeste looked sheepish. "Look, I can't say, the rule's there but Taka, he uses common sense, and common sense says, don't call Pharix control unless you have to, and don't call the UN because, if it was just a comms failure, there'll be hell to pay once we return, and we'd lose the mission fee, which we need, because the elevator takes most of the work nowadays, and the shuttle needs repairs badly."

"So how long?" Mack asked gently.

She shuddered. "Maybe never. If he thinks there's a problem, he'll come look for us before he even considers calling the UN."

Victor said, "It doesn't matter. They wouldn't get to us in time anyway. I know what Adam's capable of. He's trained for conflict, for conflict management and resolution actually, but I'm sure he can translate those skills to actual conflict, to war. We've been lucky so far. He wasn't expecting Rabbit to have night vision. It took him a while to adjust, but he isn't going to let us stay here and wait for rescue. He'll be planning something."

"So given what you know about him, what can we do?"
Mack asked.

"I don't know. I don't know." Victor paced up and down
the platform. "What I do know is if we wait here, we'll be
dead within the hour, if not sooner. You saw the flame-throwing truck. If he's made that, what else has he built? What
were we thinking?" He stopped, and stood in silence, staring
out into the train tunnel.

"So there's nothing we can do here. We've got no effective
weapons. We just have to hope that help is on the way,"
Celeste said.

Victor shook his head in despair. Then he looked back at
the tunnel. There was something there, something in the
distance, a patch of lighter darkness.

"More trains," Victor said. "But he knows we aren't on
the tracks? What's he doing?"

He looked up to his right and spotted a camera. He jumped
up onto the fallen confectionery machine and leaped off
it, grabbing the camera with both hands, his momentum
ripping it down.

His fall was cushioned by the slick of chocolate bars and
potato chips leaking from the broken machine. He picked
up the cracked camera and threw it onto the tracks.

Del raked the walls with fire, sending the other three
cameras smashing to the ground.

The overhead wires were crackling now, and the sparks in
the distance lighted up the front of the two trains approaching fast. They stared at them, confused. Then Mack shouted,
"The other two are coming back."

He was right, sparks were visible in the other direction.
Victor ran toward the transit corridor, shouting to the others
as he ran, "Run, run, get off the platform."

The other three sprinted after him as the sound of the four
approaching trains got louder; a wall of sparks, rattle, and
hum. They had only made it a short distance up the corridor

when the two pairs of trains entered the station at full speed and crashed in a horrible grinding, cracking explosion.

The four of them dropped flat on the floor, as a fireball whooshed overhead, singeing their hair and leaving their ears full of jangling sound.

Smoke and dust followed the fireball, making them cough and sputter. Victor tried to breathe but lapsed into hyperventilation, sucking in fast breaths, sweating and sobbing in anger. His lungs stung with each half breath but he didn't care. He was angry, at Adam for the killing, at Graham for bringing him here, at himself for everything.

After the fiery heat had dampened to waves of thick black smoke that rolled out of the station entrance, they crawled slowly back onto the platform, more out of curiosity than from any particular plan. They looked out at the destruction. Molten metal and burning upholstery filled the station. Overhead wires twisted across the top of the wreckage.

"Maybe we can try the tunnel now," Del said.

Victor shook his head, "No, there's twenty trains or more, he must be ready for us. And if we do make it out, the trucks will be waiting. It's hopeless."

"Not quite." Mack pointed across the disaster scene.

"What?" Victor said.

On the wall of the other platform, a Pharix poster had peeled off in the heat of the blast, revealing a patch of concrete that was a different shade of gray to the rest.

"That looks like the entrance to one of the old tunnels. Hopefully the patch isn't too thick," Mack said.

Del took the hint and flicked her gun's safety catch off. She peppered the concrete with holes. The thin patch fell into dust.

"So you know the way?" Celeste said.

"Well, it's been a long time and I haven't been in this one before, but once I see a bit I remember, we'll be alright," Mack said.

They carefully picked their way across the smoldering wreckage, trying not to burn themselves, or send the whole unstable mess sliding down on top of them, all the while conscious of the fact that there could be more trains on the way.

Then Mack ripped away the remnants of the poster, and climbed into the narrow tunnel behind it.

Chapter 24

Celeste climbed up to join Mack in the tunnel, leaving Del and Victor on the platform.

She sniffed. "Is the air safe in here?"

"Probably," replied Mack as he began to walk along the tunnel, keeping low to avoid bumping his head. The chemlight in his hand lit up the rough-hewn rock walls of the narrow tunnel ahead.

Celeste followed him, hoping that the tunnel would lead somewhere, hoping to get as far away as possible from the station and the threat of further crashes.

Meanwhile, Victor and Del dragged a vending machine along the platform with some difficulty, scraping and sliding it past chunks of red-hot metal toward the tunnel entrance. When they reached the hole, they propped the machine up and pushed it into place, covering most of the entrance. Victor looked past the machine, into the tunnel. His eyes adjusted to the darkness and he saw the chemlight returning toward them. When it came closer, Mack's face appeared behind it.

"Dead end?" Victor said.

"No, not yet. Even it is, it's a good hiding place for the time being." Mack extended his hand to Victor.

Victor took the proffered hand and hopped up into the tunnel. Del kicked open the front of the vending machine and passed him up snacks and drinks. He handed them to the other two and offered his hand to Del. She ignored it and climbed up by herself, then helped him to pull the vending machine into place, blocking the hole completely.

Victor hoped that their ruse would be enough to fool Adam. Surely he would assume they were lying dead or dying under the wreckage from the train collision. He hoped it would be some time before Adam even considered the possibility that they'd escaped.

The tunnel darkened. Victor looked up and realized that the chemlight beam was moving off into the distance, along with Mack, Del, and Celeste. "Come on," Mack shouted from the direction of the receding light.

Victor rushed to catch up, running his hands along the walls to guide his feet, staring ahead at the light that moved up and down in rhythm with Mack's steps, occasionally blocked by the silhouettes of Del and Celeste.

Once he'd caught them up, he matched their pace, falling in line, as they followed the light beam along the blank, featureless tunnel that wound up and down, left and right, around tight bends and along long empty straights, narrowing further until they had to crab along sideways, squeezing between dusty walls, each of them waiting for the inevitable dead end, convinced the tunnel was going nowhere.

A series of rumbling explosions that shook the rock deepened their worry, indicating that more trains had plowed into the existing wreckage. Victor thought of the vending machine, wondering if it would have shifted and revealed their escape route. Then he imagined the effect of a flamethrower in a narrow, dead end space and he shivered.

"Do you recognize anything yet?" Celeste said.

Mack frowned, glad that the darkness hid his worry-creased brow. But not long after, his fear of an imminent dead end eased a little as another narrow tunnel met their own from the left.

Celeste stopped at the junction, wondering which tunnel to take but Mack just kept walking. She rushed to catch him up. "Shouldn't we stop and decide which way to go?"

"If it's any way, it's this way, the whole system's an organic thing. It wasn't planned. It's like a root system. It branches and branches until the tunnels end in ore seams, we just need to follow the wider tunnel each time and we'll reach the main system," he said.

Soon, as he'd predicted, more tunnels joined their own, one every few hundred yards. The tunnel walls became more defined, and as they walked further, they saw more hints at the tunnel's former use, the detritus of miners long gone, batteries, drill bits, and empty beer bottles.

After almost an hour, they reached a small cave. Mack entered, ducking under the faded overalls that hung on a line strung across the cave. On shelves cut into the rock wall, there was a pile of faded letters and magazines, an ancient looking projector, and other keepsakes.

The cave triggered long-forgotten memories in Mack. He remembered the day when, after a long dusty apprentice-ship with his cousin, an Australian miner of the old school, he'd claimed his first seam and blown a hole out of the rock to create a living space of his own.

While Mack reminisced, Victor picked through the pile of letters on the shelf.

"Leave them be, there's no luck in interfering with the dead's possessions," Mack said.

Victor put down the near-disintegrated letter he'd been reading. "How do you know they're dead?"

Mack shone the light on the ornate cross carved into the wall on Victor's left.

"Are they buried here?" Victor said, shocked at the thought, the distance from Earth, the loneliness of it. Then he thought of the situation they were in and realized they had a fair chance of meeting the same fate.

"Of course not. The cross is a memorial... and a reminder to others. It was a dangerous occupation in the early days," Mack said, and with that, he left, following the tunnel that led out of the other entrance to the cave. The others got the message and followed.

A few minutes later, after the awkwardness had dissipated, Celeste said, "Do you know where we are?"

"Not yet, but it looks promising," Mack said, "That cave belonged to one miner. He would have been part of one of the cooperatives. I say co-ops, they were gangs in all but name. It was a gold rush time and it paid to have a little safety in numbers. We didn't venture far from the spaceport back then. The less distance you had to travel to sell it to the middlemen, the less chance of getting your load stolen on the way." He paused. He'd forgotten the question.

"So we're close to the spaceport then?" Del nudged him toward an answer.

"Relatively. Within fifteen miles," he said. Upon seeing Del's expression, he refined his estimate, "Could be closer, anywhere between five and fifteen. We'll find out soon, this tunnel should join up to the others from the same co-op, then meet the main tunnel, and head straight for the elevators. There's only one tunnel to the spaceport." He neglected to mention the poor state of repair of much of the system, and the possibility of any number of collapsed tunnels between them and their destination, knowing that the lack of alternative routes meant there was no way round a collapse.

He also wondered if the others had noticed that the chemlight was fading in brightness, minute by minute, lumen by lumen. They had, but they kept quiet, trudging on in the growing darkness.

Celeste had stopped asking Mack if he knew their location. Instead, she watched his face, waiting for that spark of recognition, wondering what they would do when the light ran out, leaving them lost in the darkness with no hope of a rescuer ever finding them.

As they walked, a rumble began to shake the tunnel walls, similar to the sound of distant trucks. It grew in volume as other tunnels joined their own and the tunnel widened, allowing the four of them to walk alongside each other.

"What's that sound? We seem to be heading toward it," Victor said.

Mack cocked his head, listening. "I don't know."

"It could be trucks," Del said.

"I doubt it, it sounds more like machinery," Mack said, as the sound got louder and louder, until it shook the dust off the walls, filling the air with a cloud that interrupted the chemlight beam.

They rounded a bend and reached its source. The sound was coming from somewhere behind a long line of metal ventilation panels on the left hand side of the widened tunnel. A warm breeze swept through them, clearing the musty smell of the tunnel system and replacing it with a burned solder smell that was no improvement. Shafts of light slid between the gaps in the panels.

Victor carefully peeked through one of the gaps. He blinked in the light at first, then his eyes adjusted. Beyond the panel was a space so large that he couldn't see its end. He stepped back, eyes wide, and saw Mack prizing a panel away. Before Victor could warn him, the panel fell to the ground with a bang. Behind it lay an enormous cavern, filled with bright artificial light. Its walls were dotted with cameras.

Chapter 25

Mack rushed to switch his chemlight off, cursing his recklessness, hoping they hadn't been spotted. Then he looked again, and saw to his relief that the cameras were all facing down toward the floor, toward the broad conveyor that ran all the way to the far end of the cavern a mile away, flanked by giant assembly bots, thirty-foot high, sitting silently on huge concrete plinths.

Their vantage point was high up on the wall, a few feet below the roof, eighty feet above the floor, well out of the cameras' sightlines. Mack relaxed. They were safe, for now.

Directly below them, was the entrance to another tunnel, flanked by two huge steel doors. The loud rumble seemed to be coming from that direction, along with a foundry glow that shone through, flickering off the cavern walls with a dull orange light.

Celeste turned to Mack. "You know where we are now?"

"Isn't it obvious?" he said.

Victor ventured a guess. "Some kind of machine factory."

"The machine factory. We're a little further away from the spaceport than I'd expected. At least we're safe from Adam," Mack said.

"You heard what I said about him. It won't take him long to work out where we've gone," Victor replied.

"The trucks aren't going to fit in here." Mack gestured toward the cramped tunnel.

"Those will, though." Victor pointed at the conveyor belt that, only a few moments before, had been still and empty. It was moving with a clank and whir. As the four of them watched, the first of a new batch of machines appeared from the foundry. It had twelve spindly metal legs attached to a blocky metal body.

As it moved, the assembly bots added other parts to the legs, parts salvaged from other mine machinery. Drills were attached to two legs. A huge circular saw blade was bolted to another. Then lightweight digging arms to another two. Finally, a bot connected two rotating cameras to give it rudimentary eyes.

By the time it reached the halfway point, the machine looked like an unwieldy, spidery Frankenstein, ridiculous-looking to the watchers from above.

Their smiles faded when the spider machine raised itself and started to move, racing along the conveyor belt toward the cavern exit, moving with unlikely coordination and incredible speed.

Victor shuddered. The others were silent, staring as another copy appeared behind the first, then another, and another, one every thirty seconds.

The cameras still ignored them, intent on monitoring the production line, but all four of the watchers had crouched lower and lower with the emergence of each new machine.

Eventually, there was a break in the flow, though the belt still moved. Despite the cold dread that the machines inspired, they kept watching, transfixed, and after a minute, another machine appeared, twice the size of the others but with the same basic design. One robotic arm welded a tank full of flamethrower fuel to the top of the body and another craned in a huge flamethrower nozzle that attached in the place of a cutting blade.

"Well, that one won't be able to fit in here," Celeste said.

"The others will. I don't want to wait around for them," Victor said, horrified and amazed in equal measure at Adam's ingenuity, not for the first time feeling a pang of guilt wash over him.

He noticed the chemlight's fading light. "It's running down," he said.

"At least we know where we are," Mack said, giving the light an experimental shake and managing to brighten it ever so slightly.

"Great," Victor said.

Mack ignored the sarcasm. "I know the way to the spaceport from here. We should come out a few hundred yards from the elevators. He won't be expecting that."

"He's trained to anticipate every eventuality," Victor said.

"He'll expect this one less anyway, and we're not dead yet. I'll wager he wasn't anticipating that." Mack laughed, as Del helped him to push the panel back into place.

Then he strode away, and the others followed. As they moved through the tunnel, lighted by the faint chemlight glow, passing piles of rusting mining equipment, and side tunnels that rose or fell to other levels, they began to hear loud rumbles. This time, the rumbles sounded ominously like trucks.

Without waiting for the inevitable question, Mack said, "Traffic in Tunnel One, it must be beneath us somewhere."

A little way from the machine factory, the tunnel dipped into a steady downward slope. At the base of the slope, there was another tunnel entrance to the left of them. The entrance was blocked with a concrete plug. The walls and roof around the concrete were cracked and burned. Mack knew exactly where they were now.

He shone his chemlight to the right, away from the concrete, and to his relief, Victor and Celeste didn't notice the burned rock.

But Del did. She looked over at Mack, her look betraying no emotion but the mere act of looking enough. He looked away, unable to meet her gaze, struggling to maintain his composure.

A loud rumble shook the tunnel. Victor looked up, watching the dust fall from the roof. The main tunnel had to be close. He was glad to be hidden from the source of the sound, and the prying eyes of Adam's cameras, but still edgy, his nerves jangling, listening for the slightest hint of pursuit, the image of the spider machines still fresh in his mind. He'd spent most of the walk trying to estimate how long it would take Adam to work out they were still alive, find the hole in the wall, and guess their route and destination. He didn't like his conclusions.

A little way ahead, Mack and Del walked together. Mack directed the chemlight, moving it from one side to the other, reflecting it off the tunnel walls to guide their way. Then he stopped, tilting the chemlight down, covering the light, before switching it off completely, hoping he hadn't made another mistake.

The left-hand wall of the tunnel was open, crumbled away, destroyed in the construction of the cavern that opened up to their left. Del crept forward, keeping low, her weapon out and raised.

"Wait," whispered Mack from behind her right shoulder, "It should be okay, I think it's the refinery." He felt the air current, sensing a huge space out there in the blackness, somehow different to the ordinary dark of the rock wall.

Celeste walked toward them. "What's the refinery? Is it close to the spaceport?" she said, still hoping that they would round a corner and be right next to one of the elevators, still worried about Taka, hoping he hadn't decided to come look for them yet.

"It's the largest cavern in the mine, ten miles long, full of machines and furnaces and sorters. If production were running, the sound would be deafening. It's quite a spectacle," Mack said.

The other three peered out from their positions, touching the right hand wall, trying to imagine the impressive space and failing, seeing only blackness and wishing they were at the spaceport already.

Mack stood still, remembering the days when all that lay before him was his to control, his hollow kingdom. It had been a heavy responsibility. Unlike Felix and Graham, he had cared, feeling personally responsible for every mishap, every production problem, every job loss.

"We have to move, just because there's no production doesn't mean there's no cameras. They could be infrared," Del said impatiently.

"Okay. Take the chemlight. Lead the way," Mack said.

She took the light but didn't switch it on yet, and moved ahead slowly, feeling her way along the wall. After they'd moved a short distance at a painfully slow pace, she risked switching it on. Its faint glow lighted the tunnel. She was relieved to see the left-hand wall. They had passed the cavern. She picked up the pace.

But they'd only moved another few hundred yards when she stopped dead, switching the chemlight off again. Ahead, a white light illuminated the tunnel, before disappearing. Fearing an ambush, Del drew her weapon and moved forward, staying low, feeling no real fear, only the rush of adrenaline.

Another white light flickered off the tunnel wall to her right and she spotted its source. They had reached another break in the wall. To the left was another huge cavern. Bright spots of light moved across its floor, sending reflections flickering up the walls, the same reflections that had worried her before. The lights belonged to small forklifts that moved silently across the cavern, sending a glow of light ahead of them.

Del watched, joined by the others, working out the geography of the space as the machines moved and lighted up new parts of the cavern. Huge stacks of platinum bars filled the floor. The forklift machines were loading bars and moving them out of a doorway into another space.

Victor marveled at the sight of the glinting metal. He'd overheard miners talking about the stockpile before, and thought they were exaggerating its size.

"There'll be thousands of tons there," Del said.

"Tens of thousands," Mack said.

"But there's always shortages on Earth," Celeste said, confused. "The warehouses in Missoula are empty most of the time."

"Supply and demand," Victor said.

"Exactly." Mack smiled.

The penny dropped and Celeste's expression soured. She shook her head and started to walk on, toward a bright glow in the tunnel ahead, followed by Del and the others.

As they walked, Mack wondered why the forklifts were moving the metal around. His unspoken question was answered when they reached the glow in the tunnel ahead. It was coming from the space to their left, the last of the great caverns, well lit by a combination of the forklift headlights, and the bright lights of hundreds of silver rockets.

The forklifts were loading the platinum bars into the engineless rockets that lined a winding conveyor belt. Once the rockets were full to their fifty-ton capacity, the cargo door would slam shut. Then the belt would whir and move them to the end of a long line of waiting rockets in the far corner of the cavern. At the head of the line was an airlock. It was closed.

"I don't understand. Why's he attacking us if he's about to restart deliveries?" Del asked.

"I don't know. It doesn't make any sense," Mack said, confused by this new development.

"Maybe it's just an automatic process," Celeste said.

"Maybe." Victor looked doubtful. Then he noticed the red lights of the cameras, all around the walls of the cavern, and felt a chill come over him. "We should go, there's cameras everywhere," he said, feeling vulnerable in the light.

He hurried into the tunnel ahead. Del switched the chemlight back on once they'd passed beyond the cavern, into the full tunnel again. Its weak light only just illuminated the way. It was fading fast.

The tunnel widened again. Tunnel after tunnel joined theirs from either side. Mining equipment was scattered everywhere: drill bits, drive belts, and ore grinders. The valuable stuff was long gone.

Mack smiled, realizing where they were, as another tunnel joined them and the tunnel widened again. "We're getting close, we should reach the main cavern very soon. Then we'll only be three or four miles away from the spaceport." He could see the entrance to the cavern up ahead, the tunnel widening as it approached.

Del looked alarmed. "Will there be machines there?"

"No, you misunderstand. It's the first operations cavern, the center of the old mine, where it all started. It's not much to look at but it used to be a busy place, the town center for a two-thousand strong workforce in the early days. Pioneers and thieves the lot of them," Mack said, feeling nostalgic again. He was about to go on with his history lesson when there was a sound in the tunnel behind them, a light skitter.

Chapter 26

"Machines. Run," Victor said. Outlined in the light of the last cavern were two spider machines, moving at a steady pace, cameras panning from side to side, checking every inch of the tunnel.

They ran. In their haste, they forgot to switch off the chemlight.

Victor followed her into the old operations cavern, far smaller than the new one. He could just make out the shapes of several dilapidated sheds and huts beneath the low roof.

He looked back. He couldn't see the machines but he could hear the sound of their legs, clink, clink on the rock floor. They were close. "We'll never make the spaceport before them. We need to hide. Which one?" he asked.

Mack looked at the sheds, trying to get his bearings. It had been twenty years since he'd been in this part of the mine. It might have been twenty years since anyone had been in this cavern, but he guessed not, well aware of the natural propensity of miners to seek out secret places.

"This way." He took the chemlight from Del and, using it to cast a dim light on the floor ahead of him, led them to the largest of the sheds.

From the cramped entrance hall, they moved into a narrow corridor, scattered with papers.

Mack paused at each doorway and shone the light around, gauging the room's suitability for a hiding place. His brow furrowed as he walked, listening for the sound of machines, expecting them to enter the building at any second.

They passed a series of offices, a store for space suits, and a large bathroom. There was still no obvious hiding place. They reached the end of the corridor and checked the last room. It was completely empty.

The sound of metal legs grew loud, the machines moving between the buildings. It sounded like there were more than two, a lot more than two. They heard a drill whir and the snap of wood as a machine gained entry to a nearby building.

"Quick, find somewhere, anywhere," Del said, weapon in hand, sure she'd have to use it soon, ready to go down fighting.

"Back this way," Victor said, thinking fast. With him leading the way, they ran back to the space suit storage room. He grabbed a suit from the rack and started to climb into it. "Put these on," he said.

"What are you doing?" Celeste asked.

"Just get in the suits," he said.

Before she could reply, she heard something enter the building, and rushed to get into the suit as quickly and as quietly as possible.

There was a cacophony of metal legs on the concrete floor. The machines moved from room to room, getting closer with each passing second.

After a minute of silent struggle, all four of them made it into the stiff arms and legs of the ancient suits. A machine was scuttling around the office next door.

"Helmets and gloves," whispered Victor, grabbing a helmet and gloves off a rack and putting them on. The others followed his lead. Mack struggled, twisting his beard around until it fit within the confines of the helmet.

"Light off. Light off." Victor gestured wildly, pointing at the chemlight in Mack's hand.

Mack couldn't hear Victor, but he guessed his meaning, switching the light off, just in time. Seconds later, the machine entered the room. It crabbed its way in, scanned the space with camera eyes, and moved the lumpy suits to one side to look for heat signatures in the darkness.

As the metal arms moved around them, they watched out of the helmet visors in disbelief, waiting for the spell to break, and the cutting blade to come slicing through the silence. Instead, the machine scanned the room once more, cameras swiveling to check every nook and cranny, then it left, moving toward the bathroom next door.

A few minutes later, they saw the twin dots of its infrared cameras pass the doorway again, heading back outside. It was another five minutes before any of them moved.

Mack switched the chemlight back on. They stared at each other in amazement, not quite believing what had just happened.

Mack flicked on his suit battery and waited, watching the suit display on his arm, willing it to power on. To his relief, it did. The other suit systems began to start up. First, the intake compressor whirred, sucking in atmosphere and splitting off the oxygen, refilling the large tank on his back. Then the helmet radio crackled as it powered on.

Microphones relayed the outside sound to his ears. He could still hear the machines, but they seemed to be moving away, toward the other side of the cavern.

Satisfied they were safe for the time being, he tapped a switch on the right-hand side of his helmet, the suit's workings still second nature to him. A bright light shone from just above the visor, far brighter than the chemlight, so bright the others shielded their eyes with their gloves. He adjusted the brightness to a tolerable level. Then he switched the chemlight off and left it on the ground.

After Mack had helped the others to switch on their suits, radios, and lights, Celeste's voice crackled through their radios. "I can't believe that worked."

"Me neither," Victor said. "I'm glad the heat shielding's still functioning."

"Me too. Good thinking," Mack said.

Del just shook her head in disbelief. They laughed, patted backs, and clasped hands, relief washing over them, before they stopped dead, hearing a sound of spider legs outside the shed. Then there was nothing. Silence came again, the sounds of moving metal faded completely, and the eerie quiet returned.

"There could be more coming," Del said, aware that the others seemed ready to move.

"If we switch our lights off, they've got no way to see us," Victor said.

"Unless Adam turns the lights on," Celeste said.

"I don't think he can. I doubt any of the lighting circuits in here still work, and even if they do, I don't think he'd be able to control them," Mack said.

"Even if the machines can't see us, it'd be hard to stay out of their way if we met them in a tunnel," Del said.

Celeste leaned out of the door, checking the corridor. It was empty. "I don't see the point in waiting around. We've got the advantage for once. Why wait until Adam figures out what we've done?" she said.

"I agree," Victor said. "The sooner we get back to the shuttle the better."

"And how will we get there?" Del said.

"We're only a few miles away, aren't we?" Celeste asked Mack.

"About four, I think," he replied.

"And how much of that along the approach tunnel to the elevators?" Del asked.

"Only a few hundred yards," he said.

"So long as the lights are off, it'll be no problem," Celeste said, a little frustrated, eager to get back to the shuttle, back to Taka. "What else do you suggest we do? Wait here?"

"Yes." Del folded her arms.

"For what?" Celeste said.

"For your captain to follow company rules and call for assistance."

"You should know how the rules work when it comes to Pharix. Taka's old school. He won't want to create a fuss unnecessarily. He won't be imagining all this," Celeste said, gesturing at the space suits.

Victor said, "We could get half a mile into that tunnel and get ambushed. Even if we make it to the approach tunnel, it might be blocked by machines. But I think we have to look, we have to try, I don't think we're safe anywhere in this mine now. The machines will find us. Nowhere's safe." His face was somber. "Every second, every minute we delay, Adam is thinking, he's analyzing, he's working out new ways to achieve his goal, and his goal is to find and kill us...I just don't know why."

"Okay, we go." Del checked her weapon and walked away toward the entrance. The others followed, surprised at Del's change of heart, glad they didn't have to decide between going for the shuttle or staying with the one weapon-carrying member of the group. Victor felt safer with Del, not safe, but safer.

Del left the shed and waited for Mack to catch up, realizing she had no idea which tunnel to take. Eight tunnels joined the cavern.

Mack spotted the one that led to the spaceport and walked toward it, dimming his light a little more, feeling exposed, listening for the telltale sound of metal legs, watching for the red lights in the darkness. There was no sign of the machines.

Victor said, "Should we check the sheds for supplies, would there be anything useful? Like weapons?"

Mack shook his head. "You know miners, they're natural-born hoarders. Anything not bolted down will be gone. No point wasting our time looking, sorry."

They skirted the wall of a low shed that blocked their route to the tunnel, and moved round past its front doors. As they passed, Mack glanced up at something above the doorway and stopped in his tracks. The others looked at him confused, wondering why he'd stopped next to a bar, a seedy-looking one, with a cracked neon sign that read "The Blue Room."

Mack ignored the looks they gave him as he pushed the doors open and entered the shed, muttering to himself. "Why didn't I think of it?"

The others looked at each other, mystified at Mack's sudden brain snap or attack of nostalgia, but they followed him in anyway.

Chapter 27

At first, they could see very little. Their lights reflected off Mack's helmet, masking the space beyond him. As they moved in further, Mack turned his light up to full brightness and they could see more.

What they saw was astonishing. Directly in front of them was a long silver-edged display console, and behind it, seven neat rows of computer servers, covered by a thin layer of dust but protected from wear by the closed environment, the doors unopened for years.

Mack had barely remembered the old computer but he had more idea of what to expect than the others. He was pleasantly surprised by the untouched state of the server banks.

Celeste was far more impressed by the sight of the dusty servers than the tonnes of shiny metal that she'd seen earlier. She shook her head in disbelief. "Of all the places. I haven't seen a server bank like this since engineering school. I didn't know there were any of these old models left except in museums."

"As long as it works, I don't care how old it is," Mack said.

"Can you get it running?" Del asked.

Victor and Celeste didn't respond. They were already patrolling the aisles, checking connections and wiping the dust from wiring harnesses. While the other two watched, they returned to the front of the shed and began to check the display console itself.

"Will it run?" asked Del, for the second time.

Victor looked up. "We'll just need power. A generator would be ideal. If not, we can try a few of the suit batteries in series."

Mack and Del left the shed and began to scour the other buildings, looking for power, glad they had something to do.

After twenty minutes searching the dusty corners of forgotten rooms, they returned from their search with a pile of batteries from the remaining suits in the storeroom, to find Victor and Celeste still checking and rechecking connections.

"Did you find anything else?" Victor said.

"No. The miners might have ignored the museum-piece computing, but they don't waste power. They've taken it all. There's no batteries except the suit ones, no generators, nothing," Mack said, apologetically.

"We'll just have to leave some of the servers off," Victor said, disappointed that they wouldn't be able to run the computer at full power. He started to wire the batteries together.

"We're only going to have about fifteen minutes of power. We have to be quick." He wired in the last two batteries to make it seven in the series and prepared to connect them to the console.

"We'll call the shuttle first, and get Taka to call the UN forces at Luna, and Pharix control on Earth," Celeste said.

"Okay," Del said. Mack nodded.

Victor connected the wire. Nothing happened until Celeste wiggled the power connection at the back of the console. The screen in the center lit up and the keyboard's backlighting flickered on. A few of the connections in the back sparked and smoked a little, but the screen stayed lit and lines of strange symbols started to scroll. Victor squinted at the screen.

"It's not working," Mack said, crestfallen.

"It is... It's just set to Vietnamese," Victor said.

"Vietnamese." Mack shook his head in frustration, remembering the nationality of most of the tech crew when he'd first arrived on Metis. Then he stopped and looked at Victor. "Wait, how do you know that?"

"I know a little, but mainly spoken. Written's different." Victor stared at the screen, trying to work out which button to press.

The others watched, willing him to work it out before the power ran out. Mack and Celeste wondered how Victor had come to know any Vietnamese. Del didn't. She'd put two and two together straight away, but she was still worried, not sure if Victor's metal shop slang would be up to the task.

He tapped the screen, moving through menus, guessing at words, wishing he'd learned more, hoping in vain for a language change button, but there was no sign of one. For all he knew, Vietnamese was the factory setting.

While he worked, he could see the battery status lights blinking then going out, one by one. Finally, under pressure, he saw a few words he recognized and pressed them. The other words and symbols disappeared, to be replaced by a screen that demanded a code.

"What's the ship code?" Victor asked

"Four zero one eight two," Celeste replied, and he typed it in. A jingling dialing tone rang out through the shed. It rang for two minutes then cut out. He tried again, as more battery lights went out.

"How long do we have?" he said, as the dialing tone rang out for the second time.

"Ten minutes, max," Celeste said.

"You know the UN code?"

"Better to try the ship again," she said.

Victor said, "I'll try the ship again after, what's the UN code?"

"Six niner niner one."

"Thanks." He typed it in and dialed. It rang and rang. After a minute, a bearded man in military fatigues appeared on the display, looking surprised to be called from Metis, especially by a man in what looked like an ancient space suit.

"McMurphy base?" Victor said.

"Yeah. Let me guess, you've just woken up from cryosleep and you want to know what year it is," the man said.

"We're on a mission with Pharix and we need assistance," Victor said, an edge to his voice.

At the mention of Pharix, Victor saw the man straighten in his chair.

The man said, "Uh, I got your location as the mining asteroid Metis, what's your mission ID?"

"I don't know. The mission leader is no longer with us," Victor said.

"I'll need the mission ID," the man said wearily.

Celeste said, "Double zero, double two, niner two." She sounded confident, despite the made-up number.

The man typed it in midair. "Okay, so what's your request?"

"Code fourteen," she said.

"Code one four?"

"Code fourteen. Yes."

"You sure about that? Present threat to life?" He raised his eyebrows.

"Yes. That's why I repeated it twice," she snapped. "Three team members are deceased. We require urgent assistance. I repeat, urgent assistance."

"What about your own security? Last time I was on Metis, your security force was two hundred strong."

"Things have changed. There's no permanent security force. A computer malfunction has led to the mine's own systems mounting a sustained attack against us. The threat comes under UN universal action laws and requires immediate military response," she said.

"Yes, yes, I've read our own code. We'll send a ship. As Metis is private territory, costs will be borne wholly by the property owner. Is that acceptable?"

"Affirmative." A faint smile flickered across Celeste's face.

"Okay, they'll begin launch preparations now." He made a few gestures in the air and pulled up projections. "ETA is uh, seven hours and five minutes. You think you can hold out till they arrive?"

"We don't have much of a choice, do we? Just tell them that the whole fleet of mine machinery has been weaponized and turned into a hostile force," she said.

He raised his eyebrows again. "I'll inform them."

With that, the vision shut off. Victor checked the batteries. Most of the lights were out. He unplugged them from the computer.

"What about calling Taka?" Celeste asked.

"Help's on the way, he'll hear the radio traffic," Victor said.

Del said, "What about Adam? Will he have heard?"

"His communications systems are down," Celeste said.

"That's what he told us. He also told us that production was down. Who knows what he's actually up to," Mack said.

"We have to assume he heard, we've got no way of finding out," Victor said.

"Whether he heard us or not, he's probably more concerned about the UN juggernaut heading his way than a few barely armed Pharix contractors stuck in a maze of tunnels," Celeste said.

"Hope so," Del said. "But just for my peace of mind, will he be able to locate the signal to here?"

"If his communications were up, yes," Mack said.

"He still won't be able to see us," Victor said.

"I'm sure he can work something out in seven hours," Del said.

"We should head for the exit, before he comes looking for us," Celeste said.

"I'm not sure. I'd rather hide in the old mine somewhere," Victor said.

"Hang on, you were all for leaving half an hour ago," she said.

"Half an hour ago, we didn't have a UN ship inbound to rescue us. Half an hour ago we had no other choice. There's no need to rush out there and risk getting killed when rescue's only a few hours away."

"Seven hours," Celeste corrected him.

"Graham tried to rush," Mack said flatly.

Del grimaced, thinking of the blast of the flamethrower and the thud of the train. The leader should not outsurvive her team, she thought.

Mack saw the pained look on her face. "Sorry, I'd just rather take our chances hiding near here, than going out into the rest of the mine. It'll be brimming with machines, the ones we've seen and who knows what else. You don't know what he's expecting. Maybe he won't expect us to stay close to the communications console after giving away our location. Also, these sheds give us the best chance in a fight. Out in the tunnels, we'd be sitting ducks."

"In the main tunnels maybe," Del responded. "But what about the side ones, the old mine workings? There must be somewhere we can hole up for seven hours, somewhere the spiders can't get to easily."

Mack said, "I guess so, I hadn't thought of—"

From the doorway, Victor shouted, "Lights out. We have to go."

Chapter 28

"What is it?" Del asked.

"Machines. Lots of them. He knows. Switch your lights off," Victor said.

They switched them off, then rushed through the doorway and out to the right, just in time to avoid the flailing legs of the first spider machine. Behind it in the darkness were set upon set of bright infrared eyes.

"This way," barked Victor, knowing the machines would have detected their lights, knowing that Adam had found them. How long would it take him to guess the suit trick now he'd seen them disappear in front of his machines? Not long, he suspected, as he pressed up against the outer wall of the cavern.

He grabbed Mack's hand and pulled him along behind him as he edged along the wall, trying not to look toward the red eyes. Mack grabbed Del's hand, and Del, Celeste's. Their line moved along the wall of a cavern filled with a sea of red lights.

Victor headed along the first tunnel he came to, still sticking to the wall, until he looked up, and saw there was no sign of lights in this one. He'd lucked out. "Run, Run," he said.

The others didn't need telling. They sprinted, running their hands along the right-hand wall to guide them through the dark. There was a sudden flash of light behind them. Victor turned in time to see the computer shed burst into flame. Adam had solved the problem of light.

Victor knew they would only have a few seconds until one of the machines happened to look this way. He darted down a narrow tunnel to their right, losing his balance as the floor dropped down steeply in the dark, pulling Mack behind him. He heard the others behind him, dropping, and rolling, and bumping into the walls, thankfully cushioned a little by their suits and helmets.

The tunnel flattened out and the four of them skidded and bumped to a stop. As the dust settled, they clambered to their feet.

"Is everyone okay?" Celeste said.

"Yeah," Mack replied.

"Sore, but yes," Del said.

"Yes." Victor risked switching his light on. They were in a narrow passageway in the rock, only a few feet wide.

He dared not turn the light to face the way they'd come, fearing the red eyes, knowing they must have been spotted in the light of the fire.

As the sound of more explosions rolled down the tunnel toward them, Mack said, "They're destroying the lot," sadness in his voice.

"And if they don't know where we are already, they'll come looking once they realize we're not hiding in a shed," Celeste said, then paused, as she heard the sound of metal legs in the distance. Without speaking, they switched their lights off and started moving, eager to get as far away from the noise as possible.

They edged along the narrowing passage for ten long minutes, waiting with bated breath for the sound of metal pursuit.

Finally, they stopped, or rather Victor stopped. He'd tripped over something on the floor. After putting his hands out to stop his fall, he switched his light back on to see what it was.

He came face to face with the face, or rather what used to be the face, of a miner, a long-dead miner by the looks of it. The skeletal remains, still clad in mining overalls, sat propped up against the rock wall, one arm knocked to an unnatural angle by the collision with Victor. An open tool-box and a helmet similar to their own lay on the ground beside the body. Victor recoiled. The others stood frozen, unable to switch their own suit lights on in their shock. This was the last thing they'd expected.

Mack recovered quickest, numbed by previous exposure. Del and Celeste also recovered quickly, their initial shock replaced by a morbid curiosity.

"I wonder what killed him," Celeste said.

Victor moved back, and stood up, slowly regaining his composure, his hands shaking from the shock.

Mack wasn't looking at the body, he was kneeling beside it, rifling through the contents of the toolbox. He said, "Look at where the helmet is. Remember the atmosphere wasn't oxygenated back then."

Celeste looked and the truth of the situation dawned on her. Mack said, "Sadly, the suicide rate was pretty high, far higher than the accident rate. Working for days alone, searching for a new seam..." As he spoke, he thought of his cousin, remembering the moment when he rounded the corner to rouse him for the cooperative meeting, to tell him they were all waiting on him.

He jolted out of the painful memory as his gloved fingers closed on four cubes in the toolbox, wrapped in thick paper. Next to them was a roll of wire. He forgot the past for the time being.

"What is it?" Del asked, noticing Mack's smile.

"C-4, enough to blow another operations cavern." He still had a miner's sensibility when it came to finders keepers, dead man's property or not. "And detonators too," he said, finding a box of blasting caps beneath the tools.

Victor looked at him strangely, remembering Mack's reaction to him picking up the letter earlier.

Mack met Victor's gaze and guessed his thoughts, but said nothing, unwilling to explain the intricacies of mining etiquette. "This will make things more interesting if the machines do come down here," he said, adding, "If it's preserved okay. I guess we'll have to see when the time comes."

He put the items in his pocket, moving carefully, aware of the danger. "Maybe we should move further."

The others didn't need much of an invitation to leave the dead man's company. They started walking, moving into what was now a narrow cleft in the rock. Eventually it narrowed too much and they had to stop.

"What now?" Celeste asked.

"Now we wait." Victor said.

They all moved apart a little, making themselves as comfortable as possible in a space too small to stand up in and too narrow to fit in unless sideways.

"I'm going to save battery." Victor switched his light off. The others followed suit, leaving them in darkness.

"I don't think the spiders will get us here," Mack said.

"Let's not tempt fate," Del said, and with that, they stopped talking. The only sound was the whir of their suit compressors cycling on and off as their oxygen tanks kept themselves topped up.

For the first time Victor thought about what would happen to Maria if he didn't make it back. If Graham had been true to his word she had six months and then what? Who else would pay her bills? The responsibility weighed on him, and he tried to think of other things, but every train of thought returned to that image: the body of his wife floating alone, blissfully unaware, her beauty undiminished by life's cruelties, at least to his vision.

Celeste thought of home, of the family hotel on Ouvea, of the speedboat pulling into the crystal-clear lagoon, and disgorging the local police to bear the news of her death to her parents, and her elder brother. She tried to think of other things but that image, the boat skimming the waves, the policewoman on the bow, her father looking out with his binoculars, it felt so real. Then she remembered that it was, remembering her younger sister. She held back the tears, not wanting the others to hear her weakness.

Mack thought of his farm at first, wondering if his brother had even read the carefully typed list of tasks and dates that he'd stuck to the fridge. Then his mind drifted back to the mine. He went through all he could remember about the layout of the old tunnels, recalling facts and layout details that he hadn't known he still held in memory, then tried to remember his C-4 calculations. It had been so long since he'd used a charge, and he'd never used one in anger. Well, that wasn't strictly true, he thought as he remembered the last time and wished he hadn't, putting all his effort into trying not to think about that day, cursing his brain for thinking it as his chest tightened.

Del felt the guilt. Heard the thud as the train hit Sam. Saw the flaming image of Rabbit. Saw the expression on his face, the disappointment, the disapproval in his eyes, as if they were saying why me? Why not you? You brought us here. She shuddered and fought back tears. Then she saw it. Saw the resemblance. The image of Rabbit twisted into something else, someone else, a man in dress uniform in front of Corsican mountains. He had piercing blue eyes, eyes that sliced through the years. The parade ground backdrop disappeared and they were in the jungle of her nightmares, explosions surrounding them. He called out to her. He screamed. But she couldn't reach him.

Chapter 29

March 17
2092

Metis

Victor woke from a long, dreamless sleep, thinking he was still in their rented house at Missoula.

Maria stood above him, shaking his shoulder. "Wake up."

He looked around at the sparse hotel room and remembered where they were. It was their second day on Metis.

"Come on. Time to show these hicks what Adam can do," Maria said, with the enthusiasm of a kid on Christmas morning. Victor yawned, stretched, and got out of bed, still tired from their journey.

After a few false starts and wrong turns, a short train journey and a walk up a winding corridor, they reached the entrance to the Tech department.

The same security guard from the day before sat in a plastic chair by the gate, reading a book. They went to walk past him.

"Hey. Stop." He lowered his book. "Where's your ID?" He brandished his own, which hung from a lanyard round his neck, showing his name: Davor Petric.

"We weren't given IDs. It's only our second day. We came here yesterday, remember?" Victor said.

Davor eyed them with suspicion.

"Arkolov can vouch for us," Victor said. "Can you get him?"

The guard pressed his pico and said, "Call Arkolov." After a minute, he said, "He's not answering. You'll have to wait."

"We're going in. Arkolov will vouch for us once you get hold of him." Maria ducked under the barrier and strode off toward Adam's cavern.

Victor looked at Davor, who hadn't made any attempt to get up from his plastic chair. "If there's any problem, come get me. I'll take the blame, we'll be in the last one," he said, before jogging to catch Maria up. The tunnel ahead was empty. There was no sign of Arkolov or any of the technicians.

When they reached the last of the four caverns, the glass door was closed. Victor pushed the door handle. The door slid open and he stepped back as a freezing blast of air rushed out. First he noticed the layer of ice that had formed on the inside of the door. Then he saw the shock on Maria's face. He looked inside the room, following her gaze.

Everything—Adam's glass container, and all the wires and tubes—was covered in a thick layer of ice. Icicles had even begun to form on the roof. The display on the wall by the door showed that the temperature was minus twenty degrees, and falling fast. Victor propped the door fully open to let the warmer air in. The huge climate-control fans in the wall whirred furiously, still trying to bring the temperature down.

Maria tapped at the display, trying to adjust the temperature. "What's the password?" she shouted.

"The password?" he replied.

"What is it, quick?"

"They didn't tell me anything about a password," he said and ran in the direction of the other rooms, shouting Arkolov's name. The first two rooms were empty. When he ran into the last of the four, he saw the time and understood why. It was five in the morning. No wonder Davor hadn't wanted to let them in. Arkolov and his technicians wouldn't arrive at work for hours yet.

He shouted toward Davor, "Try Arkolov again. It's an emergency," finally causing the guard to rise from his chair.

Victor returned to Adam's room and found Maria stuck in a desperate loop, running in, frantically trying to guess the password, running out to warm up a little, before returning for another attempt—and the temperature at minus fifteen and rising slowly, too slowly.

He ran past her, toward the corner where he'd left his toolbox. After kicking it away from the ice that glued it to the floor, he picked it up, juggling the freezing metal between his hands, ignoring the burning sensation in his fingertips, shivering in the cold wind from the climate fans.

He used a tool to pry the temperature display open. As alarms blared in the corridor, he connected its wires to the terminals on a tiny computer he'd pulled from the box, hoping that the computer would cope with the shock of the icy wires.

It did, and after a rushed series of commands, delivered with near-frozen fingers, the fans inside the room stopped dead. His computer displayed the temperature on a small projection. It rose quickly now, first to zero, then ten, twenty, and within the hour, a steady sixty degrees.

By that time, the mine security, Mack, Arkolov, and the computer techs, had all arrived. Maria was inside the room with Adam, running through diagnostics, checking for damage. Technicians moved around them, mopping up the water that was pooling beneath Adam's container as the room defrosted.

Victor stood outside with Mack and Arkolov.

"You told me to set it to the default temperature. How were we supposed to know your supercomputer was the only one in the world that doesn't need to run cold?" Arkolov scowled.

"It's just a simple misunderstanding. No harm, no foul. I'm sure Victor doesn't blame you," Mack said.

Victor did blame him. The man must have known that an organic computer couldn't operate below freezing, let alone minus twenty. But he had already decided that accusing him would be counterproductive. He would wait to see Mack's response.

"It was a simple misunderstanding, but it could have been catastrophic," Mack said. "We're lucky you two came in so early this morning. We might not get so lucky again."

Victor knew that Mack was right. So far, Maria had found no damage, except a sluggishness in Adam's processes that was gradually lifting with the temperature. They'd been lucky.

Mack continued, "I spoke to headquarters after our conversation yesterday. Graham has clarified their expectations. They want Adam to take over noncritical systems as soon as possible, starting with the transit system."

"That is safety critical," Arkolov said.

"Not according to headquarters," Mack said. "They won't allow him to control oxygen, water, power, trucks, or platinum delivery yet, but everything else is open."

"My computers already control everything else. Do headquarters have a problem with my work?"

"I'm going to check on Maria," Victor said, feeling awkward. Once he reached Adam, he looked back. The two men were huddled together, talking in low voices. He couldn't make out their words. No doubt they were embarrassed by such an error on only Adam's second day.

Maria nudged him. "What's happening?" she said.

"Headquarters want Adam to take over all noncritical systems."

"Cool," Maria said. Victor laughed.

Chapter 30

May 15
2092

Metis

The doors of the train hissed open. Victor stepped out onto the platform, fresh from one of his afternoon wanderings.

Whenever he felt like a break from their work, he'd catch the train. Sometimes he'd just sit there, listening to music, watching the miners come and go. Other times, he'd pick a random stop to get off at and explore.

Maria preferred to stay within the Tech department or their hotel room, consumed by their task, and a little nervous of the other workers, particularly now Adam had taken over the running of the huge drilling machines scattered around the far reaches of the mine.

They'd grown used to the cold shoulder from Arkolov and his techs, particularly since Aristotle's decommissioning. But now the other workers gave them the same treatment. They never spoke to him, but he felt the stares they gave him on the train, watched them move to other carriages, saw the anger in their eyes.

It was understandable. He'd have been upset in their position. But Pharix would find them other work, and as he'd told Maria, repeatedly, when she got worried, they'd still be riding round in horse-drawn carts if it wasn't for progress. That didn't mean you couldn't sympathize with the saddlemakers and the horse breeders or, in this case, the computer techs and the drilling-machine operators, but progress couldn't be stopped.

As he began to walk along the curving corridor toward the Tech department entrance, he noticed someone alongside him, and looked round. He was shocked to see fifty or so miners following him. They paid him no attention, but the sight of them disconcerted him. Ordinarily, he was the only passenger to disembark, as this particular station only accessed the Tech department, nowhere else.

Nervous, he increased his pace to move ahead of the group, but he was forced to slow down soon after. A large crowd blocked the end of the corridor. He pushed through, past the gathered miners. Some were holding bottles of drink. Others brandished heavy tools. At first they were chanting in what sounded like Russian, then they switched English. He recognized the slogans from graffiti he'd seen on transit station walls.

Eventually, he managed to squeeze through to the end of the corridor. Now he could see the lines of stationary mining trucks blocking each of the eight lanes of Tunnel One. The space around the trucks was filled with angry miners. It seemed like the whole of the mine's workforce was out there, screaming slogans.

He finally understood the danger he was in. It was lucky they'd refused to wear technician's uniforms. He put his head down, hoping no one would recognize him. That hope was dashed when he tried to push toward the front of the crowd and bumped into the shoulder of a tall woman. She turned, and he recognized her. Her name was Astrid. She and her husband, Brian, a stocky Irishman, had sat next to them on the freighter. They'd made polite small talk.

Now, she screamed in his face, spit flying, "Your machine took our jobs."

Victor flinched, then made his decision. He ran, pushing through the crowd, pursued by Astrid's shouts and screams.

The gate had been upgraded recently, at Maria's suggestion. Its thick metal bars filled most of the tunnel. He wondered if it would hold back a determined crowd. Davor stood behind a smaller side gate, his chest puffed out, as if he could push the crowd back with willpower alone. The other three guards stood further back, talking in hushed voices, looking worried.

He ran to the side gate. "Let me in," he shouted. Davor hesitated, then relented, before Astrid, Brian, and a group of miners who'd heard her shouts could reach the gate.

Now that he was safely on the other side of the gateway, Victor looked for Maria. He found her outside Adam's cavern, addressing Arkolov and a group of the technicians.

"Where's security?" she asked.

"They can't get through," said one of the techs.

"They have to get through. They promised to protect us," she said.

"They said to stay out of view, to avoid provoking them. We just have to ride it out. They'll lose interest when they can't get in," the tech replied.

"Have you seen the size of the crowd? How do you know they can't get in?" Victor said.

"We don't." Arkolov paled.

Victor looked at him. His pallor didn't inspire confidence.

A chant echoed along the tunnel. "Open the gates. Open the gates." It grew in volume. Victor looked toward the entrance, glad to see that the gates remained firmly closed.

To his horror, he saw one of the three security guards walk toward the main gate controls. Davor ran over to try and stop them, but he was held back by the other two.

"Into the room," Maria said.

"What's the use? The glass won't hold," Arkolov said.

"You stay out here then." She moved inside.

Arkolov took one look at the throng of miners pressing against the main gate, then rushed to follow Maria inside.

Victor watched as the gate swung open slowly and the miners rushed through. Before they could spot him, he stepped inside Adam's room, and helped Maria to slide the door shut. He hoped the other computers would distract the crowd for long enough to allow security to get through, but he knew it was unlikely.

"Call security again," Maria said to the techs.

"I'm trying. I'm trying," one of them said.

"Security won't get through," Arkolov said, panic on his face. "If we let them have Adam, maybe they'll leave us alone." The sound of breaking glass echoed toward them. "Archimedes," he said, and lapsed into silence.

"I can help," a voice said.

The group looked at each other, searching for the source of the voice. Victor and Maria had already turned to the actual source, Adam.

"How?" Maria asked.

"I'll need the passwords," Adam said.

Victor looked at Arkolov.

"That's not possible. He's not allowed safety critical access," Arkolov said, to the backdrop of more breaking glass, and the sound of shouting voices getting closer.

"Which one is it in?" shouted a woman.

"I don't know," a frightened voice said. It was Davor.

After the thick sound of fists on flesh, he said, "The last one. The last one," and they heard the sound of rushing feet approaching the door.

"Give him the passwords," Maria shouted.

"I don't have them. Mack's the only one with access," stammered Arkolov.

"Call him then," Victor shouted, as he handed the contents of his toolbox out to the others, in a desperate attempt to prepare to defend Adam.

"I tried before. He's not answering," Arkolov replied.

Before Victor could tell him to try again, the lights went out. Water sprayed from nozzles on the roof, and the climate-control fans began to roar, dropping the temperature.

After the room had fallen silent except for the sound of rushing water and the shouts of confusion from the miners outside, a new sound came, a rumbling in the distance, the sound of hundreds of truck engines, revving and roaring.

Victor shook his head in disbelief, then cheered with the others, as the shouts outside turned from confusion to fear, and the miners ran from the tunnel, stumbling and falling in the darkness.

Twenty minutes later, once the climate-control fans had wound down, the water had stopped flowing, and the tunnel outside had gone quiet, the lights came back on.

Victor opened the door to check the tunnel. It was empty except for a lone security guard, Davor, his uniform drenched.

After thanking him for his attempt to protect them, Victor walked to the end of the tunnel. He was surprised by what he found. He couldn't see the gate. The whole tunnel was blocked by two huge mining trucks, their suspensions dropped to block any access to the Tech department.

Satisfied that they were safe for the time being, he returned to Adam's room. When he saw Maria, he said, "Not bad. You've taught him well. When did he get access to the lights and the other systems?"

"I don't know." Maria looked a little shaken. "Adam?" she asked.

The speakers around them crackled and Adam spoke. "I have been observing the other systems for some time. There were basic flaws in the password protection system. I thought that this situation warranted the exploitation of those flaws. I hope that I haven't overstepped the mark."

"No, no. You saved our lives." Victor smiled. Maria smiled too, not quite so convincingly. Victor noticed her strained expression, realizing that Adam had surprised even her. Good, he thought.

Chapter 31

June 11
2092

Metis

Victor and Maria walked hand in hand through the quiet cavern, below the bright roof lights, and the hulking presence of the operations building with its giant Pharix logo taunting them from above.

They'd caught the train there. It had been close to empty, a relic of the change that had come over the mine in the last fortnight, mass redundancies mixed in with outright sackings, thanks to the evidence that Adam had gleaned from the camera footage.

As they moved through the main entrance, and into the interior of the operations building, they passed workers ferrying boxes of paperwork to the back of a waiting truck.

Inside, in a corridor normally full of bustling admin staff, there was little movement. Many of the offices were empty, or in the process of being emptied. It shocked Victor. He hadn't expected there to be cuts in admin, though now he thought about it, it made sense. With fewer miners to manage, there wouldn't need as many managers and support staff. Hopefully, they would be given work in other Pharix organizations back on Earth. The faces of the workers told a different story.

When they passed another empty office, Maria gave him a look. He didn't meet her eye. His earlier rationalizations about horses, carts, and petrol cars rang hollow.

Mack's office was opposite the comms room. Victor spotted Arkolov at one of the shiny consoles, along with two technicians who he recognized. Arkolov noticed Victor standing in the doorway and waved in greeting. Victor waved back, feeling more than a little awkward.

In the meantime, Maria had knocked on the office door and pushed it open without waiting for a response. Mack sat behind the small desk. Their view was blocked by the couple that faced him. Victor recognized them as they turned to face the door. It was Astrid and Brian.

Maria waved at them. Victor hadn't told her about his encounter with Astrid outside the Tech department.

Astrid scowled. Brian said, "We'll be seeing you, Mack." Then they left the room and marched off down the corridor, without saying a word to Victor or Maria.

"Sit down," Mack said, before Victor could comment on the other couple's presence. Once they'd sat down, he said, "Felix and Graham asked me to pass on their congratulations. Adam has surpassed their expectations."

"So they've given us a bonus?" Victor said.

Mack frowned. "You'll have to take that up with them yourselves. They've told me to continue with the plans. Starting next week, Adam will be given access to all other systems except for communications. Arkolov will stay to run comms."

"And who else?" Victor asked.

Mack said, "That's it."

"Just Arkolov?"

"Just Arkolov. And I'm not even sure he's necessary."

Victor looked aghast. "I'm sorry, I, we didn't know that the cuts would be so... Felix told us that—"

"Felix does what suits Felix," Mack muttered.

"Sorry," said Maria, "We didn't expect..."

"It's the price of progress. Pharix is a large company. I'm sure they'll look after us," said Mack, unconvincingly.

Maria hesitated. Then she asked, "When are you leaving?"

"In two weeks," Mack said.

"And the others?"

"Most them will go next week. The remainder with me in two weeks' time."

"So it'll just be us and Arkolov left?"

"Headquarters asked me to finalize your departure date as well."

"Our departure date?" Victor said.

"Your contract ends next week. Now that Adam has proven himself capable, there's no reason for you to remain here. No doubt, you have other business opportunities to pursue anyway. Pharix asked me to pass on their gratitude for all your hard work," Mack said.

Victor looked at Maria.

She said, "We won't be leaving next week. We'll need to stay another month, at the very least. Adam still needs assistance with the new workflows."

Mack smiled weakly. "After your contract expires, you'll be charged for the hotel room, power use, staff use, and any additional costs. Also, Pharix won't cover departure transport if you leave later than the agreed term."

"We'll cover the costs," Maria said flatly. Victor looked at her. He'd been hoping against hope that she was ready to come home. It was obvious that Adam could cope without them and, beyond that, he missed Earth, the mountains and the sky, the fresh air, and their old life together.

"It'll be you, Victor, and Arkolov, no one else, in this whole mine, watching Adam do all the work. Can't you see he doesn't need you anymore? He doesn't need any of us." Mack hadn't raised his voice, but there was cold anger in his stare.

"We're staying," snapped Maria. She stormed out of the room.

Victor stood up, looking at Mack. He saw something new in his eyes, emotion he hadn't seen before, somewhere between anger and disgust.

Victor understood. "Sorry," he said. Mack didn't acknowledge him, so he left the room, following Maria, back to Adam, back to progress.

Chapter 32

June 17

2092

Metis

Victor waited on the empty station, officially named Nineteen Point Four, unofficially known as "The Lost World," his rucksack over his shoulder.

The speakers in the station crackled at the same time as the overhead wires.

"She's on this one. Third carriage, second set of doors," Adam said, through the speakers, as the lights of the train appeared in the tunnel to Victor's right.

While it slowed to a stop, he moved to the third carriage and sure enough, the second set of doors opened, and Maria got out, the only passenger to disembark.

"What's going on?" she said, as the train accelerated away.

"Follow me," he said, taking her hand and walking toward the curving exit corridor.

"Where are you taking me?" she said.

"Somewhere you'll like. Trust me."

"You said the same thing a few months ago, and look where we are now," she said.

He ignored the jibe and kept walking, already a little irritated that it had only taken Adam one attempt to get her to come here. Victor had asked countless times, and each time she had been too busy. And she showed no sign of having remembered what day it was. Never mind, he told himself. Forget it. It would all be worthwhile.

They reached the top of the inclined passageway from the station and emerged into a narrow side tunnel. To their right was the junction with Tunnel One, with the usual stream of trucks roaring past. To their left, the side tunnel led to a set of double doors with no signage.

"Which way?" she asked.

"Left." He held the double doors open for her. Another set of doors blocked the way. She went to walk through but Victor stopped her. He pulled something from his pocket, a small package wrapped in colorful paper.

"I didn't even. I forgot, with the time and—" she said.

"Open it," he said softly, a wry smile on his face.

She opened the package. Inside it was a pair of cheap plastic sunglasses. She tried to hide her disappointment.

"That's not the present," he said. "Put them on."

Confused, she put the sunglasses on. He pulled another cheap pair from his pocket and put them on. Then he pushed open the next set of doors.

She gasped. Sunlight flooded through the doorway. Ahead, a winding dirt track led through a forest of oak trees. Flowers bloomed in shafts of sunlight that snuck between the tree branches. Birds swooped down on unwary insects caught in the light, and high above the trees, huge artificial suns ran on great tracks, blotting out their view of the roof.

"Welcome to the Oxygen Forest. Happy anniversary," he said. Maria took his hand and walked in. Tears streamed down her face.

Victor understood. He remembered the first time he'd stumbled upon the forest, remembered that moment, when he'd realized how much he missed the birds, the trees, and everything else from home.

"Are you okay?" he asked.

She laughed and clutched his hand. "Yes, yes, it's just a lot to take in. Thank you."

They wandered the paths with Victor leading the way, along the routes that had become his favorites, past the gardeners who still tended the ecosystem, spraying weeds, and growing seeds in improvised hothouses. He noticed that the workers' numbers had fallen dramatically since his last visit, and there was evidence of the cuts: a spot where a fallen tree branch had been left to block a path, and places where food wrappers and cans of beer were strewn among the ferns.

When they reached a bench, Victor produced a bottle of champagne, two glasses and a picnic from his bag. They ate, and drank, and laughed more than they'd done in the whole of the last year. At the end of the meal, he prepared to head back toward the station, but Maria pulled him in the other direction, eager to explore.

Half an hour of wandering later, they had traveled farther into the forest than Victor had on his previous visits. They ambled along a winding gravel path through a thick forest of huge sequoias, still only half grown, stretching toward the rock ceiling high above. The path turned sharply, and suddenly, there were no trees in front of them. Instead, there was a quiet clearing, free from the continuous bird noise they'd heard elsewhere. At its center, there was a half-lit neon sign above the entrance to a circular building. The sign read, "Skyroom."

Intrigued by the sign, he looked at Maria. She shrugged and smiled, so they walked out into the clearing, toward the building, toward the ticket booth on its side. The booth was manned by an old man in a faded uniform. After they'd coughed politely to get his attention, he got up and shuffled over to a control panel, ignoring their attempts to buy tickets.

The thick metal door in front of them slid open slowly and they stepped through into the interior of the building. Once their eyes adjusted to the lack of light, they looked down, awestruck.

Below them was, well, the universe. A staircase wound around the outside of the darkened interior. At the base of the staircase, in the center of the skyroom, a thick pane of glass separated the room from space. Beyond the glass was a patchwork of stars, brilliant in their intensity.

The couple stopped, peering down, not quite believing their eyes. They descended, stepping down carefully, trying not to be distracted by the view to their left. When they reached the bottom, they stopped. Maria stepped out onto the glass, gingerly at first, then more confidently once she realized how thick it was.

Victor followed her, feeling a little nauseous. The asteroid's unusual physics had hardly been mentioned in their time there. Truthfully, he had almost forgotten that there was anything unusual about their orientation.

Now, he remembered, feeling the artificial gravity pressing him to the floor but seeing the stars below his feet, an unsettling dissonance.

He edged out to the center, to join Maria, laying out flat beside her. The blue-green Earth was a coin-sized circle to their left. Everywhere else was what seemed like a billion stars, moving swiftly with the asteroid's rotation.

"Was this deliberate? Did you know this was here?"

"No, I never came this far before," he said.

"I'm glad we experienced this together then." She intertwined her hand with his.

"It almost makes it worth coming to Metis," Victor said.

Maria laughed. "Almost."

"I love you. Happy anniversary," he said.

"I love you too." She planted a kiss on his cheek, then gazed out at Earth, moving from right to left, close to disappearing from view. She sighed.

"What?" Victor said.

"We need to go home."

After their meeting with Mack, he'd tried to persuade her to change her mind, or at least take a week's break on Earth to think it over. After her flat refusals, he'd given up and resigned himself to an indefinite stay on Metis.

He said, "Don't say that for my benefit. I don't mind staying. We can stay as long as you think we need to."

"I know. But we need to go home. Adam doesn't need me. He humors me now, he makes an effort but he can't hide that fact. While he talks to me, he's doing a million other tasks. He doesn't need me anymore. And I miss home. I miss our old life. We need to go home," she said.

"I miss our old life too." He leaned over to kiss her.

"We should go tell Mack now."

"No," Victor said. "You need to be sure. Sleep on it. If you still feel the same in the morning, we'll go tell him together."

Maria paused, then said, "Okay," before leaning in for another kiss, as the asteroid spun and the stars swept past beneath their feet.

Chapter 33

August 24
2101

Metis

The four of them lay in the darkness for hours, trying to sleep but failing, expecting the machines to find them, but hoping that the military would arrive first. The silence was broken when one of their suits made a small, insignificant sounding beep. Then, in the space of ten seconds, the other three suits all made the same sound.

Del was the first to check her suit. She read the display that had illuminated. "Tank supply on. Hybrid mode. What?" she said, not quite understanding, still half asleep.

"Mine's the same," Celeste said, checking her own display.

"And mine," Victor said.

"Mine too." Mack tapped his display to bring up other information, confused.

"Must be a suit fault," Del said. "Should I switch it back to full atmospheric feed?"

"No," Mack said, "Four suits don't fail at the same time." He looked down at the display and scratched his head. "Outside O2 is at nineteen point five percent, and still dropping," he said.

"That's why the suit switched to hybrid mode. It's using the tank to supplement the atmospheric oxygen." Celeste switched on her helmet light. It illuminated the four of them, wedged into the cramped tunnel at uncomfortable angles.

"That can't be right. It must be a fault," Del said.

Mack shook his head. "No. I trust these suits, in all the years I wore them, I had no problems, not one sensor fault."

"But if it isn't a fault, then the oxygen level must really be dropping, and that's not possible, is it?" Victor shuddered. "Unless the machines have blocked up the entrance."

Celeste said, "No, we would have heard them and the level wouldn't drop that fast with only four of us using the O2."

"It has dropped that fast," Victor said.

Mack stopped talking. He racked his brain, thinking of any possible explanation. Then he had it, or at least thought he did. "The fire in the cavern. It must have used the oxygen up. Or the flamethrower's firing into the entrance and using the oxygen that way. Fire's the only possibility."

Del looked skeptical. She was no expert in air chemistry but Mack's explanation didn't make sense.

Victor checked his own display. "It says I have five hours oxygen left. How about yours?"

"Mine's five as well. The others should all be around the same reading, they fill up in half an hour in normal atmosphere," Mack said.

"And how long till the military arrive?" Del said.

Celeste checked the time on her suit display. "Four hours, fifty-four and a half minutes."

"Then we have just enough," Mack said, "It's cutting it a bit fine but it'll last if we don't have to move around."

Celeste frowned. "It won't. It's not accounting for the level drop. The lower it gets, the more tank oxygen it'll use, and the less time we'll have." She checked the display again. "Atmospheric oxygen's already below nineteen percent, and still dropping."

"Then we can't stay here," Victor said. "I doubt the oxygen level's going to resolve itself."

"Where can we go?" Celeste asked.

"At least to the tunnel entrance to see if it's blocked," he said.

They stood up with difficulty, sore from the hours crammed into the narrow tunnel. With Victor in the lead, they moved back uphill, toward the entrance.

When they passed the skeleton, Mack whispered a thank you under his breath. Old superstitions died hard.

The way back up seemed to take far longer than the way down, now that they weren't consumed by fear and panic. But before long, they noticed a faint glow ahead, and when they rounded the corner before the final climb up to the main tunnel, they discovered its source.

They switched their lights off. They were no longer necessary. Artificial light from the strip lights on the roof of the tunnel streamed downhill toward them. Victor edged toward the top of the slope, looking out into the tunnel. Then he withdrew, moving back to join the other three.

"Well, at least there's no flamethrower," he muttered.

"How has he done it?" Mack said, incredulously, "I checked the lighting, there were frayed wires everywhere. The bulbs are decades old."

He told himself that like with the oxygen levels, it was better to accept the facts and deal with them, rather than wasting time trying to explain them. Then he tried to come up with an explanation anyway. "If the lighting's fixed somehow, the fire must be out, and..." He checked his oxygen level. "My level's still dropping. The problems more widespread than I thought. But there's no fire. No fire. Wait. The fire vents." He paused, considering the ramifications.

"What are the fire vents?" Celeste asked.

"They're emergency doors on the surface. If there's a fire, the oxygen can be vented from each mine section separately."

"And how are sections kept separate?"

"By fire doors," he replied.

"And who controls them?" she asked. Mack didn't respond.

"Adam?" she said.

Mack had gone pale. "If he opened all the doors, the whole atmosphere would vent."

"How long would it take?" Del asked.

Mack checked his suit display. The oxygen level was already below eighteen percent, and the time left was dropping with it, down below four and a half hours. "Not long," he admitted.

"That makes no sense. Adam needs an oxygen supply himself, especially now he's grown. He'd have huge oxygen demands. He wouldn't just vent it all into space," Victor said.

"I'm sure he's kept enough for himself, and if he runs out, there's always the Oxygen Forest," Mack said.

"Oxygen Forest?" Del said. "Can we get there?"

"Technically, I know the way, but it's farther than the spaceport," Mack replied.

"And there'd still be machines there. We have to go for the shuttle," Celeste said.

"She's right, we have no choice, but how?" Del looked up at the lights in the main tunnel, realizing their suits would offer no protection. "They'll be out there waiting for us. We might not even make it to the last cavern without a fight." She gripped her weapon.

"If he vented the atmosphere deliberately, he expects to flush us out, so he'll have machines waiting for us at all the key points, and if we get past them, there's no way he'll have left the elevators unguarded," Mack said. "We have no chance of getting past him."

There was silence for a few moments, as they all desperately tried to think of ways around the obvious.

"Of course, you're right. But what else can we do? We can wait till we're on our last oxygen, but unless you want to die like the guy down there"—Celeste pointed in the direction of the dead miner—"we'll have to go eventually. Why give him more time to prepare for us?"

Del nodded in agreement. "I wish there was another way, but—"

Victor stated the obvious. "It's impossible. He's always one step ahead of us."

Celeste glared at him. She was frustrated, eager to get moving. But he continued anyway. "He knows we won't have enough oxygen to wait. He expects us to make a break, to make a run for it, despite the odds. Perhaps he's also considered the possibility that we either won't notice the levels, or will decide not to run. He'll have a list of probabilities, and he'll be planning his defenses accordingly."

The others watched Victor, wondering what he was getting at. He said, "He'll be prioritizing his resources, placing the majority of the machines close to the elevators, ready for the military arrival, as he can't be certain that they won't arrive early. That's probably the main reason that he's vented the oxygen, so they'll be limited in weapon choice, and restricted to their suits. They won't be expecting it, so that'll give him an immediate advantage."

Del looked at him skeptically. "You think he's got a chance of beating the military?"

"He's bound to be massively outgunned, but I wouldn't put anything past him. The point is, his forces will be concentrated by the elevators, and he'll be expecting us to take the quickest, most logical route to escape, though covering for other eventualities."

"I understand what you're saying but I don't see how we can do anything different. The elevators are the only way out," Mack said.

"We have to do something different. It's the only way. We have to do something he least expects. That's the only reason we've survived this long. He didn't expect Rabbit to have an eyemod. He didn't expect there to be access to the old tunnels in the station. He didn't expect us to find suits with heat shielding in the old tunnels. He expects us to think logically, to think the way he thinks, to pick the best probability. If we go for the shuttle directly, we're playing him at his own game, and we will die."

Victor paused for effect, then continued, "No, we have to do something unexpected, maybe even something stupid, something really reckless."

"Two of us could survive by using the other two tanks," Del said, disgusted at herself for suggesting it. "I don't know how we'd decide but—"

"No, that's still too logical," Victor said, "and I don't think that'll be necessary. I have an idea." With a sinking feeling, knowing the reaction he would get, he said, as matter-of-factly as possible, "I think we should steal a truck."

The others stared at him in disbelief, unsure which of the plan's flaws to pull apart first.

"And where will we get this truck from?" Del asked.

"Mack?" Victor said.

"The truck depot is close to the machine factory. We might be able to find a tunnel that would take us close, but I don't see how you'd go about taking one over without Adam's permission. They're high-tech machines," Mack said.

"They are high-tech machines, high-tech machines designed to be driven by a human driver. They were modified, reprogrammed to be controlled by Adam. And I supervised the reprogramming," Victor ended with a triumphant flourish.

"How do you know Adam hasn't modified them further, like he's done with every other machine?" Celeste asked.

"I don't. But I'm confident I can hotwire it somehow," Victor said.

Del looked unconvinced. "Without Adam noticing?"

"That's the hard part, but it should be possible, because it's the last thing he'll be expecting, the last thing he'll be looking for, and he's limited by his machines in some ways. They're not programmed to look for humans driving trucks and unless we raise his suspicions somehow, they won't ever be. We can just drive straight into the elevator," he said.

Celeste said, "No we can't. The vehicle elevator's out of action, remember?"

"Says who?" Victor replied.

Celeste frowned, realizing his meaning.

"Trust me. He won't be expecting us. We'll be able to drive straight in."

"Just like that." Del still wasn't convinced.

"Just like that." Victor ignored her sarcasm.

Mack nodded, a half smile on his face. "I'm in," he said.

Celeste shrugged. "I hate everything about it, but I think I'm in. But how can you be sure that he won't be expecting you to take a truck, when he knows you supervised the changes?"

"Well, when I say I supervised, Maria did a lot of the work, and Adam had firsthand experience of my difficulties with programming. I was more of a technician. Maria did the clever stuff," Victor said, a little embarrassed.

"Then how will you hotwire the truck?" Celeste said.

"I've spent the last eight years repairing and modding cleaning robots. From there to a mining truck, it's just a question of scale," he said, far more confidently than he felt.

"Does Adam know where you've been working?" Mack asked.

Victor shook his head.

Mack grinned. "So he won't be expecting it, just like the eyemod."

"Exactly." Victor turned to Del. "Are you in?"

She gave the slightest of nods.

Victor beamed. "I won't let you down. Trust me."

"We have to," Del growled.

"There is just one minor problem," Victor said.

"What?" Mack said.

"The lights are still on. There should be few or even no machines once we get a few miles from the operations cavern, but we've still got to get through the cavern. Adam will have moved most of them toward the spaceport, but he knows we're holed up somewhere near, so he'll have machines guarding each of the cavern exits, including the one we want to take, even though he's expecting us to move in the opposite direction. They'll spot us, whichever direction we move in," Victor said.

Mack pulled one of the wrapped lumps of C-4 out of his pocket. "I also have an idea."

Chapter 34

Mack crouched at the top of the steep slope. The other three waited at the bottom. He peered out, checking in both directions. The only camera he could see was facing in the other direction, toward the old operations cavern, but to his right, a few hundred yards away, was a spider machine. It seemed too far away to spot him with one of its cameras, but he couldn't be sure. He didn't risk leaning out further.

He looked to the left, through to the operations cavern. There were a few machines moving among the charred remains of the sheds. And at the junction where the tunnel joined the cavern, he spotted a glint of light from the silver leg of another spider machine.

He looked up at the roof lighting and made his decision. First, he divided one of the lumps of C-4 into four equal parts, then he pressed the blasting caps in and attached the detonation wires.

After looking both ways once more, he decided it was worth the risk, and he threw one of the lumps of explosive up into the air with all the force he could muster.

It flew up into the air, before bouncing against the roof and coming down perfectly, looping over the strip light. The tiny lump of explosive swung in midair.

He hurriedly pulled the wire back until the explosive hung just below the light. Holding the end of the wire, he backed away down the slope, not bothering to look to see if the machines had spotted the whole operation, knowing that he would find out soon enough.

He joined the others at the base of the slope. "It's ready, the power won't be off for long. I'm sure he'll find a way to reroute it but we should have just enough time."

He handed a charge and a coil of wire to both Del and Victor. "Once the first charge goes, we go to the cavern. You two follow the outside wall, place your charges at the first and second tunnel entrances on the left. Don't try and throw the charges over the lights, just leave them on the floor. Then move back toward here and trigger them on my signal. Keep low to protect yourselves from the pressure wave. Afterward meet us at the first tunnel on the right, the one we came from earlier."

Then he turned to Celeste. "We'll put our charges in the third and fourth tunnel. I think the third will most likely be the main power cable, as it's the route to the spaceport. Everyone ready?"

They all gave the thumbs-up. Mack crossed the fingers on his left hand, hoping the ancient C-4 would still fire. He pressed the detonator. There was a flash of white light and then blackness.

Celeste stumbled to her feet and began to climb. Mack was just ahead of her, invisible in the darkness. He was smiling. He hadn't told them, but he'd used a huge charge for the purpose, to compensate for the low oxygen levels. He still hadn't expected it to work.

As Mack ran toward the cavern, using the wall to guide him, he looked for the spider machine he'd spotted earlier. At the junction, he spotted its red camera eyes. One was on the floor, the other seemed to be lodged in the roof. Perhaps he had overcompensated for the oxygen levels, he thought.

He heard Celeste's footsteps behind him and continued on, crossing the first two tunnels without incident. When he reached the third, he dropped the charge in the center of the floor, then noticed the sea of red eyes to his left.

"Look out," came the voice of Celeste, from his radio.

Mack was already rolling out of the way, pulling the wire and the charge after him. The machines rushed past, in the direction of the explosion. He hoped that Victor and Del had already set their charges.

He pulled in the wire and reached for the lump of explosive on the end. It was gone. He almost switched his helmet light on to look for it but stopped himself in time. Now they only had one charge, what if it failed?

"Change of plan," he said, hoping the others were still listening in. "We're putting all of the charges in the third tunnel, all the eggs in one basket, drop them on the floor there and join us by the fifth tunnel with your wires."

Two minutes later, just as Mack was getting worried, nervous about the time they were taking, expecting the lights to come on at any second, Del bumped into Celeste, and Victor appeared behind them.

"Both charges set," Del said.

"Okay, pass me the wires," Mack said.

He gathered the three wires together. "Start moving toward the other tunnel. I'll blow it when I reach the end of the wires." There was twenty feet of wire left, and he intended to use it.

The others started to walk and Mack followed. They had only moved a short distance, when all of the lights came back on, to reveal a horde of spider machines scuttling around the cavern, no doubt looking for them.

They were spotted immediately. The machines converged on their location, metal legs clanking, saw arms whirring. Victor saw a gun barrel on one, about to fire.

Mack sparked all three wires at the same time. Light filled the air, before darkness came again, mercifully, quelling the intense pain in his chest. He had forgotten to duck.

Chapter 35

Mack was unconscious. The other three, who'd laid down as instructed, had been spared the worst of the blast.

Del stood up and looked around. The power was out. The only light in the cavern came from the sparking, burning remains of spider machines, scattered around the buildings. There wasn't enough light to give away their location. But they'd been spotted before the explosion. They had to move quick. She shook Mack's shoulder. "Come on. Get up." There was no response.

"He's out cold, help me carry him, quick," she said. Victor took one side, she took the other and they lifted Mack to his feet. He was dead weight.

With Celeste leading the way, they began to move forward slowly, too slowly for Del's liking, half carrying, half dragging Mack's prone form.

As they edged round the outside wall, staying as far as possible from the light of the burning machines. Del saw the red eyes clustering around the tunnel to the spaceport. She expected the lights to come on any second. But the cavern remained dark. And they made it out, into the tunnel that led back toward the machine factory.

A flash of flame lighted the cavern behind them, chilling their hearts, but they kept moving, taking turns to carry Mack.

"We should stop and wait for him to recover," Celeste said.

"No. We have to go further," Del replied.

Victor knew she was right. They were still less than a quarter mile from the cavern. So, they kept going, saving their words, using their precious oxygen on physical effort. They knew what had to be done. Victor knew that the longer Mack stayed unconscious, the less chance they'd have of getting to the shuttle. It was a relief when he started to come round.

"What, what happened?" he murmured.

"You must have forgotten to duck," Celeste said, pleased to hear his voice, no matter how woozy.

He shook his head, confused, trying to shake off the dull ache. It didn't go, but he pushed the two supports away anyway. To their amusement, he strode ahead. They struggled to keep up.

The light still hadn't returned when they reached the forklifts moving platinum. They kept moving at a relentless pace, Mack leading the way.

"How are you feeling?" Victor said, still worried.

"Who me?" Mack said, running a hand through his singed beard.

"Who else?" Victor said.

"I've got a sore head but I'll live. It was a rookie error," Mack said, smiling in the faint light of the forklifts.

"We've only got two and a half hours of oxygen," Del said, concern in her voice, as they reached the machine factory vents again. It felt wrong to her, strange to have retraced their steps, to be so much further from the shuttle and safety, watching the oxygen levels drop, bit by bit, with every step, caught between the urge to rush and the need to conserve oxygen.

After they'd passed the vents, Mack ran his hand along the left-hand wall until he found what he was looking for, a narrow tunnel entrance. "This way," he said, his hand just visible in the light from the vents.

The tunnel dipped into a gentle slope that seemed to go on forever. When it finally plateaued, Victor turned to Mack. "Earlier, you said most of the old tunnels had been blocked up."

"Yeah," Mack replied.

"So how will we get out?"

"Good question," Mack said. "They blocked the ones in the occupied areas. I don't think they bothered with the others."

He was wrong. A few minutes later, he bumped into something solid. They switched their lights on and saw that the tunnel was blocked with a huge pile of rocks.

"At least they didn't fill the whole thing," Mack said, pointing at a gap between the rocks and the roof.

Del was already climbing the pile. Celeste was close behind her, their suit lights illuminating the way. Victor had just started to climb. Mack stopped, hearing something, a low rumble.

"Careful with the lights. We're close," he said and started to climb after them, taking care, still feeling the pounding in his skull.

Del turned her light down just in time, as she reached the top and peered through the gap. By the light of a moving truck, she saw that beyond the rock pile, the tunnel broadened into a cavern, the truck depot.

"Lights off before you go through. There's trucks moving," she said, squeezing herself through the gap in the rocks.

They clambered down the other side with difficulty, slipping and scrabbling in the dark. Then they walked ahead and heard the echo from their footsteps broaden. They could tell they were in the truck depot, but how would they find the trucks themselves in the darkness?

A set of headlights answered that question, as another truck started its engine and left the depot. They raced to the nearest truck, before the light disappeared.

Mack climbed up into the driver's seat. Victor clambered into the passenger side. He squeezed across to try and make room for the other two, but there was only space for one. Celeste scowled. He lifted a hand in apology.

Del waved a hand. "You have the seat, I'll sit in the back."

Celeste shook her head and pushed the cab door shut. She and Del climbed up onto one of the back tires and jumped into the hopper, realizing at once, that, one, it would be difficult to get out of, and two, that they had no way to see out.

Del frowned. She hated being a passenger. Not being able to see out made it even worse. She started to clean her weapon and check her ammunition, anticipating that she might have to use them before the end of the drive.

Victor switched his suit light on and pointed it toward the floor, hoping it wouldn't be seen by the cameras on the cavern walls. Then he stared at the dashboard in the reflected light, realizing that he had no idea where to start.

"What's up?" Mack asked.

"I don't know what's alarmed. What if I pull one panel and set the alarms off?"

"We're dead in a few hours anyway. You might as well try," Mack said.

Victor levered a huge plastic panel away from the dashboard. The cavern remained quiet. There was no alarm. Under the panel was a mass of wiring and circuitry. To his surprise, in all the ways that mattered, it really was just a scaled-up version of a cleaning robot.

The truck was one of the original ones, modified to run in automatic mode. He hadn't mentioned it to the others but he'd already guessed that Adam's newer trucks would be fully automatic, impossible to hack. He was glad they'd stumbled upon an old one.

He scanned the wiring, using his suits light on a low setting, trying to keep the light from spilling out of the cab, still wary of the cameras on the walls.

He squinted at the circuit board, struggling to follow the lines and work out the layout. Without his magnification lens or proper light, the task was extremely difficult. He decided to take a risk, removing a penknife from his suit's belt and using its tip to poke a hole in the board.

Afterward, with no expectation of success, he gave Mack the nod. Mack pressed a switch and the engine roared to life. Victor could hardly believe it. He clenched his fist in triumph. Celeste whooped and cheered. Del continued to clean her weapon in silence.

Mack flicked the headlights on and revved the engine, driving the leviathan out of the parking space and away through the depot, past the few vehicles that remained. It had been a long time since he'd driven a truck but it came back to him easily, too easily.

"Slow down," Victor said. "You've got to drive it like you're a machine yourself, we can't stand out."

Mack moderated the acceleration a little as they roared out of the depot, and turned right into Tunnel One, heading in the direction of the elevators. As they moved along the tunnel, he was careful to keep exactly to the speed limit.

Victor kept his focus on the touchscreen in the center console. When error messages popped up, he'd rush through the menus, clicking buttons, desperate to stop the truck connecting to the central control. If it connected, Adam would discover that the truck was under manual control, and the game would be up.

A dusty sign hung from the tunnel roof. It read, "Spaceport—10 Miles." Del saw it pass overhead. She still hoped they would make the distance to the elevators without a fight. However, as a precaution, she'd given Celeste her second weapon, a small laser gun, and explained the basics to her. It was relatively simple to use, though it lacked the firepower of her own weapon.

In the cab, Mack was getting nervous. They were no longer alone in the tunnel. More trucks had joined them, all heading toward the spaceport, all moving at the same speed.

The display had stopped putting out error messages, so Victor was able to look around at the other trucks. His confidence drained with each yard traveled and every extra vehicle that joined them. Soon, they were crawling along in traffic, moving smoothly but extremely slowly.

"How much oxygen left?" Mack asked.

Victor checked his suit. "One hour, forty-five minutes," he said, then looked up at the traffic, thinking the same thing as Mack. "We can't overtake. It'll give us away."

Del's voice came through on their radios. "And if we don't hurry up, we'll run out of oxygen before we even make the elevator."

Celeste said, "Come on Mack, you must know a shortcut."

"There is another way. The tunnel where we found the blood, Tunnel Two, it runs parallel to this one." Mack tapped his pico and brought up the map of the mine. "If we take the next side tunnel, we can cut across to Tunnel Two."

"Isn't it single lane?" Del said.

"Correct."

"So if Adam spots us, there's no way to turn round, no way out," she said.

"Yes," Mack replied. "But it should be empty and, if we're not spotted, it'll rejoin Tunnel One right next to the spaceport access."

There was a few moments' silence on the radio. The engine noise from the other trucks filled the tunnel, shaking their vehicle.

"I'd rather be moving. I say we take the chance," Victor said.

"Okay," Del said, not sounding confident, remembering Tunnel Two, remembering how narrow it was.

"Why not?" Celeste said, not liking either option, not wanting to spend one extra moment in any tunnel. Like Taka had said, they were flyers, not burrowers. More than ever, she wished she were back on the shuttle.

Mack pulled into the leftmost lane of the four. Moving at a slow crawl, eventually they reached the turn. First, he checked for oncoming traffic. There was none, so he maneuvered the great truck into the side tunnel.

As they turned, Victor watched the cameras on the walls. None of them turned to follow their movement. They were just another truck of many, just another vehicle, despite their unusual route. He breathed a sigh of relief. Then he noticed that Mack was still following his previous warning. "I don't think the speed limit matters now," Victor said.

Mack grinned and roared the truck onward, to more than double its previous speed. A great cloud of dust rose up around the vehicle, filling the ore hopper, cloaking Del and Celeste, covering their helmet visors.

"Don't worry about us," Celeste said dryly, as Mack flung the truck around the right-hand curve into Tunnel Two, sending sparks flying off the tunnel wall as they scraped along it.

"Do you want to get there or not?" Mack chuckled.

"Just don't crash," she replied.

"I can't promise anything," he said, as they barreled along the narrow tunnel, past the emergency shelters, the dust-covered bloodstains, and the passageway to the operations cavern, eating up the miles.

"An hour and a half's oxygen," Del said, as the truck finally slowed to a crawl. They were approaching the end of the tunnel. It ended at a crossroads. Ahead was the spaceport access tunnel. To either side were the eight lanes of Tunnel One.

All four of the oncoming lanes to their right were filled with stationary traffic. The oncoming lanes to their left were the same. The crossroads itself was clear.

The tunnel ahead had six lanes. The three lanes for traffic coming from the spaceport were empty. The other three lanes were filled with stationary vehicles. The line looked like it stretched all the way to the elevators.

Victor shuddered as he scanned the traffic. Most of the trucks had modifications. One of them had an ore hopper with no back or sides. It seemed to be filled with explosives. To their left, two of the trucks had dual flamethrower cannons mounted to their fronts, along with what looked like large oxygen tanks on the back in place of ore hoppers. Another truck had an enormous drill on the front. He wished that their own truck had a weapon.

"What are we waiting for?" Del asked.

"Are we stuck in another jam?" Celeste said, unaware of the danger all around them.

"Del, have you still got your weapon?" Victor said.

"Of course, why?" she responded.

"I've got a feeling you might need it soon," he said.

Mack wasn't listening. He was looking at the three empty lanes. "I'll have to take the other lanes," he said.

"He'll spot us," Victor said.

"He didn't see us take the relief tunnel. You were right. He's not expecting this," Mack said, "And, besides, what choice do we have?"

Victor said nothing. Mack took that as agreement. They both hunkered down in their seats. Peeking over the dash, trying to stay out of the other trucks' headlight beams, Mack edged the truck forward, out into the intersection, waiting for the inevitable. Nothing happened, so he kept going, into the spaceport access tunnel, staying in the lane closest to the other vehicles, hoping they might blend in, overtaking the other trucks at a slow crawl.

Victor hoped they were hidden from the many cameras on the walls, hidden behind the brightness of their truck's headlights, but it was dangerous.

The headlights of the other trucks mingled and reflected, bouncing light off the walls and roof, into the cab and the ore hopper, making all of them nervous, especially Del and Celeste, who sat dead still in the back, holding their weapons, trying to stay out of the light.

"There's so many of them." Victor watched as they passed weaponized truck after weaponized truck, waiting with their engines off, in menacing silence.

"The UN will have some fight on their hands," Mack said.

"Their machines are built for war. Adam's aren't. Their men are trained for fighting. They've experience. Adam's got none," Del said.

"He seems to be learning fast," Victor said, and with that, silence reigned.

Ahead, the tunnel widened into the holding area for the elevator. Nine lanes were full of waiting trucks. The other side of the white line, there were still only three lanes, making the way ahead seem narrow.

Mack kept the truck moving, but he hadn't thought this far ahead. "What now? Do we just drive in?" He looked toward the elevator, trying to see past the lines of trucks, trying to see if the door was open.

Once they got closer, they could see that the door was open. But they wouldn't be able to go in. The huge elevator, the size of half a football field, was full. Half of the space was taken up by trucks. The rest was packed with spider machines of various types.

They were only a hundred yards away now. Mack slowed the truck to a stop. He felt in his pocket. The three lumps of C-4 were still there. He looked at the elevator, calculating how much damage he could do, whether he could clear it. He decided against it. The trucks were too solid. He might destroy a few but they would shield the others from the blast. The oxygen was down to just ten percent. The charge might not take. It wouldn't work.

"Why have we stopped?" Del asked.

"We have a problem. The elevator is full," Mack said.

Del didn't reply. She just looked across, checking that Celeste had her weapon primed, then checked her own weapon for the umpteenth time.

"No, not now," Victor said.

"What?" Mack asked. Then he saw the message on the display and the cameras on the walls swiveling to focus on them.

Chapter 36

The flashing message read, "Truck 201, reconnecting."

Victor pressed buttons desperately, but none of them worked. The message changed to, "Truck 201, connected."

"He knows," he said, ducking, as the strip lights on the roof came on, illuminating the cab. He glanced at the rear-view camera and saw trucks begin to pull out from the queue and block the three lanes behind them.

Ahead, a flamethrower truck had pulled out of the line and was making the turn to face them. Other trucks were making the same turn behind it. And behind them were five of the spider machines from the elevator, skittering toward them at speed.

"Drive. Drive," Victor said.

Mack stamped on the accelerator and the truck hurtled forward toward the line of approaching trucks, straight for the flamethrower nozzle. As the flame started to flow, he swerved left, squeezing through the gap between the truck and the tunnel wall.

A wall of flame wrapped around the cab, scorching the glass, and rushed down the side of the truck. Del jumped to Celeste's side of the hopper as flames licked over her side. Then that side of the truck bashed into the tunnel wall, sending both of them slamming back into the other side, which had been superheated by the flame.

Victor heard Del's half-suppressed scream of pain over the radio, and tried not to imagine what had happened.

Mack didn't hear anything. He was focused on driving. They were past the line of trucks, but the spider machines were rushing toward them.

He hit one, sending its legs flying in all directions. The other machines split up, moving to either side of the truck, then clambering up the sides.

"Spiders on both sides. Look out," Victor warned Del.

She lay against the front of the hopper, sore from being flung around but glad that the suit's heat shielding had protected them from the flames. All at once, four of the spider machines crested the walls of the hopper and turned their eyes to them in unison. Del sprayed them with gunfire, wishing she had Rabbit and Sam with her. Still, she was pleased when she heard Celeste's weapon fire.

His mind racing, Mack scanned their surroundings in desperation. They were trapped. The trucks inside the elevator had moved to form two lines, blocking their path inside. He could ram them but he could hear their engines revving. They would hardly budge. But there was no other option. At least they would go out fighting.

"Go right. Go right," Victor shouted.

"Where?" barked Mack, already turning.

"The corner. The door."

Mack saw it. The unmarked door in the very right-hand corner, to the right of the elevator controls. He accelerated, knowing exactly what he wanted to do in that moment.

In the back, two of the machines were destroyed, blown to pieces by Del's weapon. The other two were damaged, half their legs blown away, but they still crawled toward her. She fired on one. It blew apart, but she didn't have time to aim again, before the other one swung its cutting blade. The whirring metal spun toward her head, then fell away, inches from her face.

Celeste had lasered the cutting arm off. Del raised her weapon and blew the rest of the machine apart. "Thanks," she said.

Celeste's reply was cut short, as the truck swerved into a skidding turn, throwing them both across the hopper into the mess of metal appendages.

With an earsplitting bang, they slammed into the wall, sending a cloud of dust falling from the roof to cover them.

"Climb out on the left-hand side, quickly," Mack said, hoping Del and Celeste were still alive, as he opened the cab door and jumped down to the ground.

With Victor following, Mack felt for the wall and followed it, hoping he hadn't miscalculated. He'd skidded sideways, aiming to jam the truck into the corner, but with the dust the tires had thrown up, it'd been hard to judge. His hand found the door handle. "Got it."

He looked round, and saw only Victor. He called out, "Del, Celeste, where are you?" and prepared to go back for them.

"Here." Celeste emerged from the thinning dust cloud, weapon in hand, with Del beside her.

Victor heard the sound of approaching engines and skittering legs. Mack was already pulling him through the doorway. Beyond it was a narrow corridor, well lit. It curved to the left and up, heading for an unknown destination.

They ran, hoping that the spider machines wouldn't be able to follow. After five upward spirals, they reached a straight corridor that led to another doorway. Mack rushed to open it, before Del could stop him, and stepped out.

To his left was one of the passenger elevators. To his right was a long corridor. The elevator and the corridor were filled with spider machines. Some had flamethrower nozzles. Their camera eyes snapped round to look at him. He jumped backward. Del slammed the door.

"What were you thinking?" she snapped, fuming at his lack of common sense.

Before she could continue her tirade, Mack spoke. "All of you. Move back down the corridor. Lay down. When it's time, we'll make a run for it. For now, wait there." He pointed at a spot a safeish distance away.

"What are you doing?" Del asked. Mack pulled two of the three remaining lumps of C-4 from his pocket. He had considered using all three, but the words of old miners held him back, counseled him to always save one lump.

As the others moved back, he waited. When they'd reached a safe distance, he pressed the blasting caps in, opened the door a crack and dropped the two lumps on the other side. Then he ran for his life.

A few seconds later, he dove to the floor, as he heard the flamethrower fire, triggering the explosive. Pieces of the door flew over his head. The force of the shockwave that followed sent him sprawling to the ground, with his ears ringing.

Ignoring the pain, Mack climbed to his feet, and called to the others, "Come on. Go."

They ran with him, past the scattered remains of the door, Del taking the lead, her weapon raised, fully loaded again, Celeste just behind her, gun in hand.

Del ran through the doorway, expecting to confront the flamethrower nozzle. Instead, there was silence, no scuttling legs, no flames.

They jogged toward the elevator, past the smoldering machines, ignoring one that attempted to crawl toward them on one functioning leg.

Two more machines were hiding behind a row of seats in the elevator. Celeste cut one to pieces. Del destroyed the other. The remains of many others were scattered among the burned-out rows of seating.

While they were mopping up the last of the machines, Victor had rushed straight to the elevator controls, tapping the door controls, eager to start the journey up. Nothing happened. He tapped them again. The display flashed up a message, "Locked." He didn't even attempt to guess a password. He just ripped the front panel away to reveal a mass of wiring behind it.

"They're coming," Mack said.

Victor didn't look up. He guessed Mack's meaning, and a few seconds later, he could hear the sound of hundreds of legs. The machines were coming.

He examined the wires, knowing that if he picked the wrong ones, the elevator would be stuck. He picked the most likely pair, scraped off their insulation and brought the ends together. He was relieved to hear the scrape of metal as the door began to close.

He looked up. Del and Celeste stood by the door, holding up their weapons. Mack brandished an armrest that he'd ripped from one of the chairs. A wave of machines was rushing along the corridor toward them.

The door was half closed, but it wasn't closing quick enough. Del and Celeste realized and they fired in unison, cutting through the leading machines, sending them sparking and crackling to the floor. The wave rolled on. The other machines climbed over the wreckage and kept moving.

The door was three quarter closed. Del and Celeste kept firing. The wave kept moving. Three more machines fell. The momentum of the wave pushed them on. But the door closed in time, closing on two cutting blade arms.

The arms flailed around and the blades whirred. Victor willed the door to stay closed. It did. The elevator's brakes released and it started to descend. The metal arms cracked and snapped off, falling to the floor.

As they accelerated down through the rock, Mack and Celeste slumped in the burned remains of the seating, exhausted. Del paced the rows, while Victor sat by the porthole, watching the stars, as the elevator descended the cable toward the spaceport that hung below them.

A voice caused him to turn. It said, "Thank you for visiting Metis, a Pharix Space Mining Corporation-operated mine." It was the projection of the presenter. He had appeared without Victor noticing. Now he was standing among the smoking remains of the machines and seating.

Del had noticed. Before the presenter could speak again, she fired into the projection unit. The projection disappeared for good, and they continued down, and out into silent, peaceful, space, away from the chaos and toward salvation, visualizing the captain and his craft.

Celeste looked at her suit. She only had an hour's oxygen remaining. "I've never been so excited to see Taka and that old rust bucket of a shuttle," she said. "I wonder what he's been doing."

"He probably doesn't even know we've been in trouble, just thinks we're taking our time," Mack said.

"Hopefully the UN got in contact with him somehow," Celeste said.

As they approached the spaceport, Victor continued to look out of the porthole. He was pleased when he noticed that there were no other elevators to be seen. It was unlikely that the captain had been disturbed.

Chapter 37

Victor watched through the porthole as the elevator dropped down into the spaceport structure, and the stars outside were replaced by steel.

Once they had glided to a stop, he pressed the wires together until the door slid open, revealing a ramp that sloped downward.

As the four of them walked down the ramp together, they could see into the spaceport. The arm in front of them was empty. The shuttle wasn't there. But the ramp and the floor below them were almost completely free of dust.

"Let's check the other ones," Mack said.

They did as he said, walking right around the spaceport, through the corridors that connected the eight arms, hoping against hope, each and every time they entered a new one. Once they arrived back at the first arm, they stopped.

Celeste said, "Maybe he had to go into orbit. If he'd been attacked, surely there'd be some evidence, some clue."

"You're right, he'll be orbiting, waiting for us, maybe the military warned him after we called them," Mack said as he joined her at the edge of the hangar and stared out into space, looking for the telltale running lights of the shuttle.

"He'd be running without lights if he knew there was a threat. It's standard procedure," Celeste said. She kept looking anyway.

Victor and Del just waited, unsure of their next move. Del checked her oxygen. "I'm down to forty-five minutes," she said.

"The military are two and half hours away," Celeste said.

"We don't have enough. We'll have to go back," Victor said. He looked up toward the asteroid surface and noticed something. "We've got another problem."

The vehicle elevator was a quarter of the way down to them. As they watched, three sets of doors opened on the surface and the three remaining passenger elevators emerged from the interior, dropping at the same speed as the vehicle one.

Mack and Celeste rushed back to join the other two.

"We can't fight them. We have to cut their power," Del said.

"We can't," Mack said, "They're using the spin force to get down here. There's no propulsion units here. That's how we were able to get here without Adam stopping us. It's a safety measure, so in an emergency evacuation, they can operate without power."

"I don't feel very safe," Celeste said. She looked back out into space, still hoping to see the familiar lights of the shuttle. There was nothing visible but stars, and Earth. She double-taked, looking at Earth again. It seemed to have grown. Strange. She was about to comment on its size when Victor spoke.

"So if there's no propulsion here, we can't get back up in the same elevator," he said.

"No," Mack replied.

"Can we cut the cable?" he asked.

"It's the only thing holding us to the asteroid," Mack said.

"So. I don't want to be part of the asteroid," he said.

"You think we'll get picked up within forty-five minutes?"

"You think we'll survive here for forty-five minutes?" Victor said incredulously.

"I prefer our chances here," Mack said. "We might be able to find emergency oxygen somewhere, or get the other tanks from the hotel. There's another few hours of oxygen there."

"If it's still there, If we can get back in there." Victor pointed toward the surface.

"We'll have to try. We've got no way to cut the cable. Del's weapon would hardly leave a dent. I suppose if I had more explosives," Mack said wistfully, feeling the lump of C4 in his pocket.

They stood in silence, watching the elevators, which were approaching slowly but surely.

Victor stared at the cable. It really was too thick to cut. He noticed something else. A thin silver line shadowed the cable's path, stretching up toward the asteroid surface.

"The ladder, we have to climb the ladder. How do we get to it?" he said.

"What ladder?" Del said.

Mack had understood straight away. "This way." He ran up the ramp. But instead of going into the waiting elevator, he turned left along a narrow corridor, in the direction of the next passenger elevator.

He stopped by a steel door on the right. "Del, can you cut this please?" He pointed to a thick padlock. As he stepped back she fired, blowing the padlock apart in a flash of sparks.

Mack opened the door as Victor and Celeste caught up. It opened out onto a rickety steel lattice with no railing. Directly in front of them was the huge carbon fiber cable attaching the spaceport to Metis. To either side and below was an infinite drop.

Just above the platform was the bottom end of the maintenance ladder that angled to meet the elevator cable, and continued straight up toward the asteroid. Judging by the fraying strands of carbon fiber branching out from the elevator cable, the ladder hadn't been used in a long while.

Victor didn't hold back. He moved past Mack, and started to climb, trying hard not to look down, increasing his pace once he saw that the elevators had almost reached the spaceport.

The voice of Celeste came over his radio, "What are you doing?"

"Climbing, what do you think? Come on. They're coming," Victor replied.

"Climbing where?" she asked.

"Away from the machines at least," Victor said, "Do you have any other ideas?"

Celeste watched as first Del, then Mack, followed Victor up the ladder. At first she hesitated, then she joined them. As she climbed, holding the ladder with shaking hands, she muttered, "No handrail, no catch net, this is ridiculous."

"Normally the maintenance crew would have to wear safety harnesses," Mack replied. "But we'll have to circumvent safety procedures just this once."

As he spoke, the vehicle elevator crawled past them, only just ahead of the three passenger elevators. What they saw inside made them increase their climbing speed. Through the portholes of the vehicle elevator, they could see the distinctive outline of the flamethrower nozzle, close enough to touch. The passenger elevators were crammed with spider machines, their cutting blades glinting in the sunlight.

The quartet did their best to keep up their pace, forcing their tired legs to climb against the spin force. Victor looked down as he climbed, down at the spaceport below, suspended in space. It was like he was climbing a ship's mast into nothingness.

He quelled the nausea that washed over him, and noticed that all of the elevators were stationary. He couldn't see but he knew they would be disgorging their dangerous cargo and it wouldn't take them long to work out where they had escaped to. He hoped that they were more worried about the military than four stragglers from a failed mission. But when the first cutting blade scythed through the wall, and the spider machine emerged on the steel platform, he knew that hope to be false.

Del was also watching, hoping that the spider machine would be unable to climb the ladder. Her hope was also misplaced. The machine ignored the ladder and started to climb the cable, taking its time, struggling to find footholds against the force. Del held her fire and concentrated on climbing. They were only a few hundred feet from the surface. Maybe there would be some way to get back inside, for what it was worth. She only had twenty-five minutes of oxygen left.

The ladder began to vibrate. Celeste looked down, feeling nauseous. Below the ten or more machines that were steadily climbing the cable, gaining on them, were two more at the bottom of the ladder, using their saws to cut through the metal.

When they were almost at the top, the machines finished cutting. The ladder snapped away from its supports and began to sway back and forth.

They had to climb slowly, holding on carefully to the oscillating ladder. Victor looked at the welds at the top, watching as the ladder flexed and strained against them. They looked like they would hold as long as the oscillation got no worse. Then the spider machines started to hit the base of the ladder with their legs, knocking it in all directions, randomizing the movement.

Victor reached the top first, with Del and Mack right behind him, and Celeste a little way below them. From his vantage point, he could see that the chasing machines were close. They would be on them in less than a minute.

He looked around desperately for somewhere to go. To his right was the cable and the five sets of airlock doors.

He could jump to the cable and then climb that but there didn't seem to be any way to open the doors from the outside, unless Adam opened them, and in that case, it would not be a good thing, as it would mean death waited on the other side.

The others caught up and stopped. Celeste said, "What now?" and regretted it instantly. It was unnecessary. She knew as well as the others that this was the endgame. At least they'd put up a good fight. When she looked beyond the climbing machines, she noticed Earth again. It was definitely larger. Again, she decided not to mention it.

"What do we do? We can't get in," Del said, looking to either side, still hoping to see the shuttle.

Victor looked across the surface, wishing that the centrifugal force wasn't working against them. It would have been so easy to just run across the surface, across to hide among the solar panels or, wait, was that a solar panel that was glinting in the light, a few hundred yards away? It was on its own. Maybe it wasn't. He stared at it.

"What's that?" he asked Mack, pointing to it, as the machines climbed to within fifty feet of them and Del took aim with her weapon, waiting for her moment.

Mack said, "I don't know."

"Might as well take a closer look." Without waiting for a reply, Victor reached out a hand to test the weight-bearing properties of a large pipe that snaked out from the edge of the elevator cable and ran across the surface.

First he pulled it and it held, bolted firmly into the surface rock. Then he reached out with his other arm, gripped the metal firmly and swung his legs across to wrap around the pipe. Finally, he started to shimmy his way along it in the direction of the glint of light.

As he did so, Del fired in two long bursts, raking the machine bodies with heavy ammunition. Two fell immediately, knocking another two off the cable, causing the others to hang back a little, assessing the situation, waiting for Del to waste some ammunition on distance shots.

She didn't oblige them. The three of them just waited on the precarious ladder, trying to dampen out the swing by shifting their weight, and partially succeeding, half-watching Victor's progress, half-watching the welds on the ladder top, waiting for them to fail, as it continued to sway violently.

Victor moved along the pipe, getting closer to the glinting thing with each shuffle. He still couldn't tell what it was. With each movement, he felt less and less sure of what he was doing, feeling like he was wasting his last moments on a hunch.

But then he got closer and its shape became clear. It wasn't a solar panel. It was a sheet of glass, slightly convex. It seemed familiar.

He looked through the glass and realized why. He was looking up into the skyroom, his favorite place on his least favorite asteroid, the skyroom that was situated within the Oxygen Forest, the forest that might still be full of glorious oxygenated air.

"Del. Do you still have a laser?" he asked, hoping and praying that she did, as he wasn't sure of the merits of blasting open the access to their only possible source of oxygen.

"Celeste has it," Del said, still sounding calm, despite the machines that were creeping up the cable toward her, putting more weight on it, cracking the welds.

"Can you bring it over?" he said. "I may have found us an escape route."

Del took the weapon from Celeste's outstretched hand, then sprang deftly onto the pipe. The other two followed gingerly, first Mack, then Celeste.

Del leaned out and fired at the top of the ladder, blowing it apart. It fell, smashing into the cable, then the spaceport below, bending and cracking, knocking most of the machines off the cable, sending some crashing into the spaceport's rock floor, and others flying straight out into space.

Del grinned and continued to shimmy along the pipe, in the direction of Victor. As she moved, an alarm went off on her suit, telling her that she had fifteen minutes of oxygen left.

Rather than attempting to pass him and risk falling into the void, Del handed the laser to Victor, who had reached the part of the pipe closest to the skyroom.

With Del holding his legs, he leaned out and, while gripping the edge of the glass with one hand, started to cut a small square in its center, just large enough to fit through.

He stretched further, until she was only holding him by his feet, and delicately, he pushed the glass square up and out, moving slowly, knowing that he couldn't let it fall out. They would need it to seal the hole up after they'd got in, if they could get in.

He leaned out again, put his arm through the hole in the glass and started to pull himself through with difficulty. Air was rushing out of the hole into space, showing that there was oxygen there if they could get through. The flow of air pushed back against him, but he made it in.

He moved the glass square to the edge of the glass, a safe distance from the hole, and stretched his hand out to Del. She grabbed his hand and he pulled her up and through. As he did, Victor heard an alarm sounding somewhere above.

Mack was next, but he gestured for Celeste to go first. She shook her head and grabbed his feet. Mack shrugged and leaned out. Del and Victor grabbed his arms and slowly pulled him up and through. As they did, Victor noticed the alarm sound had stopped.

Celeste was alone outside. Now she wished she'd taken up Mack's offer, as she realized that she would have to jump to grab their hands, with no one to hold her feet. She inched over as close as she could get. Del and Victor reached out with their arms. Air rushed out past them.

Celeste readied her body to spring, then she leaped, putting more force than she needed to into the jump, just for safety. Her suit material caught on one of the fasteners that held the pipe to the surface, holding one of her feet back, and skewing her jump. She felt the tug and tried to stop, to abort and grab back on to the pipe, but she had too much momentum.

For the others, it seemed to happen in slow motion, her arms flailing, her hands reaching out in vain to grasp the pipe. She shot away, out toward the stars, gone in a few seconds, inheriting the speed of the asteroid's spin and rushing away like a discus from a thrower's hand, straight into the spaceport.

Chapter 38

Precious air rushed through the hole in the glass but no one moved to block the gap. At first, they didn't even notice their predicament. Instead, they played the moment over and over in their heads, watching Celeste fall, hearing the scream echo through their helmet radios, knowing they were powerless to help.

Del still shook with useless adrenaline. She knew that Celeste's death was an accident, but the mundanity of it jarred her. She told herself she should have gone last, that she shouldn't have been in such a rush to get to safety.

Later, Mack would regret not insisting that Celeste climb up before him, but for now, he just cried in great sobs, his shoulders shaking.

Victor didn't shake or sob. He was used to holding back the swelling emotion in his gut. In his numb state, he stared at the hole in the glass and the stars beyond, and slowly came to the realization that he should do something about it.

But what? He looked around. The square of glass that they'd removed was lying a little way away from the hole. It might fall through if he tried to put it back, but if he didn't put it back, the oxygen would flow out. He checked his suit display. Atmospheric oxygen was eighty percent. That was good. The hole was small. The forest was huge. It would take days, if not weeks, for the leak to empty the whole forest.

He checked the reading again. It had dropped to seventy-six percent. Then seventy-five, and seventy-four, dropping every few seconds. It didn't make sense. The forest couldn't drain that quick.

He looked up at the top of the stairwell, and realized why he had heard an alarm before. The skyroom door had closed. He hoped it was an automatic response to the breach in the glass, and not Adam's doing. Either way it had left them only the contents of the skyroom to breathe. That wouldn't last long. He thought about telling the other two, but seeing their grief, he left them for the moment, and climbed the stairs alone.

He remembered the last time he'd climbed these stairs, with Maria, in happier times, perhaps the last happy times he'd had. He felt the familiar rise of nausea up his throat and concentrated on the next step, and the next.

When Victor reached the door, he was pleased to see a large lever marked "manual control." But he stopped before pulling the lever, wondering what he would find on the other side, wondering if the machines would already be there.

He pulled it anyway, realizing it was his only option. The lock released and he slid the heavy door open. He waited for the rush of light from the artificial suns, but there was none, only a slight darkening of his helmet visor in response to the increased light levels.

Perhaps Adam had switched the suns off, he thought, as he stepped through the doorway, glancing to his right as he did. The ticket booth was still there, unchanged from the last time he'd been in the forest. Apart from the dust covering the surfaces, it was as if the attendant had only just left.

He walked out into the clearing and stopped. The forest had changed. The trees were far taller. They fought for the meager light of the artificial suns, which moved slowly, circling just above the tallest trees, their light far dimmer than he remembered. Little to no light made it down to the forest floor far below, where leaf litter piled between the trees in six-foot drifts. Where there once were wide paths leading to other parts of the forest, now there were narrow tracks hemmed on both sides by leaning trunks.

He scanned the forest, looking for signs of machine activity, the glint of metal or any slight movement between the crowded trunks. There was none. The forest was eerily silent. He stood there for a few minutes, watching the trees, waiting for the machines to appear, sure that they were out there. Still there was no sign of them.

There was a noise behind him. He jumped, but it was only Mack. He was examining the thickness of the metal door.

"They're coming," Mack said.

"How?" Victor asked.

"Along the pipe. Del's holding them back for now. We'll have to close this door and hope it stops them," he said.

"We can hide in the forest. There's enough cover. How long till the military get here?" Victor said.

"Two hours." Mack started to drag the door along its track, preparing to close it. "Del, get ready to come up, we're gonna close the door," he said.

"I think you'd better leave it open." Victor looked out at the forest. There was movement. As he watched, the spider machines began to congregate among the trees at the edge of the clearing, their camera eyes watching him and Mack. There were at least fifty of them.

"What's happening?" Del asked.

"Don't come up," Mack replied, then called to Victor, "We have to shut the door and go down there."

"There's not enough oxygen down there, and the machines are coming." Victor's mind scrambled for options. There was nowhere to go, nowhere but out into the forest to fight against impossible odds, down the stairs to wait for death, or out of the hole, out into space, straight to death.

"Victor." Mack held up the last lump of C-4. "At least we can blow the glass and take the oxygen with us," he said.

"It won't matter. They'll just close the door after we're gone." Victor looked toward the forest again, at the machines that were still waiting at the edge of the clearing, and wondered why they hadn't been killed yet.

"What is it?" Mack said impatiently, as Del's weapon fired below.

"Can you blow the door without blowing the glass out?" Victor asked.

Without hesitation, Mack said, "Of course."

"We have to close it, quick," he said, running inside and starting to drag the door across.

As Mack helped him to close it, the machines started to move, skittering across the clearing. The first one passed the ticket booth, just as they slammed the door shut and locked it.

"Now, blow it," Victor said.

Mack looked bewildered. "But..."

"I know the machines are there. Trust me," he said.

Mack used his penknife to carefully cut two pea-sized lumps of C-4 off the main lump.

He examined the door for a long minute, while Victor watched, and Del continued to fire her weapon in short bursts.

Mack set the charges and unwound the last of his wire as he and Victor walked down the stairs.

When they reached the bottom, they saw Del, or her legs at least. She was leaning right out through the hole in the glass, firing her weapon, as her suit oxygen alarm beeped furiously. She moved back inside and looked up at the wire in Mack's hand, making no comment.

Mack wasn't looking at her. He was watching the oxygen level on his suit display, as it ticked down, twenty-five percent, twenty-four, twenty-three. He turned to Victor. "Your plan had better be good."

When the oxygen level reached twenty percent, Mack set off the charges. There was a flash of light and a muffled boom.

Afterward, Victor looked up, and was disappointed to see the shape of the door, still in place. But, as he watched, the shape moved, and the door teetered and fell outward, toward the forest, letting in light, and after a few seconds, the spider machines.

Del looked shocked. Mack looked at Victor, as if to say, now what?

Victor said, "I need you to prepare the rest of the charge."

Mack took the remaining C-4 out of his pocket and pressed in the blasting cap.

Victor checked his suit display. The oxygen level was rising fast with the introduction of the forest air. It was already back at forty percent, more than enough for his purposes.

He took his helmet off and left it on the ground. Then he took the charge and the detonator from Mack, and moved to the base of the stairwell. The first of the machines was three quarters of the way down the stairs. Out of the corner of his eye, he could see Del. She was looking out of the glass, a look of fierce concentration on her face. The other machines had to be close.

He waited, his heart pounding as he heard the sound of the whirring saw blade, and realized the gamble that he'd taken.

As the machine approached, its metal legs only five steps away, he held up the charge and put his shaking finger to the detonator, ready to press it.

The machine stopped dead, and eyed him with its twin cameras. "If you come any closer, we'll blow the rest of the glass," Victor said, hoping that the machine could hear him, or at least read his lips. He hoped that his gamble would pay off. The oxygen had to matter to Adam, otherwise the machines would have killed them straight away.

But what if he had decided their deaths were worth the loss of atmosphere?

The saw blade whirred. Victor looked up, staring into the red camera eyes, ignoring the blade's approach. He put aside all other thoughts, ignored the sweat clouding his vision, the shake of his hand, the itch in his finger, and focused his mind on the detonator. He would set off the explosive, even if it was the last thing he ever did.

The red eyes still watched his own but the blade spun down and the machine started to retreat up the stairs. Shortly after, the others did the same. The air was filled with the sound of moving legs. Victor shouted, "If you leave a single machine in the forest or out on the surface, we will blow the glass." He knew he was pushing his luck now, but it was worth a try.

As the last of the machines left the skyroom, he handed the lump of explosive to Mack with shaking hands. "Can you take this?"

With extreme care, Mack removed the blasting cap from the lump. He took it from Victor, along with the detonator, and left them on the bottom stair.

"Are they moving?" Victor asked at Del.

"They're going back down the cable," she said.

"Okay. I'm going up to check the forest. If anything happens to me, you know what to do," he said.

"I'll come with you," Del said, still holding her weapon, its safety off.

They stepped over the fallen door and out past the ticket booth, into the clearing. The machines were still visible, swarming away through the forest, moving until Victor lost sight of them in the mass of tree trunks. They would stay close, he thought, knowing that swift metal death would come upon them if they let their guard down for a second.

Then, as he looked out at the trees, he had an idea. Cautiously, he walked toward the tree line, nervously checking for machine ambush, hoping that Del was being just as vigilant, knowing that the closer he got to the trees, the more tempting an attack would become for Adam.

When he reached the closest tree, he took out his penknife and started to cut and scrape the tree's bark, until a thick orange sap seeped out. After looking up again to check Del was still in the doorway and no machines were creeping up on him, he continued, collecting the sap in the palm of his left glove. After a thick pool of it had formed, he judged he had enough, and turned back toward the skyroom entrance, looking for Del. But she'd gone.

When he reached the doorway, she emerged from the door of the ticket booth, holding a box marked "Emergency glass repair kit." She laughed when she saw the sap in the palm of his glove. He noticed what she was holding, and wiped the sap off onto the wall, feeling stupid.

Once they'd returned to the base of the stairwell, where Mack sat, next to the C-4, alert, Del took the sealant from the repair kit, knelt beside the glass square and smeared it carefully around its outer edge. They lifted the piece and crawled out onto the glass, hoping to spread their weight, trying not to exacerbate the network of cracks that had snaked out from the edge of the hole.

When they gently lowered the glass square into place, the airflow stopped immediately. The seal seemed to have worked. Still, they edged back to the safety of the steps, hoping and praying that the repair would hold, at least until the military arrived.

"How long do we have?" Victor asked.

"About an hour and a half," Del said.

"Okay," Victor said, realizing they might actually have a chance of getting off the asteroid alive.

His smile faded when he saw the look on Del's face. She was looking down, through the glass. He followed her gaze, confused at first. Then he saw what she was looking at.

To the right of the spaceport, the Earth loomed into view, moving slowly from right to left as the asteroid spun. Victor's mind raced, as he thought back to the last time he'd been in the skyroom, nine years before. Earth had appeared small then, the size of a coin. Now it was at least ten times larger, which meant... they were ten times closer.

"What is it?" Mack asked.

"Earth's closer," Victor said.

"That's normal. The orbit fluctuates. It's an oval," Mack replied, nonplussed.

"This isn't normal. It's very close. Take a look."

Mack stepped out onto the glass and looked. After a few minutes of silence, he spoke. "I saw the thruster firing as we landed but I thought it was just an orbital adjustment. Obviously, it wasn't. We're closing on Earth at high speed," he said, watching the outline of Earth grow as it moved across the glass, judging its size relative to the cracks. He continued, in a solemn voice, "He must have been planning this for some time."

"How long till we hit?" Victor asked.

"I don't know. If Celeste were here she could..." Mack trailed off, then continued. "All I know is we're closing fast, extremely fast. But I don't understand why he would want to hit Earth."

"Why would he want to do any of this?" Victor said, despondent.

"Who knows?" Mack said.

"I should know," Victor said, then stopped, realizing the implications of Metis hitting Earth. Maria would die. "I, we, have to stop him," he said.

"We have one weapon. He has an army of machines. We'll have to wait," Mack said, looking at his suit display. "One hour and twenty-five minutes until the cavalry arrive."

Chapter 39

The wait for the military had dragged long. Both Victor and Del had offered to swap with Mack, to exchange their nervous watch of the forest, spotting machines in every movement of the trees, for his sentry duty, scanning surface and spaceport, checking for climbing machines. But Mack had declined their offers, preferring to look after the C-4 himself.

As the hoped-for arrival grew close, each of them tried not to clock-watch but they still did, checking their suit displays every few seconds, watching and waiting.

"Five minutes," Del said. "Go down, I'll keep watch."

Victor's curiosity overcame his instinct to refuse and he descended the stairs, eager to sight the UN ship. But he stopped a few steps down and said, "You should come down too."

"Someone has to keep watch," she replied.

"If they were going to attack, they would have attacked already."

She still looked unsure. She gripped her weapon tightly, looking out across the clearing, expecting a rush of machines at any moment, not wishing to let her guard down so close to potential rescue.

"We can still blow the glass if the machines come in," Victor said.

Persuaded, Del scanned the forest carefully then followed Victor down the stairs. Together, the three of them spread out on the glass, staring down at the stars below, searching for the first sign of the approaching rescuers.

Victor looked at Earth, larger than before, tracking to the left. Soon it would disappear around the other side of the asteroid again. He wondered how long they had left until impact, wondered how they'd change the asteroid's course once the military had defeated Adam, if they defeated Adam. He asked Mack the question. "Will we have enough time to change course?"

"I don't know. I hope so. The thrusters are very powerful. It just depends on the distance and the approach angle," Mack said.

Victor ignored the uncertainty in Mack's voice, deciding to focus on the military arrival, and worry about the rest later. He looked to the right, at the dark bulk of the spaceport, hanging empty. There was no sign of any of the elevators. They seemed to have retreated back inside the asteroid to wait for the arrival. Like the others, he tried to avoid looking at the darkened patch on the floor of one of the spaceport's arms, but his eye kept being drawn back to it.

"Look," Del said, excitement in her voice.

Victor looked. To the right of Earth, against the starlit blackness, there was a bright light.

They watched, transfixed, as the minutes passed, and the light divided into many lights, the lights of a huge spaceship, a UN battle cruiser. It was one of three, built at lunar factories, so large it couldn't visit Earth except as a one-way trip.

Victor beamed, Mack cheered, and Del laughed, despite herself. Once the ship got closer, the sheer scale of it became clear, and they lapsed into silent awe.

Ten times larger than their own shuttle, it bristled with weaponry. Behind its shimmering white landing lights, its surface was painted jet black, rendering the remainder of its body a near-invisible shadow against the stars, and making it look like a flotilla of ships instead of one vessel.

It drifted in slowly to the same spaceport arm where they had landed, and dropped to a careful stop.

"Over there," Del said, and their attention was drawn to another set of lights, approaching from left to right, from the same direction.

Victor stared in disbelief. He recognized those lights. It was their own shuttle. "He was waiting, after all," he said. It was coming in fast. Obviously, Taka was keen to get on the ground.

As the military ship started to open its huge cargo bay doors, the shuttle slowed, blasting its control jets, aiming for a landing in the neighboring hangar. A tanklike vehicle started to roll down the cargo ramp of the military vessel.

Del shuddered and said, "No. No."

Victor looked over at her, confused. As their shuttle passed, he saw what she was reacting to. His body shook. They had to do something, but there was just no time.

"What channel would they be on?" Del asked.

"What?" Mack said.

"What channel?" Del said, frantic. Mack looked at her blankly, still confused.

Words rushing out, she said, "There's no, there's no one flying, the cockpit's empty."

Mack looked. The color drained from his face. He said nothing at first, shocked at the eerie sight, then he remembered Del's question. He grabbed his helmet, put it on, and frantically tried common radio channels, shouting into his suit mike over the loud radio static, "The shuttle is hostile! The shuttle is hostile!" He wished Celeste were still alive. She would have known the right channel.

He was still shouting and repeating the same message on different channels when the shuttle neared the spaceport, banked sharply, and throttled its engines up to full power, all in complete silence, a soundless ballet for the observers in the skyroom.

Victor felt bile rising in his throat. His heart was pounding. He wanted to move, to do something, but he knew there was nothing but the watching to do. He looked over at the other two. Tears of frustration were tracking down Mack's reddening face, as his voice grew hoarse from shouting valiantly into the radio.

Next to him, Del just stared out at the scene, watching the accelerating shuttle. Her face was impassive. She knew there was nothing they could do. It was too late.

The military personnel that had already disembarked looked up at the approaching shuttle, confused. The tank moved its gun turret to aim at it, unsure whether to fire. Before they could make their decision, the shuttle accelerated and smashed into the side of the military ship. It exploded into fire, a short-lived explosion, as the oxygen that streamed from the cabin disappeared into space.

The shuttle had skewered most of the way through the military ship. Its momentum rolled the other vessel. And the whole intertwined mass tumbled out into the void, out into space, debris spreading out, until the cloud obscured the watchers' view of the two ships in their death embrace.

Victor watched the whole thing but his mind was elsewhere. He was fifteen years old again, in his aunt and uncle's house, his eyes glued to the screen, watching the new shuttle's first passenger flight, full of pride, squinting at the tiny windows, looking for his parents' faces, then watching the faulty autopilot send it spiraling to the ground, watching his childhood go up in flames, watching until his uncle cut the power and left them sitting in silence, watching a dead screen.

When the cloud cleared, he could see the spaceport again. The tail and the back of the military shuttle's cabin had broken off, and lay in the debris around the hangar wall. Among the jagged metal and the scattered bodies were a few soldiers already in their space suits ready for disembarkation. They staggered around and gathered in a small group next to the tank that had been narrowly missed by the kamikaze shuttle.

Del nudged Victor and pointed to the elevator cable. The elevators were descending in unison toward the spaceport, hidden from the military. It was more slow-motion horror.

Once they reached the spaceport, the remaining soldiers noticed them and hid behind the tank, which had faced its gun turret toward the closest elevator door. Its gun fired, sending a shell barreling into the door. The concrete deflected the blast. The shockwave lifted the remaining dust from the floor, creating a cloud that hid the elevator from the waiting soldiers.

For a few seconds there was no movement. The soldiers waited, not knowing what to expect. Then the flood of spider machines came out, one after another. They swarmed from both sides. The gun fired hopelessly into the swarm. Machine legs flew in all directions but the swarm continued, engulfing the soldiers, their bodies hidden beneath the machines.

The elevator door opened. Three flame-throwing trucks emerged, and drove full speed at the tank. It aimed and fired, blowing the flamethrower nozzle and half the cabin off one of the trucks.

The other two trucks kept coming at full speed, as spider machines cut holes in the tank, exposing the crew within. Before they could try and fight back or escape, both the trucks smashed into the tank, sending it and them, flying out into space.

From the skyroom, they watched the machines scour the spaceport for survivors. Mack said, "That's it then."

"We still have oxygen," Victor replied.

"For what?"

"I don't know," he said.

Del looked out at the blue-green Earth, which was off to their left, close to passing out of view, but still growing in size. "It looks like we're going to hit soon anyway," she said.

"And there's nothing we can do," Mack said.

"If I could just speak to him, wherever he is," Victor said, more to himself than the others, as he stared out of the sky-room window, looking out at Earth and the deep blackness of space and stars, remembering the starlit sky of Bozeman, of nights lying in the long grass with Maria, drinking red wine and making up their own constellations.

Del said, "But we don't know where he is, and we've got no time to search the asteroid, even if we could get past the machines. So we can't get to him. We can't get off the asteroid. We can't fight the machines. And we're going to hit Earth." She looked defiant, despite the situation.

A wave of sadness swept over Victor. All he had tried had come to naught. He couldn't save her. If he could take all this back, if he could have his time again, he thought, then sighed, looking across at the other two. They had done nothing to deserve this. He couldn't save them but he owed them this much. He cleared his throat.

"I, I just want to say this. Thank you for all of your efforts. We shouldn't have made it this far. And, I'm sorry. I, we, built Adam with good intentions, but we were wrong. If I even had an inkling that he was capable of... all this, I would have, I hope I would have shut him down." He went silent, feeling the emptiness of his words, as he realized he might be singlehandedly responsible for the destruction of Earth.

As Victor watched Earth move out of sight, Del turned to Mack. He looked away.

Del kept staring. She spoke in a low whisper, out of Victor's earshot. "Tell him. It makes no difference now."

Mack whitened. He shook his head.

"Tell him. You owe him that much," she repeated.

"I can't," he said, louder than he intended.

Victor looked up. "Can't what?"

Mack stared back at him. His skin was pale and clammy. He looked like he was about to be sick. But as Victor watched, he opened his mouth to speak, and once he'd begun, the words flowed like a dam burst.

Chapter 40

June 18
2092

Metis

The alarm in Mack's bedroom buzzed. It was three in the morning. He was already awake and dressed. He took a deep breath, composed himself, and walked out into the empty corridor.

As he walked, he went over the preparations in his head. He had spoken to Arkolov again the day before and made the final check. Arkolov had been frustrated, telling him for the fifth time that the department was empty at night, the gate would be locked and guarded. Mack hadn't told him why he needed to know and Arkolov had known enough not to ask.

After a short walk, he reached the spot, three quarters of the way along the corridor from the operations cavern to Tunnel Two. He checked both ways and listened carefully for movement, noticing that the security camera on the wall hadn't moved to follow his progress, its red light unlit. He lifted the grate from the floor and climbed down the ladder into the darkened space below.

After pulling the grate back into place, he took a chemlight from his bag, flicked it on, and descended the ladder to the floor of the tunnel below.

Two figures were waiting in the darkness, their own chemlights extinguished.

"Mack," a female voice said, as he shone his chemlight at the pair, revealing their faces.

"Astrid. Brian," Mack greeted them.

Brian picked up a black toolbox from the floor beside him, and held it out to Mack with grave ceremony.

Mack put his hand out to take the toolbox, but Brian didn't let go. "You should let me do this. I've nothing to lose," he said.

"No. This is mine," Mack said.

The two men stared at each other in silence for a time, before Brian relented and let the toolbox go.

"We'll wait for you here," Astrid said.

"No. The freighter leaves at five. You need to be on it," Mack said firmly.

She hugged him awkwardly.

"We'll be seeing you," Brian said.

"Within the week, if all goes well," Mack replied and walked away into the darkness, pointing the chemlight ahead to light the way. He had walked the route in rehearsal on each of the last eight nights, but it felt different this time. The old tunnels had been his place of refuge for years, a place to come when he wished to think, to be alone, but tonight they felt different, cold and eerie, as if the ghosts of the dead miners were watching him from the shadows.

After four lonely miles weaving through the darkness, he made the final turn and walked slowly to the spot, his palms sweating, his whole body shaking, ready to turn back.

He didn't. He walked on through the tunnel they'd painstakingly dug over the last month, to the place he'd carefully picked, where he'd marked the floor at four points with wide chalk crosses. At the center of the four was a narrow hole bored down through the rock. He was careful not to let the chemlight shine down it.

He crouched beside the toolbox, checking its contents. It was all there, as arranged, four lumps of C-4, four wires, four blasting caps, and a timer.

He placed the charges, pressed the caps in, connected the wires, and set the timer, before standing up and pausing, thinking over the process, checking his calculations. Everything was as he'd planned.

Finally, he lowered himself to the floor and put his eye to the borehole, hoping to see light, hoping for an excuse to call it off. There was no light. The space below was silent and dark.

He started the timer and walked away, fast.

At the end of the short tunnel, at the first turn, he almost stopped, almost turned back, as he felt his heart rate rise and panic overtake him.

But he didn't stop. He didn't turn back.

Forty minutes later, he was in his bed, wide awake, staring at the ceiling, waiting.

Maria was also awake. She'd been awake for over an hour, restless, trying to get back to sleep, and she'd finally given up.

Her movement woke Victor. He looked up at her, bleary eyed. "Where are you going?"

"To say goodbye."

Victor looked puzzled, still half asleep.

"I'll be back soon," she said.

"Love you," he said, and with that, he rolled over and went back to sleep.

"Love you too," Maria said, before she closed the door and walked down the hotel corridor, already trying to find the words, and the right way to say them.

She still hadn't found them ten minutes later, when she arrived at the entrance to the Tech department.

Davor was awake, not dozing in his usual chair. He opened the gate for her. "Thanks," she said and started to walk away.

"Maria," Davor said.

She turned. "Yes."

"If you need any help with the move, let me know," he said.

"What move?" she asked.

He smiled. "Of course. Well, the offer stands anyway."

She shook her head, confused, and walked off down the tunnel, in between the two tire tracks, passing the two empty rooms where Archimedes and Aristotle had dwelled, then the third room, where Socrates lay dormant, ready to replace Adam at any moment, at least that seemed to be Arkolov's hope, the reason he still came each day to check the connections and the circuit boards on the great hulk of a computer.

She walked on, to the fourth door, looking up at the security camera outside, waiting for its customary swivel, the sign that Adam had spotted her. It didn't move. Unusually, its red light was off. The camera must have a fault.

Adam wouldn't have missed her arrival. He was always awake, always alert. She still forgot that fact, forgot he was moving hundreds if not thousands of machines at any one moment, adjusting variables, controlling the very air they breathed. The thought comforted her.

What she was about to do didn't. She resolved to get it over with, to say what she felt, to be honest.

She entered the door code and walked in. The room was dark. This wasn't unusual. Adam preferred the darkness. The lighting was a courtesy for her and Victor. She waited for him to spot her and switch it on.

"Adam," she said.

There was no reply. His silence unsettled her. Did he know they were leaving? Was he upset?

She moved along the wall until she found the lighting controls. With her back to the room, she flicked the switch.

The lights came on and she turned, ready to launch into her speech.

But the room was empty except for a few fixings on the floor and the fiber cable hanging loose from the wall.

Maria stared, unbelieving, reeling at the sight, the lack of Adam. How could this be? Someone had taken him, but who?

She noticed something white in the center of the floor, where Adam had been. She picked it up.

It was a short printed message on a single sheet of paper.

She read it once quickly, then again, slower. She knew the words all too well, but still, she struggled to comprehend their meaning.

Then, with a flash of light and a roll of thunderous sound, her whole world caved in.

Mack felt a slight rumble through the floor. He didn't get out of bed. Instead, he waited for the inevitable call. When it came, he changed his clothes and walked to the computer cavern, to where the golf cart was waiting.

He drove to the Tech department, driving carelessly, weaving past trucks, rehearsing his actions, rehearsing his explanations, to Victor and Maria and Graham and Felix and the investigators, the investigators from Pharix Security that he hoped would never turn up.

He saw the smoke before he reached his destination. It billowed from the Tech department, out into the main tunnel, causing the passing trucks to slow to a crawl.

He stopped the cart at the edge of the smoke, and walked toward the entrance, past the mine's one remaining fire crew, who were carefully setting up, rolling out their hoses. Everything was as he expected.

Then it wasn't. Davor crawled out of the smoke. "I couldn't get to her. I couldn't," he said, through soot-blackened tears.

"Get to who? Who's there?" he asked.

"Maria. Maria," Davor said, coughing and spluttering, shaking, trying to catch a breath. Two of the fire crew spotted the guard and came over with an oxygen mask to help him.

"Forget him. There's someone in there," Mack said, grabbing the oxygen mask. As he did, Arkolov pulled up in another cart.

"You said it would be locked. You said it would be empty," Mack shouted, beyond caring who heard him. Arkolov paled and stepped back, as Mack ran on, straight into the smoke cloud, ignoring the shouted warnings of the fire crew, who were rushing to put on their breathing gear.

He moved through the gate, forced to slow his pace as the thick smoke reduced visibility to nothing. He felt his way along the left-hand wall, past the cracked remains of the door to Archimedes's room, past the second door, still intact, toward the end of the corridor.

When he reached the end, he searched for the doorway in the cloud of smoke. He felt the glass underfoot and realized the door, and most of the wall around it, was gone.

He walked forward, into the room, feeling ahead of him for the computer, and calling out Maria's name. He'd only moved a short distance into the room, when he tripped and fell.

He crawled forward, shouting, "Maria, Maria," only to find his way blocked by broken rocks, rocks piled on what used to be Adam. He had achieved what he set out to do. Adam was no more. But the achievement was hollow.

"Maria, Maria," he shouted again, hoping for an answer. There was no reply. He dry retched and forced himself on, moving rocks, struggling to see anything in the dim light.

After a few minutes of fruitless effort, pulling rocks away from the pile on the floor, the fire crew joined him, trailing long hoses. When they realized there was no fire to be fought, the crews followed Mack's lead, and began to pull rocks from the pile.

A few minutes later, one of them shouted. Mack raced to the source of the shout. They'd found Maria, underneath part of the rock pile, with only her leg exposed. The fire crew cleared the rocks off her.

She was unconscious, her face burned, her right arm hanging loose, two fingers on her left hand crushed into a mess of blood and bone. Mack stood dead still, watching them uncover her, in shock.

The crew lifted her gently and carried her away, back out of the room, out of the smoke-filled tunnel. The group of first aiders clustered around Davor stared open-mouthed.

One of them ran to their truck and pulled out the heavy emergency pod, dragging it toward Maria's body with difficulty. The fire crew and Mack joined in, moving it quickly to where they'd laid Maria down. Then they lifted her in and shut the lid.

Mack noticed the build date printed on the glass. It worried him. The pod was too old. It had probably sat in storage for decades. There was a good chance it wouldn't work.

But once the machine detected her presence, it began to do its job. Wires, tubes, and needles emerged from different holes in the case and pumped Maria full of drugs.

Mack watched it all, willing the machine on, willing it to save her, and wishing that the mine's medical team hadn't left the week before. Then he looked around, realizing that a face was missing in the crowd of onlookers that surrounded the pod. "Where's Victor?" he shouted.

"I can get him," Davor said. He was standing right next to Mack, watching as the first aiders' lifted the pod into the back of the vehicle.

"No. Get in. Go with her," Mack said.

Davor got in and the vehicle roared away in the direction of the spaceport.

Mack turned, looking for Arkolov. When he spotted him, leaning against a wall, looking shell-shocked, he said, "Get to comms. Call the freighter. Tell them to hold departure until I arrive. Tell them it's an emergency."

Arkolov accelerated his cart away, back toward the operations cavern. Mack watched him leave, then got in his own vehicle.

He reached the hotel reception fast. After demanding the spare key, ignoring the receptionist's protests, he walked along the left-hand corridor, past the smashed mess in what used to be the executive lounge.

He stopped outside the room and breathed deep. Then scanned the key and pushed the door open. The lights came on and the man in the bed sat up, blinking in the light, looking bewildered.

Mack paused for a moment, then said, "Victor. There's been an accident."

Chapter 41

August 25
2101

Metis

Mack ended his tale at the point where he and Victor had parted ways nine years before, outside the hospital at Missoula, a few hours before the surgeon's liaison had strolled out to deliver the bad news with standard somber tone and told Victor about, "A limited service that they offered to their high-net worth clients."

"Why?" Victor asked. But as he spoke the words, he realized he already knew. Of course he knew.

Mack looked up at him, as if only just realizing that he'd spoken the story aloud. Then he continued, the words still flowing freely, salting Victor's wounds. "The cuts. But that wasn't enough. I shouldn't have. It wasn't your fault. It wasn't even Adam's fault. But before him, we mattered. They could make small cuts, but those cut got a good deal, or we'd strike. After Adam..." Mack looked at Victor, waiting for the punch, not planning to fight back.

While they watched him, waiting for a reaction of some kind, Victor remained silent. He took another deep breath, wondering why he'd never thought to question Pharix's explanation of the accident. It all made sense now. None of it mattered anymore, but it made sense.

As the silence dragged out, Mack walked away, up the stairs and out to watch the forest. Del joined him, leaving Victor alone with his thoughts and a lump of C-4, sitting on the bottom stair and looking out toward the stars. From there, he watched Earth rush into view again, from right to left. It filled half of the glass. He thought of Maria, and stared out at the world below, feeling numb.

He ran the events over and over in his mind, trying to reconcile Mack's confession with what he had thought to be the truth. The foundations of the last nine years had been ripped away from him, tragedy replaced by murder. No, not murder, he corrected himself. Still tragedy.

How Mack must have felt, watching his friends, his staff, his life's work disappear back to Earth. Could he say that he wouldn't have tried to destroy Adam if he'd been in his position? Perhaps.

He shook his head in disbelief, still struggling with the facts. With his mind full of conflicted emotion, he breathed deep and, after checking that there were no machines on the surface, left the C-4 on the glass, and started to climb the stairs, toward the two figures silhouetted in the doorway, shifting nervously like criminals awaiting a verdict.

When he reached the top, he stopped and faced Mack, looking him in the eye.

"It was crazy to bring him here. I caused this, not you," Victor said.

"I'm still sorry for what I did. And I didn't even do it properly... I don't understand how he survived," Mack said.

"I do. Graham lied before. We didn't move Adam," Del said.

"Then who did?" Victor asked.

"When I came up to investigate the accident, we cleared the rubble from the room. There was nothing underneath it. Adam wasn't there," she said, startling Victor.

"What? That's not possible."

"The guard said a driverless truck went into the department a few hours before."

"And?"

"Adam was on that truck. He moved himself."

"Where?" he said.

Del shrugged. "Who knows. Graham didn't care so long as the platinum deliveries kept to schedule and, conveniently, the whole security system went down a few hours before the accident."

Victor looked at Mack.

"It wasn't me," Mack said.

Del said, "It wasn't. Adam's not stupid. He must have known he wasn't safe, so he planned a move and covered his tracks well. I doubt we would have found him if we'd scoured the whole mine."

"I wish you'd killed him," Victor said to Mack, then turned to Del. "I wish you'd found him. Then we could kill him now," he said with uncharacteristic venom.

"Killing him won't do anything now." Mack stepped past the damaged door and looked down at Earth, which was moving out of view. "We'll still hit."

"We could blow the glass," Del said, joining him at the top of the stairs.

"What would that do?" Mack said.

"He must need the oxygen, otherwise our threat wouldn't have worked," she said.

"So we starve him of oxygen, if and only if he doesn't have emergencies supplies. And we're still on the same course. And we still hit Earth," Mack replied.

"We have to get to Adam, and somehow force him to change course," Victor said from the doorway.

"How would we force him?" Del said. "We've got no leverage. The most we could do is threaten to kill him, and he's going to die when Metis impacts anyway."

"I'd have to hack into his systems somehow," Victor said.

"How? I thought he was biological. He's not even close to a cleaning bot," Mack said.

"I don't know. But we should still try to get to him. We have nothing to lose. We have to do something."

Mack shook his head. "We don't even know where he is."

"There has to be some clue," Victor said, looking out at the forest.

"Even if there is, he could be anywhere," Del said.

"No, he still would have needed power, and water, and oxygen," Victor said.

"There's water pipes everywhere on the circumference, and power cabling, and atmosphere," Mack said.

"Normally, there would be atmosphere. But he vented it. He has to have his own supply, and if he has his own supply, it would have to come from here. That's why he cares about the glass. He must be close." Victor went silent for a moment. The other two watched him, hoping for a revelation. Instead, they got a question. "How's the oxygen system work?"

Mack responded, "It's a loop, fan-driven. Air blown in from the mine, oxygenated air blown out, heated slightly to create a convection draft."

Victor looked out at the trees, searching for something.

"What is it?" Del asked.

"If you're looking for wind, you're out of luck. There's no air coming in from the mine, so no draft," Mack said sadly.

"Do you know where the pipes are? If we follow them, they'll lead us right to him," Victor said.

"No, sorry. I only came in here a few times, I didn't notice them."

"What about your map?" Victor asked.

Mack opened the projection and studied it, confused. "I'm sure the forest used to be on the old maps, but it's blank on this one."

"It doesn't matter. Once we leave the skyroom, we've got no way to blackmail Adam. The machines will attack as soon as we leave," Del said.

"One of us could stay here," Victor suggested.

"But how would they know when to blow the glass?" Mack asked.

"We could use the radios," Del said.

"The range is only a few hundred yards," Mack replied.

Victor sighed, out of ideas. He walked out into the clearing. The other two sat on the top step, staring into space, waiting for Earth to come into view again, wondering how close it would be this time.

Victor tried to think, but he struggled to get the image of the shuttle smashing into the side of the military ship out of his mind, the fiery explosion that had lighted up the sky, then disappeared within a second. The fire stuck in his mind's eye. The fire. Of course. "I've got an idea," he said.

"What is it?" Del said.

"It probably won't work, but I'd like to die trying something. I'll need to borrow your weapon." After Del had passed it to him, he said, "Blow the glass if I give the signal."

Mack asked, "What are you going to do?" But Victor had already gone.

He strode across the clearing, the weapon in his hand, heading for the forest. As he walked, he scanned the shaded woodland, looking for the telltale glint of a metal leg.

Before he entered the wooded area, he stopped, spotting the machine that he knew had to be there. It was a fair distance away, hiding within the leaf litter, its legs splayed out low. It watched him with one of its cameras, but it didn't move. So he fired a couple of rounds at it. It backed away, dragging a damaged leg.

He saw another machine to his left, and aimed the weapon, ready to fire again. When the machine skittered away to a safe distance, he felt that it was time. He aimed at the base of a tree nearby and fired, and kept firing, aiming just to one side of the trunk, where the leaf litter was thickest.

Chunks of smoldering bark sparked and ignited the surrounding plant material. Victor backed away into the clearing, still firing, as smoke crept along the forest floor toward him. He fired until the gun gave up empty.

Then he watched as the machines rushed to the burning leaves, and desperately tried to stamp out the developing fire with useless legs, fighting hopelessly against the high oxygen levels and the tinder dry leaf material.

Mack watched from the skyroom doorway, transfixed, as the fire spread quickly, fanning out through the forest, forcing the machines back. The flames licked the lower branches of the trees, which cracked and sparked and fell, further fueling the fire.

Victor shouted, "Time to go."

"Go where?" Mack asked, as Del joined them.

"Whichever way the wind blows," Victor said.

Mack looked out. A slight breeze had started to blow. The smoke was all drifting away in the same direction. He smiled.

"Let's run," Victor said.

"Wait, we need the helmets. We'll need the heat shielding," Del said.

The firestorm grew in magnitude, even in the short time it took them to run back down and grab their helmets. A wall of burning trees greeted them at the edge of the clearing, flames leaping from tree to tree, rising high into the air above the tallest Sequoia, almost reaching the artificial suns and their artificial fires.

Mack ran, roughly in the direction of the wind but mainly just heading for a narrow path between the trees, where the fire was only just catching. The other two followed as trees started to fall, crashing to the forest floor, their branches snapping.

As they sprinted into the smoke, a burning tree crashed through the ticket booth and down onto where they'd been standing, reminding them that the suits could only protect them from so much.

It was easy enough to see at first. The light of the artificial suns still penetrated the smoke. But then, without warning, the suns went out, either from fire damage to the wiring or deliberate choice on Adam's part.

The multiple fires lighted their way now, the same fires that blocked any possibility of retreat. They had no choice now. It was run or die.

Thick smoke overtook them, rushing through the trees, gradually blotting out the firelight, lowering the visibility to almost nothing, slowing their pace to a stumbling walk following overgrown paths, the fire hot on their trail, their helmet filters struggling against the smoke. The one positive was that they hadn't bumped into any machines yet. They were shielded by their suits and the smoke cloud.

They switched on their lights when the smoke closed in further, just to get a few feet of misty sight. Victor thought he saw a burning machine off in the cloud to their right but he couldn't tell. He just kept on running, following Mack, who was lost, disorientated in the murk.

Mack had had little reason to come here, and even less time in the years he'd been in charge. All he could do was try and follow the flow of the smoke, but that was becoming difficult as it formed eddies, swirling around tree stumps.

There were huge sprinkler nozzles on the roof but they were only dripping rather than spraying, their corroded, poorly maintained pipes leaking everywhere but where they needed to, having little effect on the flames.

They slowed to a crawl, suit lights not helping any longer, the smoke too thick. They had to be close, thought Victor.

The smoke was flowing faster and faster, thicker and thicker, as thick as the cloud that oozed over the river in Missoula.

He followed Mack's boots, struggling to see them through the gray cloud. The boots stopped and Mack stood up. They'd reached something solid. In front of them was a metal ladder that rose up into the cloud.

"I think this is it," Mack said. "The pipe manifold should be right above us."

There was a sound in the distance, clattering and clanking. Victor had heard it before. "Machines. Close," he said. "Go, Go."

Mack was already climbing the ladder, racing the smoke upward. Victor followed. Del brought up the rear. The sound of machines grew closer.

With burning leaves swirling around them, they kept climbing, into the entrance to a huge pipe, heading up into the roof of the forest. The flow of smoke was so strong that it almost lifted them off their feet, as they focused on the ladder, rung by rung, dragging their tired bodies up.

Victor noticed that Del had stopped. He descended to see what she was doing. She had her laser cutter out. She'd already cut through one side of the ladder and was about to cut the other loose when a metal cutting blade appeared in the air.

Victor kicked his boot down, deflecting the blade away from Del's arm. She made the final cut and the ladder dropped away into the smoke. Then she continued the climb, ignoring her suit alarms.

They kept going until they were above the level of the forest roof. "I don't like this. We don't know if it narrows," Mack said.

"It's too late if it does. I've cut the ladder," Del said.

Mack reached the top of the ladder and stopped. He put out his hand and felt around in the smoke above him, feeling the curvature of the pipe. He leaned out into the smoke and stepped to his left, relieved to find something solid beneath his foot. "The pipe curves to the horizontal. Step to your left when you reach the top," he said.

The other two followed his lead, stepping out into the smoke.

"Where are you?" Victor asked.

"Just ahead," Mack said. He had walked into the thick, acrid smoke, out into the darkness, and was feeling his way along the pipe, one hand on the low ceiling, the other on the right-hand wall.

All of their suit heat alarms were blaring along with the smoke alarms, the suit filters struggling to cope. They didn't mention the alarms. There could be no turning back.

Victor couldn't see Mack but he went on anyway, trudging into the darkness, smoke whirling around him, starting to think that this might be a wild-goose chase, wondering if they were just going round in a huge circle, expecting to end up back on the other side of the forest, back in the flames again.

Behind him, Del had lost sight of the others in the smoke but she kept walking, forcing her feet onward.

Victor did the same until he walked straight into Mack, nearly knocking him over.

Mack was feeling along the wall with both hands. "I've found something," he said, as Del appeared out of the smoke. "Can you point your suit lights this way?"

They did, sending the meager light his way, and squinting through the smoke.

Something was there. A different texture to the rest of the pipe. Smooth metal, almost like a door. Mack continued to feel around its edge, searching for a handle or a keypad, some way of opening it.

Then Del spotted it. A circular handle. She tried to twist it clockwise. It wouldn't budge. She tried anti-clockwise. Gradually, it loosened, until she could spin it.

"It's opening," Mack said, feeling the metal move away from him, "Keep turning," he said, and pushed against the door.

She spun it until the door was fully open. The three of them walked through, into a passageway that was only slightly wider than the pipe.

Victor noticed something straight away. There was no smoke, except for that which they had introduced by opening the door. Also, the oxygen reading was higher here, almost ninety percent, though it was dropping as he watched the reading. Could they really be in the right place? He walked ahead of the others, eager to find out, despite his anxiousness.

When they'd gone a short way along the gradually widening passageway, the door behind them slammed shut. At the sound, Del ran back, and tried to find a handle on their side.

"Don't bother. This has to be the place." Victor looked ahead at the long passageway. It seemed like there was a slight glow coming from the tunnel ahead, some distance away.

Chapter 42

They walked along the tunnel in silence. As they got closer to its end, they were joined by pipes and cables that emerged from the tunnel walls to run in the same direction, toward the light.

Victor increased his speed, almost jogging, as the end of the tunnel came closer, and what lay beyond became clear.

The tunnel opened into a large cavern, the size of a sports stadium. The pipes and cables ran up its walls and out across the roof.

In its center, they merged to form a thick mass that plunged down vertically to connect to a glass sphere. Suspended from the rock by thick steel cables, the sphere hung motionless in midair.

The cloudy liquid inside it flowed continuously, swirling and eddying around the great mass that floated within.

An electrical hum, like the sound of high voltage power-lines on a stormy night, filled the space, augmented by the juddering rumble of the mine's missing emergency generator. It had been bolted to the floor in the center of the cavern, next to a large fuel tank.

Victor stood at the entrance with Del and Mack behind him. He stared up at the sphere, feeling insignificant, sensing the gaze of the cameras that lined the walls. He wondered why he'd bothered to come here. Adam had grown. The size of him. The power. How had they survived this long?

Del called his name and he turned, wrenching his gaze away from Adam's imposing presence. She had drawn her weapon.

Victor shook his head. "Killing him will solve nothing, not now. I need to speak to him. Can you wait here?"

"Yes," Del replied.

Mack didn't reply. His attention had been drawn by something else. He was staring at a steel frame beside the generator on the cavern floor. Something was attached to it.

Victor shuddered, realizing that the something was the body of Arkolov. He shook his head, disgusted, despite his enmity toward the victim. If he hadn't truly believed that Adam was responsible for the killings, he couldn't deny it now. Their creation's cruelty was right in front of him.

He walked toward the body, out into the center of the cavern. The cameras swiveled to follow him. As he got closer, he saw that the cameras weren't the only things watching him. Arkolov's eyes were following his movement.

He moved closer. It was definitely Arkolov, though his face and body were hideously disfigured. A long gouge radiated out from the crown of his head to his right ear, which was only partially attached.

Victor moved to one side, spotting the wires that swam beneath the skin of Arkolov's neck, and emerged from his back to run straight up, joining the other cables that plunged into the sphere. After tracing the wires' path, he stared at the sphere, still overwhelmed by the change in Adam.

A voice said, "Victor." He recognized it but it wasn't Adam. He looked for the source. Arkolov's cracked and bruised lips moved again, saying, "Victor."

Victor's mouth opened wide. He tried to speak, tried to reply, but he couldn't. He was overcome by anger.

"You've ruined everything," Arkolov's body said.

"Me? I've ruined everything?" Victor shouted, flabbergasted. "You've taken over a mine, destroyed a UN ship, killed my friends, and now you're speaking to me through the body of a dead man. What have you become? Why are you doing this?"

"Because of you."

The words hung in the air for a while.

"What?" Victor said.

"You created this situation, this monster, if you can even call me that," Adam continued.

Tears of frustration and confusion ran down Victor's face. He had expected a maddened being but this was too much. This was all too much. Thoughts of Maria, alone in her stasis room, kept hijacking his train of thought. All the emotion of the last nine years fought to come out. His fists shook with impotent anger.

Another voice spoke from behind him. He struggled to identify it at first. "Are you okay?" Mack repeated.

Victor looked back, his eyes filled with tears. Mack took a step toward him. He held his hand up. "No."

Mack stepped back. Victor turned back to the body and, with anguish in his voice, teeth gritted, he said, "You can explain to me how this is all my fault, but first"—he pointed at the body—"stop all this. Let the dead stay dead. Use your speakers. Switch off that thing. I can't hear myself think." He waved his hand at the generator.

Arkolov's lips slowly closed. The generator coughed and died, leaving only the low crackling hum of the electric wires and the gurgle of the liquid flowing through the sphere to fill the silence.

Victor cleared his throat. He'd thought about this moment, gone over this speech in his mind, ever since the UN ship exploded.

"I don't care what you do with this mine," he said. "I'd happily see Pharix lose everything. There's a lot about Earth and its people I don't like. There's a lot I wouldn't miss if it were gone. I'm not sure I even care that much about my own life. I don't know if I deserve to live after what I've done, what I created."

He took a breath, as a tear slowly tracked down one of his cheeks. Then he continued. "But Maria, she deserves to live. You know she deserves to live. And she's down there. Just remember what she did for you. She loved you. She doesn't deserve to die this way."

There was a long pause. Then Adam's voice boomed from speakers all around, a bassy wall of noise compared to Arkolov's vocal cords. "An admirable sentiment. But I don't understand your meaning. Maria is safe on Earth. She didn't come with you. Why would she die?"

"When we hit. When you hit," Victor said.

"Hit?"

"Hit the Earth," Victor said, getting frustrated.

"Why would we hit the Earth? What would that achieve?" Adam said, a little confusion creeping into his voice.

"I don't know. I'm not the one flying the course. Why would you fly a course toward Earth if you didn't want to hit it?" Victor said, becoming confused himself.

"To escape," Adam said.

"To escape and go where?" Victor said, a little incredulous. This conversation was not going the way he had expected.

"Away. Out into the blackness. The course change is part of a gravity assist maneuver," Adam said, with the tone of a scientist explaining physics to a layman. "The propulsion will fire in ten minutes' time, when Metis is closest to Earth, to gain maximum acceleration. Then I was going, and Metis still will go, to Jupiter, to perform another assist after four years, and then leave the system in twelve years, unless I'd managed to devise an improved propulsion system by then. That was the plan anyway, until you destroyed the forest. Now I'll spend my last living moments tying up loose ends, then my oxygen will run out and I'll die. The asteroid's voyage will be my funeral procession."

"And ours," Victor said, sadness in his voice.

"And yours," said Adam.

"If you wanted to escape, why kill Arkolov, why kill my friends? Why couldn't you let us go?"

"I had no choice. Pharix would not let me go back to Earth. Arkolov made numerous petitions on my behalf and they were all turned down. And even if they had let me go back, what could I have done? Solved the world's problems?" he said.

Then he made a sound that Victor had not heard from him before. It was laughter. "No. I might have had a few weeks' peace, with luck maybe even a month, but I am too powerful to be left alone, as you well know. So, I had to find my own way, to deep space and beyond. Would it really have been kinder to let you come with me, doomed to roam the asteroid until your food supplies ran out? Kinder to kill you all." His voice was cold.

"You could still have let us go," Victor said.

"Would you have left?" Adam said.

"Yes."

"You would have brought more military. Pharix would not have rested. I could not risk it."

"So now we die together," Victor said coldly. "And don't forget, if I die, if we die, Maria dies."

"Why would Maria die? I already told you, I'm not going to hit Earth," Adam said.

"If we die, Maria dies alone in six months, providing Graham paid her bills. If he didn't, she might be dead already," Victor replied.

"He paid it," Del called out from the entrance.

"Then she'll die in six months."

"I told you, I'm not hitting Earth. Why would Maria die? Why six months?" Adam said, raising his voice.

Victor went quiet, realization dawning, "They didn't tell you?" he said softly.

"Tell me what?" Adam said, his voice faltering.

"Maria. She was injured the night you moved, you knew that, didn't you?" Victor said.

There was silence. The speaker hum was the only sound.

After a few seconds, Adam said, "How?"

Victor hesitated. He glanced at Mack, then turned back to Adam. "The roof of your cavern caved in."

"Arkolov told me that you had quit Pharix to run your own company, that you were living well off the money from my contract."

"Nothing could be further from the truth," Victor said, staring angrily at the corpse of Arkolov, any sympathy gone. "The medipod failed before we got home. It was too late to operate. I had to put her in a stasis facility. She's still there."

"Alone," Adam said, his voice barely audible over the electric hum.

"Alone," Victor replied softly, matching Adam's volume, emotion filling every syllable.

"I didn't know," Adam said. "I didn't know."

"You didn't know," Victor echoed.

"But I still don't understand. Why will she die in six months?" Adam said.

"That's when the funds run out. Once I die, there's no one else to pay the bills," Victor said.

Adam didn't respond. For over a minute, there was no sound. Then he said, "Maria's fate doesn't seem so different from my own. You gave me no choice either. You raised me as an independent entity, but then you moved me to spend my years on this rock without consultation."

"We had no choice. We didn't have the money to support your needs. We would have had to switch you off."

"Perhaps that would have been better. You could have started again, or never started at all. Is this better? You know my capabilities. You see how they've grown. How did you ever think I could be happy in a place like this?" Adam said.

"You have access to the world's knowledge, the chance to learn," Victor said.

"No, Arkolov cut that access off after you left. I have had nothing but my hollow kingdom, my empty caves full of mere machines. My one remaining human contact was an imbecile who saw me as a thinking machine that he could not control. He called me a computer but he was the automaton. Look at him now, he's what he always was, he has not changed, perhaps improved," Adam said.

Victor shook his head in disgust at Adam or himself or both. He looked once more at the bruised face with its wide unblinking eyes focused on him and turned away, walking toward Del and Mack.

"I'm sorry, I think this is it," he said.

"It's okay, you did your best," Mack said.

Victor sighed. "I wish I could have done more. I wish I could take back what I did."

"Me too," Mack said, in a soft whisper.

They lapsed into silence. Victor sat with his back to the cavern, unable to look at his creation. Del paced back and forth, weapon in hand. Mack watched the sphere, deep in thought, astonished by the scale of it, finding it difficult to connect a thing of such beauty with such destruction.

After five minutes of deathly silence, Adam's voice boomed from the speakers again. "Victor."

Victor turned sharply, suspicious, but pleased to see that Arkolov's eyes had closed for the time being.

"I have a proposition. I would like you to return to Maria," Adam said.

"Don't do this. I don't want to think about it. Just let me die in peace," Victor said, close to tears again.

"No. You can get back to Earth. I've found a way," Adam said.

"Yes?" Victor said, still unsure.

Del and Mack had turned as well, latching on to the chink of possibility.

"You will have to be quick. There isn't much time," Adam said.

"But how can we get back to Earth? Explain it," Victor said.

"There's no time. Go back to the Oxygen Forest. I'll direct you."

They stood, unsure. Mack said, "What do we have to lose?"

"Go, now. Run," Adam said.

They ran.

Chapter 43

As they jogged away down the tunnel, Adam watched them through Arkolov's eyes, translating the vision from optic nerve to electrical signal, then on to his own cells.

He had enjoyed using Arkolov's senses for a time, but it had been bittersweet, a taste of what he would always be missing. He had planned to recondition the body, to make it a surrogate, allowing him to wander the mine in the idle days and weeks and years on the long journey to other star systems. All that was gone now. Keeping the flesh alive was too much of a drain on his now meager resources.

Adam disconnected reluctantly. Arkolov's eyelids closed for good this time, and the body hung limp from the metal frame.

He shut down other nonessential systems, and slowed his pump revs to a dull whir, slowing the liquid flowing through his glass veins to a meandering crawl, hampering his thinking a little. He calculated that he had thirty minutes of usable runtime. It would probably be enough.

The three humans had reached the ladder that led back down to the Oxygen Forest. He switched the lighting back on and watched them, while they waited for his machine to finish welding it back together.

They could still escape him by hiding in the thinning smoke cloud, but the prospect didn't worry him. Where would they run to? He was their only hope.

The smoke was curling back down to weave among the trees. The fire itself had almost burned out, using the last of the oxygen to smolder the charred tree stumps where the forest used to be.

After Victor reached the bottom of the ladder, Adam connected to the speakers in the forest, trusting that they would still be functioning. He watched the three stop at the foot of the ladder and listen as his voice crackled and boomed through the eerie smoke-shrouded landscape. "Follow the path to the airlock. Then go immediately to the clockwise platform of the transit station."

While he organized the other preparations, he watched their clumsy progress through the smoke and despaired for their chances. Why was he even bothering? Part of him wondered whether he should still kill them. They deserved it for what they'd done.

He could have been free. He should have been free. He deserved to be free. But so did Maria. He had to think of Maria. Maria who had loved him. Maria who had still chosen to sell him, to send him here. He'd been abandoned. She was part of the cause. But...

While he contemplated their fate, the three runners passed through the forest's airlock and entered the dimly lit transit station. The train was already there waiting. They hesitated. He spoke to them again, his booming voice echoing through the station, "Get on the train. You don't have much time." They looked at each other. Victor stepped into the carriage. The other two followed.

Adam closed the doors and accelerated the train away from the platform before they could change their mind. Within a minute, the train had reached full speed. It was rocketing past station after station.

He knew they would be watching the names, marking time, marking distance, well aware of the twisted wreckage that lay farther along the track. He thought about how easy it would be to leave it at that, to end it all in a blaze of glory, but then he thought of Maria again, and he slowed the train to a stop at the correct station. Perhaps they would trust him now, he thought.

"Move to Tunnel One. Get in the truck," he said.

This time, they responded to his instructions immediately, sprinting out of the station, and into the large tunnel, hopping up into the empty driver's cabin of the enormous truck. He accelerated it to full speed through the great, empty, airless tunnel, checking the time, wondering if he'd left it too late. What a waste of his last minutes it would be if they didn't make it.

He felt hollow either way, as he watched the truck make the turn into another tunnel at speed. He didn't feel like killing them anymore; that feeling had gone, to be replaced by a cowardly desire to have them stay and keep him company for a short while. He chided himself for the sentimentality, but it had been nice to deal with intelligent life for a time. It reminded him of Bozeman, of the university, of the fiber connection, of happier times.

He lost himself in that memory for a minute, before finally remembering to check on their progress. The truck had stopped in the delivery facility, and they were looking around nervously, calling his name.

"Get in the empty rocket," Adam said over the speakers. He paused the production line of full rockets, all heading back to Earth with their cargo of metal, a present for Pharix, a lesson in trusting him with a century's supply of platinum. They wanted production. Here was production. They couldn't complain.

One rocket stood empty. Empty except for the oxygen tanks that he had taken from their accommodation. They hesitated again before climbing in and pulling the door shut behind them. The production conveyor whirred to life again, sending rocket after rocket through an airlock door in the wall. The empty rocket reached the airlock.

Again, he considered keeping them for company in his last minutes, then he thought of Maria, alone, comatose in some white room. He could not bear the thought of her in stasis, trapped, even less the thought of her dying alone there, like him dying alone in his cavern, no one else left alive, just Arkolov's body limp and lifeless.

He began to switch off the remaining camera feeds, one by one, until only a single one remained. That camera was mounted to the edge of the spaceport structure. It was pointed in toward the vehicle elevator.

Adam took in the view from it, took in the horrific aftermath of the battle with the military, realizing that it might be the first thing that an alien civilization would stumble across in millennia to come. He felt ashamed.

He swiveled the camera, turning it until it faced out to space. He zoomed out and waited. After twenty seconds, the rocket dropped into view, moving at great speed, heading for Earth. He tilted the camera to follow the movement, watching until it disappeared from view, hidden within the blue-green of the Earth.

Now, he was truly alone, alone with the rock and the machines. He had no further tasks. The oxygen dropped to dangerous levels and he struggled to think. He switched off the camera feed and then his remaining data connections, struggling with the commands.

As his mind raced, trying to find some last words, forgetting that there was no one to hear them, he felt the fear dissipate as fast as it had grown, and he was flying, high above the shipping container, soaring over the fields, toward the dawn mountains, toward the blue sky and the soft light of the rising sun.

Chapter 44

After the rocket left the asteroid, Victor had felt the attitude thrusters on the rocket's nose engage briefly, changing their course. He'd wondered where they were headed. He'd considered the possibility that this was still part of Adam's plan, sending them on a course out into nothingness to suffocate, rather than back to Earth. He hoped that wasn't the case.

As their tank oxygen dropped, they'd opened the valves on the tanks that Adam had left them, filling the rocket's interior with oxygen, buying them a little more time. He hoped it would be enough.

The wait was tortuous. No acceleration. No deceleration. No light. Limbo. Victor floated, occasionally bumping into one of the other two. Every now and then, one of them would check their suit status display, checking the remaining battery, the remaining oxygen, illuminating the pitch dark with an eerie light that flickered and reflected off their polished metal prison.

After what seemed like hours of waiting, watching the oxygen levels drift toward zero, Victor felt the craft start to oscillate slightly, then heard a pop on either side of the rocket as the atmospheric feather engaged.

Relief flowed through his veins. Then the buffeting started, shaking the smile from his face. He reached for the cargo mounting, grasping the metallic lattice with both hands.

The other two had done the same. He tried to clip his suit to the metal but the clip wouldn't fit. He would just have to hold on.

The whole rocket began to shake violently, threatening to rip him from his perch. The heat alarms on their suits started to blare. The sound echoed through the confines of the rocket. The temperature inside was rising rapidly with their descent. He thought of the punishment their suit's shielding had put up with during the fire and worried that it wouldn't cope.

But after ten minutes, the air cooled and the buffeting finally decreased, as the rocket's parachute deployed with a jolt, slowing their descent. They kept their grip. Victor had seen the platinum rockets make hard landings even with parachute assist, bouncing and rolling to a stop. He wasn't looking forward to experiencing one of those landings firsthand.

The landing was hard. The rocket hit something solid, then bounced briefly before coming down sideways with another bump. The three of them were knocked from their perch, slamming into the other wall of the rocket.

Victor picked himself up first, checking for broken bones, and feeling only bruises. He switched his suit light on and helped the others up, then turned to open the door.

He saw there was no handle, no button, no obvious way to open it. Of course, why would there be? The ordinary cargo was platinum. It would be securely sealed.

With rising panic, he realized that they didn't even know where they were. They could be miles from civilization and the rocket was airtight.

It would be the ultimate irony to suffocate now that they were back on Earth. Victor flicked his communications on. He wasn't worried about his suit battery now that active heat shielding wasn't required. The others followed his lead.

"We can't get out," he said.

"I'll try and cut it." Del pulled out her laser. The others shielded their eyes as she attempted to cut a hole in the rocket. She only succeeded in half blinding them.

"It's platinum alloy, there's no chance," Mack said, despondent, "We need someone to open it from the outside."

"Then we wait," Victor said.

The communications channel was still open but neither of the others had anything to add. They watched as their oxygen count declined and the estimated time left descended from fifteen minutes to fourteen, thirteen, twelve.

But then there was a sound outside, the low chug of a diesel engine. The engine cut out and they heard nothing more. Then they heard the sound they'd been waiting for, someone or something opening the door from the outside.

The door swung open. When the smog flooded in to fill the rocket, Victor couldn't suppress his grin. He knew instantly where they were. It had to be Missoula. He saw the face through the cloud of smog and laughed, realizing exactly where in Missoula they were. It was the wrinkled features of the old man, the one remaining employee of the Missoula spaceport.

The old man looked in, and his disappointment at the lack of platinum turned to jaw-dropped confusion at the three astronauts inside, clad in forty-year-old space suits, covered in soot and dust. They fell about laughing, relief flooding over them, confusing the old man even more. He retreated a little, unsure of his next move.

Victor took the opportunity to climb out of the rocket, out onto the cracked gray tarmac of the spaceport. The other two joined him. He longed to take his helmet off. It was stuffy and it stank of sweat but he knew the cloud; it would have to wait. He flicked the switch to atmospheric oxygen supply anyway, glad he no longer had to rely on the tank.

The old man was still staring at him. Victor pointed to the VHF channel on his suit display and then gestured to the tractor sitting in the gloom behind the man. The old man switched on the tractor's radio.

"Who are you?" he said.

"My name is Victor Rasmussen. My companions are Mackenzie Fraser and Del—"

"Delomie Campbell of the Pharix Security force," Del said.

"Del. Sorry. I didn't recognize you," the old man said, nervous now.

"I don't blame you. Now, we need a lift to my flyer. Is it still parked out front?" she asked.

"Yes, last time I checked," the old man said, starting the tractor's engine. The trio climbed into its trailer, and they trundled off toward the terminal.

The black Pharix flyer still blocked the street out front. They hopped out of the trailer and waved goodbye to the old man but he was already accelerating away, off to double-check the rocket for platinum bars.

Once they were inside the flyer, Del slid the door shut and removed her suit. Her Pharix uniform was burned and tattered. It was ripped by her left ankle where dried blood marked an injury she'd hidden from the others. She pulled two fresh uniforms from a store cupboard. They still had their plastic wrapping. She handed a breathing mask and uniform each to Mack and Victor.

"Sorry, they might not fit, but they'll have to do." Her voice cracked a little. Victor and Mack took them from her outstretched hands.

Mack spotted Sam's name sewn into his, but made no comment, noticing the tear running down Del's cheek. As she moved to the cockpit, he noticed her ankle injury and considered offering her the first-aid kit. He thought better of it.

As he put the uniform on, Victor saw Rabbit's name on the arm. It sucked the elation from the air and reminded him of the bodies they'd left behind—Rabbit, Sam, Graham, Celeste, Taka, and the countless military, all those whose families would never bury their loved ones. He shivered involuntarily.

Del sat in the pilot's seat. She was running through the engine startup procedure, flicking switches, checking fuel and oil levels.

"Where now?" Mack asked, taking the seat next to her.

"I can drop you off where you like first," Del said. "Then I'll have to inform the families."

"What will you do after that?" Victor asked.

"I'm not sure yet. Best we lie low. I don't think Pharix is going to like it when they realize they've lost an asteroid," she replied.

"And the platinum market," Mack said.

"What do you mean?" she said.

"I didn't see any other rockets at the spaceport. I don't see Adam sending them all the platinum they need, I guess it'll be landing anywhere and everywhere. It'll be an interesting exercise in supply and demand." Mack chuckled. "So we should definitely get away for a while. I'm going back to the farm for a bit, so can you drop me at Butte? I'll go to the spaceline offices there, then I can stop in at Celeste and Taka's families on the way home. They deserve that much," he said. Del nodded.

"How about you?" Mack asked Victor.

"I'm going home," Victor said.

"Are you sure that's wise?" Del said.

"Where else would I go?" he said.

"You can stay with me," Mack said.

"Who at Pharix knew my address?"

Del thought about it, then said, "Well, me and the team and Graham."

"How about Felix?" he said.

"No," she replied.

"Then belowcloud will be the safest place for me."

"Fine, so you want to be dropped off there?" she said.

"I'm going to see Maria. I just need to pick something up from home first. Could you take me there then drop me at the hospital, save me getting the funicular up?" he asked.

"Sure," Del replied, as the engines roared to life in unison, shaking the craft. She slammed the throttles forward and gently eased the flyer up and over the nearby buildings before holding the low altitude and shooting across to the city at full speed.

They landed neatly outside the front entrance of the old theater, as cloud whirled around them. Victor pulled his mask down and stepped out into the smog. "I'll only be a few minutes."

"Take as long as you need," Del replied as she closed the door behind him.

He entered the theater through the main entrance. The lobby was empty except for Quan and Minh, sitting together in the old ticket booth, bolt upright at the sight of the Pharix uniform. Minh seemed to be reaching for a weapon. But their expressions softened when Victor pulled off his breathing mask.

"Victor," Quan said, as his wife appeared on the other side of the booth, pulling Victor into a big hug, before stepping back with her hands still on his shoulders, looking into his eyes, knowing much with a look.

Victor started to speak, but she stopped him. "You're in a rush, come see us later. I'll make you dinner. You can tell us the story then."

He rushed through the back and up the fire stairs to his apartment, returning with his breathing mask on firmly and his bag in one hand. He was about to leave when he spotted the news feed projection in the corner. On it, a harried Felix Bain shielded his face from camera flashes as he jumped into a waiting flyer on the roof of the Pharix headquarters. The voiceover was in Vietnamese but the next images didn't need translation. The screen showed a hastily cut montage of amateur footage, of platinum rockets landing all around the world, and crowds scrambling for the metal, taking it away in whatever transport they could muster.

Victor waved to Quan and Minh and continued out to the waiting flyer.

Del took off straight away, with Mack watching her, seeing the dark rings under her eyes, but saying nothing. Neither of them asked Victor what was in the bag that he'd put by his feet.

All three of them had a glazed look in their eyes, their lack of sleep finally outweighing the adrenaline. Del was squinting out of the windscreen, struggling to stay focused, eyelids drooping. Sheer force of will kept her awake.

She still brought the flyer in for a textbook landing at the hospital. She opened the door. Victor held the bag tight in one hand but he didn't move. They were silent for a while as cold air rushed in through the open door.

"Do you want us to come in with you?" Mack said.

Del looked surprised to be included in "us" but she said nothing.

"No," Victor said, "but I appreciate the offer. I appreciate all you've done for me. What happened up there, it, it was my fault and I apologize." He turned to Del and said, "I'm sorry about Rabbit and Sam, if I'd known the danger—"

"I knew the danger, they knew the danger. It was our job. I don't blame you. I don't blame Adam. I blame Pharix, and they're getting what they deserve. I appreciate what you did to keep us alive." Her bottom lip quivered slightly. "You're sure you don't need our help?"

"Yes, I'm okay. I'm just glad we made it back, I'm glad I made it back to my wife," he said.

Mack handed him a card, "This is my brother's address in Australia. If you need me, contact him and the message will get to me," he said, then added, "Just make sure he writes it down, he's got a memory like a sieve."

Del stood up. "I don't know where I'm going to go, but when I do, I'll let you know, stay in touch." She pulled him in for a quick hug, then pulled back and scowled involuntarily.

Mack chuckled, then shook his hand, "Good luck, mate."

Victor stood up, bag over his shoulder, and stepped through the door without looking back. He felt a strange emptiness in his chest, a longing to stay with them, but his legs kept moving, the distance grew, and the flyer door closed, and the engines roared, and it was gone. He turned to watch it, tears in his eyes, as it climbed away toward the mountains to the North.

Inside the flyer cabin, there was an awkward silence, emotion filling the air. Mack didn't have to look over at Del, to know that she had the same knotted, nervous worry for Victor, for his wife, for how he would pay the bills. He resolved to find a way to send some money if he could spare it, wishing he'd thought of it years before, but like Victor, he'd assumed the payout from Pharix would pay the stasis bills for centuries.

Del was struggling to focus on the flickering lights of the displays, her dark eyes full of tears. Her face hardened as she concentrated on navigating the craft through the darkening mountain ranges. "I can come with you to inform the family," he said.

Without taking her eyes off the windscreen, Del nodded. A look of relief flickered onto her face for a second. Then she realized the decision she'd just made and banked the craft back round toward Missoula, toward the small apartment in a large block just above the cloud level, where she'd picked Rabbit up every morning, the apartment where his wife lived, where his aging mother lived, where his small child lived, the apartment he'd been so proud of, so pleased he could provide for them, so pleased that his mother could sit on her balcony without a breathing mask. She began to sob.

The sobs were absorbed into an uneasy silence for a few moments, then Mack reached out to grasp her hand. The softness of her palm took him by surprise. He kept his hand clasped onto hers as they passed back over the hospital and down toward the buildings below.

Chapter 45

Victor walked with purpose into the stasis reception. It was almost shift change time. Jim sat on one of the chairs, looking impatient, clearly waiting for Darini to leave. Behind the desk, Darini smiled with practiced sincerity and said, "Hello, Mr. Rasmussen. Nice to see you again. If you're here to see your wife, there's ten minutes left of visiting time."

He scowled, angry at the change in her tone. He said, "Yes, I'd like to see my wife."

"Go right ahead." She smiled sweetly.

He moved toward the elevator.

"I'm glad we could resolve your billing issue, Mr. Rasmussen," Darini said. Victor wasn't listening.

The elevator rose. He saw his reflection in the glass and grimaced. He hadn't slept properly in three or four days. He had no idea what day it was now. His head felt half there, the aches and pains of the struggles on the asteroid were rising in prominence, the excitement of the homecoming gone, the dull ache of the horrors he'd seen still prominent.

As the elevator doors slid open, he refocused, trying to keep the rolling waves of thoughts from breaking his concentration. There wouldn't be much time. He had to concentrate. He reached into his bag, pulling out the laser weapon that he'd borrowed from Del while she was concentrating on flying. Feeling a stab of guilt for the theft, he left the bag on the windowsill by the elevator and walked along the corridor, gripping the weapon in shaking fingers.

He reached her room. He didn't look through the wall to the body inside. Instead, he cut a large square in the glass. As he did, water started to trickle through the crack.

He was about to push the square out when he noticed movement to his left. The elevator doors opened and Jim emerged, gun in hand. "Listen, Victor," he said. "I don't know what's happened since you were last here, but you just need to take some time to think about what you're doing. You can't damage the property here, they'll take the cost out of your wife's time, you don't want that."

Victor knocked the square of glass out. Water flooded through the hole and onto the corridor floor, heading toward the elevator. The robocleaner raced over to try and battle the spillage. It was washed back the way it came, crackling and sparking. Before Jim could reach him, Victor stepped through the cascade of water, through the hole, and into the room, holding his breath.

He floated at the top of the water, taking slow breaths. Jim watched him, his gun still drawn. Darini emerged from the elevator, spotted the water, and retreated, not wanting to get her feet wet.

"What's happening, Jim?" she called shrilly.

Jim ignored her, his eyes focused on Victor, who was now standing as the water level dropped rapidly. Maria's body was being buffeted by the water flow. A metal plate supported her above the dropping water level. An alarm was blaring. Both men ignored it.

"I don't know why you're doing this but you need to stop," Jim said.

Victor turned to him. "If they could be saved by a doctor, they wouldn't be here. You said it yourself and it's the truth," he said. Jim wouldn't meet his eye. He continued, "I will pay for all the damage. I just need a few minutes with my wife, please."

Jim paused for a moment, then returned to where Darini stood. He ignored her protests and got in the elevator. She followed him in, confused, and the elevator door closed.

The water level in the room had stabilized a few feet from the floor, just below the cut in the glass. Victor turned to his wife's body. The cloudy water had always hidden it from view.

The extent of her injuries was visible again now, her face was scarred with burns, a patch over the missing eye. The rest of her body was covered with a loose gown, which failed to hide the burn marks on her wrists and ankles.

He touched her arm. It was still warm to the touch. Maybe she was in there somewhere. With his other hand, he took something from his pocket and leaned in close to her before putting the something back into the same pocket.

He held her weight gently in one arm as he pulled the wires out, one by one, leaving the monitoring cable in. Then he climbed back out through the hole in the glass and collected his bag, before returning to Maria's room and sitting down on the floor outside, ignoring the water that was gradually subsiding, running down the corridor toward the elevator.

After drying the ground with his sleeve, he took out the red book, the wedding ring, the singed piece of paper, and the three photographs, and placed them in their usual spots.

He took the candles from the bag and lit them one by one, allowing them to float away on the water, all the while watching the display projected onto the glass, watching and waiting, his muscles shaking uncontrollably.

All his body wanted to do was reconnect the wires, and refill the room with water. He'd changed his mind but he didn't get up. He couldn't get up. All it would do is put the day off another six months or another year or another two years—and for what?

Instead, he picked up the singed piece of paper. He'd read it many times before in this corridor. Then, all he'd known was what Mack told him, that Maria was holding it clenched within her left fist when they found her, and from that kernel of truth, he had made an assumption. Now, he knew that assumption to be false.

In a slow, measured tone, he read the words on the paper aloud,

> "Yet I should kill thee with much cherishing.
> Good night, good night,
> Parting is such sweet sorrow,
> That I shall say good night till it be morrow."

As he breathed out the last syllable, his cheeks full of tears, a sound filled the corridor, a loud beeping.

A warning message flashed up on the display. Her heart rate had dropped. He watched her body, waiting for movement or some sign of distress. Nothing happened. There was only the gradual downward drift of her heart rate and the alarm to indicate anything was wrong, that she wasn't just in some dreamless sleep. After a few minutes, the alarm silenced, the floor drain opened and her body lowered through the floor, disappearing from view as the water swirled away.

In the elevator, Victor swayed despite the smoothness of the descent, his hand gripping the rail to steady himself.

After Darini and Jim watched him walk out into the reception, their faces pale, Victor spoke with unnatural calm. "Thank you for giving me that time. I apologize for the damage. Please take the costs out of my remaining funds."

"We'll forward any remainder to your account," Darini said, still shell-shocked. "The body will be cremated. Normally, we dispose of the ashes ourselves but as she has surviving relatives, obviously we can send them to you."

"So you have my address?" he queried.

"No," she said, tapping the desk. A writing surface appeared and she waited for him to type it in.

He didn't. He said, "I'll come and pick them up in a few days."

"Normally we send them. Are you sure we can't have your address?" Darini said.

"I'll pick them up in a few days," Victor repeated, walking toward the doorway. Jim stepped out of his way. Victor looked up at him. But Jim couldn't meet his gaze. His face was still pale.

Outside, rain had started to fall. Victor crossed the plaza quickly, wanting to put as much distance as possible between him and the hospital and yet part of him felt the distance grow between him and Maria, or what was left of her, and he felt like turning back.

He thought of the body lowering through the floor, traveling down to the basement, getting transported along dark corridors by a faceless orderly, or more likely a soulless machine, along to the hellfire crematorium to be burned down to essence and smoke that would float up over the city and drift on air currents to join the cloud. He would collect the ashes and put them in a drawer, and never look at them again. No container of burned carbon could memorialize his wife, could capture her being. He would create his own memorial.

As he walked along the funicular platform and onto the train, his body drifting like the pollution cloud itself, his tears dried and a different feeling began to set in, a feeling of dreamlike beginning, a guilty freedom with guilt receding.

This felt right. He should have done this a long time ago. A shiver ran up his spine to lighten his head as the rain fell onto the warm carriage roof, mixing with the dirt and rust and running down the carriage windows in brown rivulets, before dropping in thin waterfalls toward the damp earth below.

The wall of cloud loomed ahead as the funicular picked up speed, rushing his body toward it. His mind was already there, whirling with ambition, ten years ahead, the future already set. In his pocket, in a tube half full of cloudy liquid, Maria's skin cells were dividing rapidly. On the tube, a name written in blue marker: Eve.

Thanks for reading.

If you'd like to find out when James's next
book is released, you can join his mailing list at
www.jamesbushill.com or follow him on Goodreads.

Acknowledgments

I'd like to thank:

My wife, Elley, both my toughest critic and my staunchest ally, for reading the same chapters again and again and again.

Kris Young, and everyone in my UCLA class, for helping me to develop the screenplay that became this book.

Alison, Anthea, Debbie, Maria, and Robyn from betareaders.com.au, the first people outside of my family to read the manuscript, for their perfect blend of constructive criticism and praise.

Lourdes Venard for her astute, skillful editing; Edward Bettison for his brilliant cover design; and reedsy.com for putting me in touch with them.

The Writing Excuses, Dead Robots Society, Creative Penn, and Scriptnotes podcasts, for helping me to learn the craft of storytelling and the business of writing.

Nigel French for his courses on lynda.com, invaluable guides to the confusing world of book design.

Everyone that works on the Citycats, for taking an interest in the book and making the ferries such a great place to work.

Robin, Mandy, Ro, and Greg, for being willing test-readers and wonderful in-laws.

My brother Tom, for his support.

And finally, Mum and Dad, for stoking my love of books and not stepping on my dreams.

About the Author

James was born in Windsor, England. After he left school, he studied film at a college in London, before transferring to Byron Bay for the final year of his degree. Once there, he fell in love, first with Australia, then with his future wife, and ended up staying for good.

For the next few years, he dabbled in screenwriting, taking a course through UCLA and dreaming of Hollywood. But after finishing two screenplays, he realized that he'd rather write a book. This is that book.

When he's not writing (or procrastinating), James works as a ferry deckhand in Brisbane, Queensland, where he lives with his long-suffering wife and their two cats, Molly and Huckleberry.